To Judith

To Kill The
Truth

Callum Duffy

November 2015

To My Family

Acknowledgements

I would like to thank Dr Eric Yeaman, for his invaluable help and advice in writing my first book.

I would like to thank my family, my mother and father Gillian and Jim for moral support and my brother Christopher for all of his media and technological know how. I would particularly like to thank my aunt and uncle, Sheena and Derek Marks, without whom none of this would have been possible.

Chapter One

The Leaders of Two Governments

Nigel Braithwaite could not sleep. As Prime Minister of Great Britain, he had many decisions to make. Normally, he had no trouble, but this one was momentous. His instinct urged one course, but he was uneasy about it, especially when he contemplated the consequences of discovery. At 2 a.m., he decided what must be done, and then he slept.

By 7:30 a.m. he was up as usual, and using the phone.

Penny Carson answered on the second ring. "Good morning, sir." Her evenly modulated Home Counties accent was reassurance itself.

"Penny, sorry for disturbing you so early."

"I have been up for a while, sir, and it is my job to be disturbed by you."

"You will have read the reports I copied to you last night? I want the Referendum Group in the committee room at Number 10 at 9:30 a.m. No excuses. Penny, I would like you to sit in. Then I need you to get the Leader of the Opposition at 10:30 a.m. Tell him to leave 30 minutes for the meeting."

"Consider it done, sir."

Penny Carson allowed herself a brief smile. The Referendum Group consisted of five senior cabinet ministers who had been charged with developing and promoting the government's case against Scottish independence in the forthcoming referendum. It had always amused her that they were looking at the case against Scottish independence rather than the case for the Union.

She knew that two of the group were late risers, so she rang them first. She could start the day with a bit of fun, for the rest of it promised to be grim.

* * *

1

493 miles to the north, Alistair Morrison was finishing his light breakfast in the Scottish First Minister's residence in Edinburgh. He had read the same reports as the Prime Minister, but he had had a sound night's sleep. He was looking forward to a meeting with his Referendum Team later that morning. Ten weeks until the vote, and all was going well.

He pulled on his jacket and coat and lifted his brief case. With a nod to the security man stationed just inside the residence, the door opened. Outside Bute House, there were elegant Adam buildings all around, as well as an equestrian statue of Prince Albert in the central gardens; it certainly gave him a historic start to his morning's walk.

Morrison took the 25 minute walk, not for exercise, but because it gave him time to think, to clear his mind and prepare for the day ahead. Although his security advisors warned him of the risks, Alistair Morrison never considered travelling by car, even on the cold, wet, windy mornings that Edinburgh produced with regular monotony. This morning, however, was designed to heighten Morrison's mood. The sun shone, the sky was blue, and the outline of Edinburgh Castle rose majestically from its position at the top of the Royal Mile. Just over 300 years had passed since the Scottish Parliament had ratified the treaty of the Union, moving the centre of government to London. Morrison saw his life's work on the brink of success: ten weeks from now, the Scots people would vote in a referendum to say whether they wanted to stay in the Union with the rest of Britain, or become an independent country.

In his office in the Scottish Parliament building, he settled to deal with mail, but his mind was on the meeting with his Referendum Team in an hour.

* * *

The Prime Minister looked around the table. All members of the Referendum Group were present. They had copies of the three reports that had occupied him late into the night. No one had read them, for Nigel

Braithwaite had carefully kept the reports to himself. Until now.

They sensed a steely quality to Braithwaite this morning. None of his normal humour was in evidence. Penny Carson sat next to him. As always her outfit was conservatively neat, her hair and make up perfect. Her laptop was open in front of her. Her presence was not a good sign.

Braithwaite began, "Let me get right to the point, people. What you have in front of you are three reports, any one which would be very serious and warrant exceptional attention. Taken together, they represent the biggest threat to this country since the darkest days of the Second World War.

"First you have the report we have been expecting, prepared for the IMF. It does not, as we had anticipated, suggest that our credit rating be dropped by one point, but by three points. This is in response to our current borrowing rates and the apparent lack of growth in the economy."

Tom Albright, the Chancellor of the Exchequer, shifted uncomfortably in his seat. It was his economic policies that were being so roundly criticised by the IMF.

Not wanting to be interrupted, Braithwaite moved quickly on. "If any of you need further explanation of the implications of that for future borrowing and for interest repayments, I'm sure Tom will provide that for you at the end of the meeting. As I say, very serious for our economy.

"Next, you have the report from the EXCOL group, the world experts on international law and taxation. They confirm our worst fears. In the event of Scottish independence, between 79% and 83% of North Sea oil and gas revenues would go with them. Let's call it 80%. That is £9.8 billion every year that would be removed from our income. Taken on top of the IMF report, that puts us in dire straits."

He had everybody's attention. He took a deep breath, and ploughed on. "The third report is a preview of the latest opinion poll on how the independence referendum is going in Scotland. More bad news - 48% for independence, 34% against, and 18% undecided. And, if the damned separatists win, they go off with 80% of the oil and gas revenues, leaving us at the mercy of the IMF. The civil unrest would make the civil unrest of the 1970s seem like a Buckingham Palace picnic. I cannot, and will not, allow that to happen."

No eye met his as he scanned the faces round the table. "So here is what we do. You as a group continue. Not because you are doing well, but because the separatists would make a meal of you being disbanded. You will up your game, and report to me every 48 hours, through Richard." He nodded in the direction of Richard Hume, the Deputy Prime Minister. "For the sake of the Union, we must take on the separatists with every weapon available to us. I will take personal charge of mobilising our forces. Let me be clear. Our existence as we know it is under threat. What I intend goes beyond the use of spin. You have all tried to put gloss on the debate and it has brought us to the brink of disaster."

Never before had the members of the Referendum Group experienced such a dressing down. None of them felt comfortable, yet they wished to avoid blame. Typically, it was Sir Michael Hammond, the Home Secretary, who first looked up. Heavily built, with a florid complexion and unruly stone-grey hair, he was struggling to keep his temper under control. "Prime Minister, surely this is an over-reaction. There are ten weeks of campaigning before the referendum, and we can turn it round. True, the economy isn't looking good, but we can appeal to the IMF, and they will be sympathetic."

Braithwaite thumped his hand down on the table. "If you believe any of that, you are a fool. Do any of you even know why we are so far behind in the referendum polls?" He was answered by silence. "You don't know what you're fighting against. You can't turn the opinion polls round. Edith, you are Secretary of State for

Scotland. You are supposedly our expert on Scotland. Why are we losing?"

Edith Bannon looked forlorn. Although she was a Scot, she had lived most of her life in Derbyshire. She represented an English constituency, and it certainly showed in her accent. "I have my top advisors giving that question urgent consideration. It seems that the people just think it is time for a change, any change, and independence is a change. It is a consequence of being in a difficult financial situation for some years, with falling living standards. There is no single policy that explains it."

"Thank you, Edith, for confirming that none of you understand what is going on north of the border. The reports you have in front of you will be in the public domain by lunchtime, so prepare your responses carefully. I have a meeting shortly with Halford, who must be informed of the situation. Good morning." Nigel Braithwaite strode from the room, followed by Penny Carson leaving a stunned committee room behind him. As they left, he whispered to her, "Bring forward my meeting with Sir David Lee to tomorrow, and make yourself available."

* * *

At Holyrood, Alistair Morrison was sitting down with his Referendum Team, four senior MSPs plus Alex Watson, the leader of his party at Westminster; Donald Barrie, his Communications and Press advisor, and Reginald Small, the second most senior civil servant in Scotland. Small's role was as an observer, with a remit to advise if he thought any of their strategies were breaking rules or breaching confidentiality.

Morrison began. "I hope you all had a good night's sleep. If you didn't, I bring tidings that will ease your worries. Donald, will you pass round the copies? Let me summarise these reports for you. First, the EXCOL report, which has confirmed that independence brings 80% of oil and gas revenues. That's in line with what our own legal people have been saying, but having it confirmed by such a high profile and respected group will remove all room for debate. There is another little gem in the report. It states that, with improvements in exploration and extraction techniques, these resources will last for the next 50 years.

"Then there's the opinion poll. We're 48%, up another 3% from the last poll. So we're doing well, but we mustn't ease up."

Alex Watson, a wise old head, interrupted. "Ally, I'd be cautious with this. I don't think we are winning the debate. Sure, we are winning the polls. But people aren't seeing the benefits of independence. What they are seeing is a government in London that is not fit. Not just the present lot, but over the years. They have been sickened by scandals over MP's expenses, cronyism, failure to deal with outrageous bonuses, jobs for the boys, and the failing economy. That's why they are turning to us. It's not our positive message that is winning them over, it's the failure of the Westminster parties to put forward any kind of coherent prospect that the Union will serve the people of Scotland. Braithwaite is no fool. He will have something up his sleeve. They have ten weeks and they must have some case to put forward. I think they're biding their time, and we must be ready for when they strike."

"Thanks, Alex. Sound advice." Morrison was clearly enjoying himself. "But the third document you have in front of you will be of great interest. It's the IMF report, and it recommends reducing the UK credit rating by 3 points. That'll keep them busy, and take their minds off whatever they are planning for the referendum debate."

Alex Watson exchanged surprised glances with Christine Milne, the Finance Minister. It was Watson who spoke. "3 points. That can't be right. Things are bad in the economy, but not 3 points! Everyone thought a 1 point drop was possible, but not 3. Wow! They will be running around this morning wondering what has hit them. The referendum may have just dropped off their priority list."

Morrison could not conceal a grin. "Alex, I want you and Donald to work on a press release round the opinion polls, and try to get some TV coverage. We'll leave the EXCOL report for a day or two, because the media will be full of the IMF report, and we don't want to lose the impact of the EXCOL report. Mary, are there surprises on the horizon?"

Mary Ford, who was responsible for discipline during the campaign, was tiny, barely five feet tall, but she kept discipline as well as any regimental sergeant major. "No, Ally; no surprises. I think we all have the message that Alex was describing a few minutes ago. Everyone connected with the campaign realises that the people are comparing us with what they see in Westminster. So just competence, and no scandals or gaffes. Plus they know I've got my eye on them." That brought the meeting to a close with a laugh.

* * *

Nigel Braithwaite nodded and gestured to Stephen Halford to sit down. The two men disliked each other intensely, and barely managed to maintain a facade of civility at the weekly Prime Minister's Questions where Halford as Leader of the Opposition had the opportunity to question the Prime Minister. Yet the two were similar in many ways. Both were sons of millionaire industrialists. They had been educated at the same expensive private school, only three years apart. One had gone to Oxford, the other to Cambridge. They had entered Parliament at the same general election, and both had quickly risen through the ranks of their parties. Both looked younger than they were, and both dressed in similar fashion, with well cut dark suits and self coloured silk ties. In fact, a journalist had once remarked that if they swapped places for a month, nobody would notice.

Braithwaite said, "Thank you for coming at short notice, Stephen. What I am about to share with you is of the utmost importance. I know we have had our

7

differences, and will have more in the future, but on this issue, I think we will agree, if only out of necessity."

Stephen Halford was intrigued. He had seen the IMF report, but he would not have considered that reason in itself for a meeting such as this. He sat quietly for the next ten minutes while the Prime Minister took him through the main points from the three reports, drawing the connections and implications so clearly that they could not be avoided.

"Stephen, after the next general election I may still be Prime Minister. If not me, it will be you. It is in neither of our interests for the economy to be shot beyond repair, as it will be if the separatists get their way. Your party has been no more successful than mine in countering their progress. So we must find a different way of stopping them."

Halford nodded slowly.

It took Nigel Braithwaite another five minutes to explain what he had in mind. Stephen Halford asked only two questions, then the two men shook hands. They had agreed to trust each other on this one issue.

Chapter Two

In Defence of the Union

Sir David Lee was medium. Medium height, medium build, and medium complexion. He was also very middle aged. He wore a dark grey suit, impeccably fitted by one of Saville Row's top tailors, white shirt and striped tie. With his slim, gold rimmed glasses, he looked completely anonymous, like any city executive. He was Director of MI5, the organisation responsible for protecting the United Kingdom against threats to national security. He had been in charge for almost four years, and was widely regarded as one of the best directors the service had ever had. Under him, the service had been transformed, and their success rate, particularly at infiltrating terrorist cells and preventing attacks was rapidly becoming the envy of intelligence services over the world. He was not surprised that his monthly meeting with the Prime Minister had been rescheduled – that often happened. He was surprised that Penny Carson was sitting in on the meeting. He knew her, but not well personally. He was, of course, familiar with the file his organisation had compiled on her. She was fiercely loyal to the Prime Minister, very competent, and highly intelligent. He did not trust her one inch – anything she learned, even in total confidence would either be fed straight to Nigel Braithwaite or stored somewhere for future use.

Sir David arrived exactly on time for the meeting, and was met by Penny, outside the Prime Minister's office. She knocked twice, and both of them went in. They sat opposite Nigel Braithwaite, immaculate as ever, across the large mahogany table. He was slightly surprised that Penny sat beside him, rather than on the opposite side of the table with the Prime Minister. He noted that, unusually, the Prime Minister had no pen or paper in front of him. After some routine pleasantries, Braithwaite began in earnest. "Sir David, I am quite sure that you have seen the IMF report that was released earlier this week. I don't need to tell you that this means we will have to reduce budgets even further than we had planned. Up to now, your service has been protected, but that may no longer be possible. We are looking at total budget reductions of around 15%. I know that your workload in counter espionage remains broadly the same. However, the terror threat is reduced, in no small part due to your successes against terrorist organisations, particularly Al-Qaeda. Your work with Customs and uniformed police on drugs and organised crime has also reduced the effectiveness of these groups. Indeed, you have acknowledged that much of your activities in these fields have been passed over to others. Sir David, surely you can scale down operations, can't you?"

It was a conversation they had held often before, and Sir David had his stock reply ready. He was aware that two things were different this time. The IMF report certainly made the need for budget reductions more urgent than ever before, and why was Penny Carson here? "Prime Minister, I can understand the need for reductions in budgets, and the IMF report makes that clear. However, I would advise that our current levels of activity are essential to keep the various threats under control. There would be serious risks involved if those who could harm us believed that we were slackening our efforts. That would send out the wrong message. They would take solace from that and redouble their efforts. Then our inevitable response would cost more than the budget reductions would save. While we can say with some confidence that we have reduced the threats at the moment, we must always be vigilant, not only for known threats, but also threats that might arise from new sources."

Braithwaite paused as though deep in thought, for maybe ten seconds, then making strong eye contact with Sir David, he went on, his voice slow and very deliberate. "As you know, I am sympathetic to your service, and value its work immensely. But this IMF report is difficult. If we make the reductions it suggests, living standards across the country will reduce significantly. There will be real hardship. Let me not overstate this. We will not become a third world country, but people will definitely be poorer. They will have to forego little luxuries, and maybe some things that they would regard as essentials. Life will become difficult. There may be demonstrations, civil unrest, strike actions. These will all pose threats to our way of life. So, to prevent this scenario, I must look for budget reductions from places that will reduce the impact on the ordinary man in the street."

He waited to let the words sink in, but held his hand up in a gesture that indicated that he wanted no reply. Then he continued "You talk about new threats, Sir David. Imagine if someone was to pull £10 billion from the income to the Exchequer at this time. On top of the IMF recommendations, what effect would that have? Let me explain. That would force the IMF's hand to further reduce our credit rating, and that would cost us billions. We would have to make cuts to cover not only the missing £10 billion, but the extra repayments resulting from the changes to our credit rating. I said a few minutes ago that we would not become a third world country. If someone removed £10 billion from our revenues, that could change. I am not talking about one year, but about missing £10 billion every year. Sir David, would you say that an organisation planning to remove £10 billion like this posed a threat to our way of life? That they were a group that MI5 should be trying to prevent from succeeding?"

Sir David blinked. This was unexpected and he was unsure what the Prime Minister was getting at. He had to think quickly. "It sounds like a threat. But surely this is theoretical. If such an organisation existed, I think we would know about them by now."

The Prime Minister nodded slowly. "So you agree that such an action would be a threat. Good. If you engaged successfully in countering such a threat, you would clearly need your budget to be maintained. I think I could guarantee that. Sir David, this is a not theoretical threat, as you put it. There is an organisation that could remove £10 billion from our Exchequer, and their plans are less than ten weeks from being realised. If you were able to prevent this, you would have the grateful thanks of the nation, or at least those who knew of your efforts. That, I can assure you would certainly include whoever was Prime Minister after the next election."

Sir David permitted himself a raised eyebrow. This was a plan that had been thought through, and discussed with the Leader of the Opposition. He had to admit that it had been nicely done. The threat of huge budget reductions for his service had been followed by an alternative, a way out by dealing with a yet unknown threat. He tried furiously to think of who might have the capacity to carry out such a threat, but every name that came into his head was instantly dismissed. He could not think what organisation the Prime Minister was referring to. To his right, he was vaguely aware of Penny Carson smiling contentedly, almost purring. He had a feeling he had been manipulated into something he would otherwise have been reluctant to get involved with. He nodded to the Prime Minister in acknowledgement that he understood the deal before him, cooperate or have his budget slashed.

Braithwaite sighed and relaxed, just a little. He was sure now that Sir David was hooked. "It is not in your normal area of operations, and the intelligence comes from a report that was probably not of much interest to you professionally. It is quite understandable that this is an organisation that you do not consider a threat, as such. But let me assure you that the threat is very real indeed. You may have heard of the EXCOL report?"

So that was it! Sir David saw in a flash where this was leading. He inclined his head. The organisation in question was to be a democratically constituted political party, and one with a lot of popular support. Indeed it was the very government in Scotland. He shifted uncomfortably in his seat. Nigel Braithwaite continued.

"These separatists, if they are allowed to get their way, will remove £10 billion from our Exchequer. If they win the referendum, it will happen, make no mistake. Sir David, you agreed that a plan to remove this amount of revenue was a threat to our way of life. You must see that the separatists have to be stopped. It is imperative. We must have a means to defeat them at the referendum. Simply interfering with the count will not work. They must be discredited and destroyed. Your organisation is uniquely placed to help us negate this threat."

The Director of MI5 had never before felt so cornered. He had strong misgivings about interfering with a democratically constituted political party, particularly one that had rejected and opposed violence, and had been of assistance on more than one occasion to his staff when dealing with threats that had links to Scotland. But the alternative was worse. Apart from the effect on his own department, he understood the implications for the rest of Britain if the money was removed north of the border. Suddenly, his mind was made up. "Prime Minister, can you give me 48 hours to develop a plan? I am sure we can achieve what you ask."

"You will have your 48 hours, Sir David. You will link with Penny, here. She will speak for me and with my full authority on everything connected with this. That will save too many contacts between you and I, which might raise some suspicion that you were briefing me on a terrorist plot. Penny will be the go between. She will keep me informed. I need hardly add that there will be no record of any of this. Sir David, I look forward to hearing your plans, and I wish you every success. We both have a lot riding on this."

The meeting was at a close. There was no going back.

Penny and Sir David made an arrangement to meet in two days time at a safe venue of Sir David's choice. Sir David left, climbing into his chauffeur driven black Jaguar. His mind was racing, but one thing he knew already. Despite the Prime Minister's warning, he would keep a record of activities, and meetings with Penny Carson. He did not trust her at all, and he might just need some proof that he was acting on instruction, should anything come to the public attention in the future. It was a journey of only a few hundred yards from the Houses of Parliament to the MI5 Headquarters at Thames House, on the corner of Millbank and Horseferry Road in central London overlooking Lambeth Bridge, on the north bank of the Thames. However, by the time he had reached his office, he had made up his mind on a number of other matters, such as the size and composition of the team he would involve in this. He trusted all his staff implicitly, but he left nothing to chance, and there were numerous checks routinely carried out to ensure the integrity of all the agents. He was sure, however that a small team headed by someone close to him was required. He knew just the man for the job. The first meeting of that four man team took place within an hour of his return.

* * *

Penny Carson could hardly contain herself as she sat just outside the Prime Minister's office at Number 10 Downing Street. Her habitual grey trouser suit and white blouse looked as though she had just put them on, although it was after six p.m. and she had already worked a ten hour day. She had heard Sir David's plan two hours earlier, and while she had been able to confirm that most aspects should go ahead at once there were two aspects that she felt that Nigel Braithwaite would want to sanction himself. She was sure, and certainly hoped that he would agree. She had to admit that Sir David had produced a remarkable blueprint in such a short time, and she wondered where some of information could have come from. She made a mental note not to cross him, unaware that his file on her was already full of information that would make her shudder. There were aspects of the plan that really delighted her, and it was one such item that she was particularly keen to discuss. Just five minutes longer until the Prime Minister's prior meeting was finished. Suddenly his office door opened and out strode Sir Michael Hammond, the Home Secretary, looking somewhat unhappy, his grey hair flapping and his complexion just a shade redder than normal. He huffed as he passed by her without acknowledgement. He was followed by a junior minister that Penny vaguely recognised, and a group of civil servants laden with files, struggling to keep up. Nigel Braithwaite followed them to the door, and gestured to her to come in. She sat close to him, her excitement barely concealed, and with great restraint waited till he poured two coffees and asked her to outline Sir David's plan.

"I think you will like it, sir. His analysis of why they are ahead in the polls is much better than anything we have come up with in the Referendum Group. Knowing why they are ahead means that he can focus his attack in the right areas. It will help if I explain his analysis first. His information suggests that their appeal lies in a number of related strands. First, they are seen as competent, and that is compared with the scandals we have had down here, with MP's expenses, funding of trips by lobbyists, retired ministers taking high profile jobs with companies they had ministerial dealings with and overspends on various projects like defence procurement and computer contracts. Certainly there have been a number of examples over the last few years. You are well aware of the list, sir. On the other hand, they have built up a record of bringing in projects under budget and ahead of time. Motorway extensions, bridges, schools, a new hospital and so on. We would have to concede that they have been remarkably sure-footed in this regard. Then there is the issue of the economy and oil and gas revenues. What people see with the Union is continued austerity and reductions in living standards with no end in sight, but with the promise of these revenues they believe they can look forward to prosperity and investment in an independent Scotland. They don't see that they should share the pain for a crisis that they still blame on the bankers and stock markets, while nothing is done to curtail the wages and bonuses of those that they blame. Also the separatists have managed to sound very moderate, with no extreme or controversial policies, so there is nothing to frighten people away. Even those among them with extreme views have been persuaded to keep quiet. Finally, according to Sir David, people think that the separatists are simply setting the agenda, and we are always responding, so they are seen as more proactive while we are running to catch up. Actually we know that to be true, and you said as much to the Referendum Group.

"I've been able to agree much of the plan with Sir David, but there are a couple of things I want to clear with you first, before telling him to go ahead. It is a five point plan, and there is a safety net element that I'll describe first. One of the civil servants close to the First Minister is compromised. A few years back, he was involved in a large scale procurement deal for a computer system for the Home Office. It went spectacularly wrong, but he was protected, his name kept out of the spotlight, and he was shipped off to the Scottish Parliament. It was a difficult time, and this was seen as getting a problem out of the way. His role in the computer scandal has never come to light, but MI5 have all the details. This is a man who is now in a position of trust in Edinburgh. His political masters there know nothing of his past. He can be used to feed information back to us about their moves, and can be used to feed misinformation to them. Sir David will have one of his most trusted men ensure that the civil servant in question understands his options. In fact, he is on a flight to Edinburgh as we speak. If details of his part in the computer scandal were to come out, he would lose his job, his pension, and may well face criminal charges. Sir David anticipates no difficulties."

"Good stuff, Penny. Now, tell me what are the five points, and what was it that was so controversial that you felt I had to hear before you agreed it?"

Twenty minutes later, Penny Carson was back in her own office, breathless, but unable to conceal a smile. She had almost ran from the meeting to her office. As expected, the Prime Minister had agreed with all aspects of Sir David's plan. He had agreed with her assessment that the plan was good and was likely to damage the independence vote beyond repair. It would remove the notion of Scottish independence from the agenda for a generation. Even the fall out would be to his advantage. Now the fun would begin, and not just with the separatists. She picked up the specially encrypted phone that Sir David had given her, dialled the unregistered number and on the third ring, said only one word, "Go." She could not conceal the excitement in her voice.

Chapter Three

Edinburgh Gold

Alistair Morrison and Donald Barrie were reviewing the morning papers. It was only 8 a.m., but Donald had been up for hours, gathering in all the papers, reading blogs and reviewing the current affairs programmes on radio and television, scouring them, as he did every morning, for items that might have a bearing on the referendum. Alistair Morrison sometimes wondered if the big Invernesian ever slept. Donald was as usual, casually dressed in chinos and an open neck shirt. The designer stubble on his chin was about the same length as his closely cropped hair. Aged 30, he had built a formidable reputation for his ability to manage the media, which he did with a judicious mixture of charm and bullying. He seemed to know each journalist by name, and which ones he could trust. He knew which news agencies were sympathetic and which were hostile. Less than eight weeks to go now until the referendum, and he showed no signs of letting up. Morrison knew the importance of the younger man to the independence campaign, and valued his opinion far beyond his specialist field of communications strategy.

"Well, boss, there is nothing over the last 24 hours for us to be concerned about. The polls, as you know, are holding up, even strengthening a bit. The press is still full of the IMF report, and I think that will be the case for the next week, until the IMF central committee confirm that they are going to downgrade the UK by 3 points. We have only had a rather pathetic outburst by the Scottish Secretary, Edith Bannon, about the Scots looking to abandon their English cousins in time of need. Not many papers carried that and she got no TV time. Those who did carry it, tended to describe it as desperation, a throw of the dice from people with no arguments.

"Because of all of this, we've been able to hold back any reaction to the EXCOL report. We can use that as our trump card, but only when we need to. The Gerry Miller radio show is doing a piece on it this morning. I've got Christine covering it, and we trust her to keep it low key. She will play it down to keep it for later should we need it.

"You know boss, it's all going well. But something in my stomach tells me it is going too well. Remember Alex warning us that Braithwaite would have something up his sleeve? I've got a feeling that Alex just might be right, though I can't see what it is."

Morrison smiled at the younger man. "You are working yourself too hard, Donnie. You are beginning to see things that aren't there. Oh, you are right, of course, that we have to stay vigilant, but we are doing that. We have our eyes and ears open, and Alex misses very little of what goes on down at Westminster. We'll have none of your fey Highlander stuff. We have got here, to the brink of success, by hardnosed fact and argument. We won't let up now."

"Aye, maybe you're right, boss, but don't knock the second sight of the Highlander. It's proven right too many times. By the way, have you had time to think about why Richard Hume is being put up to oppose you in the televised debate?"

He was referring to a live televised debate, that had been arranged for the Tuesday evening before the referendum on Thursday. There were to be two speakers, one putting the case for independence, and one putting the case against. It had always been clear that Morrison would make the case for independence, and it had been assumed that Nigel Braithwaite would oppose him. Two days earlier, it had been announced that Richard Hume, the Deputy Prime Minister, would be representing the opposition to independence, and that had taken everyone by surprise.

"It is a bit of a mystery. I don't know him well at all, but Alex Watson does. We had a long chat about it. Alex thinks it might be to do with public perception.

Braithwaite is a better speaker, more oratory skills. However, Richard Hume is regarded as safer, and is more trusted by the public. If Richard says it, it is likely to be true, but if Nigel says it, it is likely to be spin. So Alex thinks it is to do with sounding sincere. But remember, too, the nature of the debate. It will be adversarial, one on one. Richard Hume was a successful barrister before he went into parliament, and had a reputation for cross examination. So maybe they are thinking that he is the best person to pick holes in our case, rather than trying to make a good case of their own. Anyway, that is weeks away, and we will work out our tactics for the debate nearer the time."

Four hours later, Donald Barrie received an urgent summons to return to Morrison's office. He covered the twenty yards of corridor that separated the two offices, and closed the door behind him. Alistair Morrison and Christine Milne were both on their feet. Morrison nodded to his Finance Minister, "Tell him, Christine."

"Donald, you know that Gerry Miller is one of the journalists who are sympathetic. Well, I got quite an easy time on his show this morning, and actually I managed to sidetrack him from the contents of the EXCOL report quite easily. But on the way out, one his researchers caught me. She said there are rumours starting in the press corps about oil companies pulling out of an independent Scotland. She has no idea where this is coming from, and thinks it might be off the record briefings from Westminster, but she seems certain that the rumours are going round. Have you heard anything, Donald?"

Donald Barrie's brow was furrowed in thought. "No, this is new. We have been in constant touch with the oil companies, and they are relaxed about it and privately would welcome independence. They reckon that with a strong economy, Scotland would be able to afford to give them tax breaks to help explore and develop the smaller and more remote fields. Let me make a few calls."

Morrison nodded, and Barrie was gone.

That night, Donald Barrie called at the First Minister's residence. "Boss, something is going on. People are aware of the rumour. Nobody had heard it two days ago. It is a rumour, and nobody seems to have anything to substantiate it. They are all watching each other to try to get a scoop on it. But nobody seems to know where it started. I spoke with contacts in a couple of the big oil companies, and they deny any knowledge of this. They seemed as surprised as we are. I spoke with Alex, down in London, and he has heard nothing. I have a few sources who will let me know if they hear anything more. This smells of underhand work, Ally."

Morrison was thoughtful. "Don't ever let me doubt your fey Highland instincts again, Donnie. You and Alex were both right, London isn't going to go down without a fight, and they have just been keeping their powder dry. We're on to this early. I want you to work with Christine to agree a strategy for keeping this as a rumour, or for dismissing it should it ever surface. Assume that it will surface sooner rather than later, so the earlier we are prepared, the better."

Next morning, there was a meeting of the Referendum Team. Alex Watson had travelled overnight from London by sleeper and was first to arrive. When Alistair Morrison sat down, everyone was present. He started by handing the meeting to Donald Barrie, to go through the prepared communications for the next week.

"We have a few announcements to release to the press this week, and they are all prepared. The relevant spokesmen have been chosen and all of them are on top of their briefs. We will talk about aspects of the campaign away from the media in a moment, but first let me go through the press releases. First, we have the update on the scheme to upgrade the A9 to motorway status from Perth to Inverness. We have reached the halfway stage for the on-site work, and it is projecting three months ahead of schedule and 8% under budget. Tom Thomson, our Transport Minister has two TV slots and four radio slots on this. He will play this as evidence that a competent government can run big projects successfully, and can work well with the private sector. He will emphasise the value to the highland economy of having improved road links, and will mention the accident rate on the old road. All good news and incontestable stuff.

"The next day, Andrew Leckie will be making a statement on crime rates. Again, pretty standard stuff. The rates are down, not spectacularly, but there is a continuing trend. It is not something we can be attacked on. Later on there is a low key announcement about upgrading the pier for the ferry terminal at Lochboisdale. Nothing controversial. The last item is also pretty safe. It is about public access to forestry walks. At the weekend, there are a couple of TV programmes where we are sending participants. The usual panel discussion formats. Alex and Christine are covering those, so we are in safe hands there.

"Moving on from the media elements, we have been doing some further analysis of the survey data we're collecting. This is the feedback that all of the branches are collecting by phoning people about their voting intentions. They are using a prepared script, so we can aggregate all the returns. The good news is that the independence vote is holding steady at 48-50%, with the no vote running at about 33%. Here is the interesting thing. When we look at the data by voter profile, we find that a lot of don't knows or weak no voters are women over 40. It is not that they are against independence, just that they have a reluctance to change. It is like they prefer the devil they know, and need reassurance about a change. Given that there seems to be no specific issue that puts them off, I'd like to propose an alternative strategy to get them on board. We have a few of our MSPs who fit the same profile, women between 40 and 60, and who look, dress and sound like typical Scots." He looked at Mary Ford and smiled. "No offence, but you know what I mean. Someone that they could relate to, as 'she's one of us'. So I thought we could get Mary Gemmell and Lorna

Wilson some media exposure in the last ten days of the campaign. Nothing too specific, just reassurance that they have thought about it, and concluded that it is a good safe option. What do you think?"

Morrison had heard the suggestion before the meeting started and had thought it over. "Good idea, Donnie. They perform well in front of the camera. I suggest you also use Jo Beattie. The more reassuring faces the better. You're right about the timing. It is the last few days that really matter. Get them as much exposure as you can towards the end of the campaign."

Just then, there was a knock on the door, and one of Barrie's assistants stuck her head round the door, "Donald, I think you had better hear this."

Donald Barrie went out with her. The others looked at each other. They knew that the meeting would not have been disturbed unless it was something of importance. They refilled their coffee while they waited for Barrie to return. When he came in, he was clearly angry, but was under control.

"We have a bit of a problem. One of our Aberdeenshire branches held a debate internally a couple of days ago on whether an independent Scotland should become a Republic. Ditch the monarchy. Now it seems that recordings of that discussion have been circulated to news agencies. It seems that some pretty extreme views were expressed during this debate, although in the end there was no vote for abolishing the monarchy."

It was Mary Ford who responded. "Let me guess. It was the Glenturrach branch. They have three or four people who are pretty anti-royalist. But they also have a number of people who are sensible enough to know that there are no votes in republicanism, and plenty of votes to be lost."

"Right first time, Mary," Donald replied. The group were constantly amazed at her knowledge of the party, and where trouble was likely to arise. "We're going to have to do some damage limitation on this. Apparently some of the content is really bad. Like taking over

Holyroodhouse and Balmoral and converting them to social housing to help with homelessness. There is an urgency, because this will hit the lunchtime news bulletins."

Morrison rested his chin on one hand. "Mary, see what is going on in Glenturrach. Why were they having that debate at all? Who recorded it? Do we know how the recording got to the news agencies? Donald, do up a release, along the lines of every party has a few people who hold views that are at odds with the mainstream. Reaffirm our policy to retain the monarchy as head of state, recognise the important role it has to play, and so on. We will probably need someone on standby to be interviewed on this. Should it be me?"

"No, Ally, it doesn't need to be you. I'll do it." It was Alex Watson speaking. "My grey hair and slightly overweight appearance always make me look reassuring, and if we wheeled you out within minutes of the story breaking it would look like a panic measure, an overreaction. I'll go over this with Donald so the press release ties in with what I'll say."

Two hours later, Alex Watson was being interviewed on live television in the first lunchtime bulletin. The interview was being conducted by Richard Barker, and he had the look of a man who had his prey in his sights. He had started off gently enough, and Watson had gone through the main points in the press statement that Donald Barrie had prepared. This was not party policy, an internal debate that reflected the views of a tiny minority, and so on. Then, Barker, peering over the top of his thick rimmed spectacles, said, "Just let me play you a couple of excerpts from the recording, Mr Watson. Then you can tell me if you think this is in any way acceptable, or does it reveal your true colours?"

Watson didn't know what was coming next, and listened intently as the recording started up. There was a clear voice. "These people are parasites. The English can keep them if they want. All their land and property in Scotland should be confiscated and used for the good of the common man. Holyroodhouse could go a long way to solving Edinburgh's homeless problem." There were audible cries of support. Then, after a cut, another excerpt was played. "We don't need a monarch. It is a symbol of all that is wrong with the country – they represent the top of a tree of privilege, the opposite of a fair society. We have to grasp the chance to dismantle this group of kings and queens, and princes and lords and earls who have never done anything for us, but just suck the money to themselves, that's where all the gold ends up. We need to start claiming back what is rightfully ours." More cheers could be heard.

Barker fixed Watson with a steely stare. "At least you do not deny the authenticity of the recording. Well, Alex Watson, is this the picture of an independent Scotland that your party really wants? Is this not your true colours? Is this the vision that you expect people to vote for in seven weeks?"

Alex Watson realised how bad the recordings sounded. He knew that across Scotland there was no serious suggestion that the monarchy be abolished, and indeed the feedback from their research had told his party that the monarchy was widely seen as one of the safeguards that would be helpful to a newly independent nation. Silently he cursed the idiots who had held the debate. "You can have my assurance that is a view held by very few people in the party. It is absolutely not our policy. I have met members of the Royal Family on many occasions, as has Alistair Morrison, at state events, on official visits and so on. We have always enjoyed very cordial relations. I have not heard this recording before, and I would be grateful for a transcript of the whole recording. We take very seriously the behaviour of our members, and while we value freedom of speech, we are also aware there are boundaries to that freedom. Therefore personal attacks on anyone, royal or not, are unacceptable. If there are sufficient grounds a full and thorough investigation into this will take place."

It was a brave attempt to mount a defence of the indefensible, but Alex Watson knew the damage had been done, even before Richard Barker ended the interview with, "Now it is for the people to consider which version of Scotland they would be voting for in the referendum, the plausible moderate one that Alex Watson would have us believe in, or the extremist one that we can hear his party members baying for?"

Back at Holyrood, Morrison and Barrie watched the broadcast with growing horror. They knew only too well how damaging it was likely to be to have such extreme views associated with their independence campaign. What else was on the recording? Was there more to come out? How to counter this? Nagging away at the back of Morrison's mind was the question of who had recorded the discussion, and why had they given it to the news agencies. Alex Watson had done well, but there was no doubt that the effect of the item overall was bad. They tuned into some other broadcasts. These were just as bad, sometimes worse, for Watson could not be everywhere to try to defend their corner. Morrison picked up the phone, and dialled Mary Ford. "Mary, I am going to announce a full enquiry into the conduct of the Glenturrach branch this afternoon, so that it will catch tomorrow's tabloids. I want you to get this organised, quickly. You know better than me what questions need to be answered, but I really need to know who sent the recordings to the news agencies. Donald tells me that even his best contacts can't, or won't tell him. They all say they were dropped off anonymously."

Donald Barrie looked at the First Minister, and was suddenly sure of something. "Boss, we've been set up. Not that many people would know the addresses of all these news agencies. Some are easy to find, but others aren't. The recording is high quality, so whoever took it knew that they were going to take copies without losing too much quality. You don't carry that sort of equipment around with you on the off chance that something interesting might happen. I am going to try a couple of the friendlier agencies to see if we can do anything to track down the origin of the recording, or at least get some kind of idea what was used to make it."

Chapter Four

London Calling

Sir Neville Hardcastle settled his colossal frame into the seat. He wasn't quite sure why he agreed to meet this man that he had never heard of. He should have insisted that one of the journalists came instead. He was the proprietor of one the largest news chains in the UK, not someone who could be summoned to a meeting like this. His heavy jowls rubbed against his collar as he studied the man already seated opposite him. There had been something quite disturbing about the man's manner on the phone, and perhaps that was why Sir Neville had agreed to meet him.

Even seated, it was obvious that this was a tall man, aged about 40, Sir Neville estimated, with light brown hair and hard, green eyes that he could feel piercing into him like cold emeralds. In front of him lay a buff coloured manila folder. The man gestured to Sir Neville. "Thank you for being so prompt. I will not waste your time." The voice had a slight trace of a Yorkshire accent that Sir Neville thought might be phoney. "You will know of Hank Warren, the Texan oil tycoon. He is in hospital in Dallas, Texas, suffering from multiple organ failure. At his age, he is 85, the prospects do not look good. I have in this folder, what may turn out to be his last interview. I want you to publish it. You will publish it exactly two weeks before the independence referendum in Scotland. As you will see, much of what Mr Warren has to say will not be welcomed by the separatists. Please read the transcript."

He passed the folder over, and sat back while Sir Neville read the two pages. Sir Neville read it twice, trying not to change his expression. "You cannot seriously expect me to publish this. It is not sourced. How did you manage to get this interview in the first place? In the second place, who are you? And in the third place, although I'm no oil expert, I do not believe that Warren said any of this."

"Sir Neville, I do expect you to publish this. You do not need to know who I am. Everything in the transcript is attributable to Mr Warren, I assure you. But I am not stupid. I know that you will need more than my assurances to encourage you to print this article. So there will be a reward. On the day that you publish you will get half of the contents of a file which contains, shall we say, some rather interesting information about a senior cabinet minister. Certainly enough to ensure his fall from grace. However, the really interesting material is in the other half of the file, which you will get the morning after the referendum. The first half of the file you can regard as a token of our appreciation for publishing the Warren interview. The second half of the file is our guarantee that you will not publish the contents of the first half of the file until after the referendum. Is that clear?"

"You can really do all of this? How do I know that you can deliver on that?"

"I thought, Sir Neville, that you would want some proof of our intent. I have in my pocket, the first page of that file. You may read it, here and now, but I require that you return it to me immediately." He reached inside his jacket and produced a single folded sheet of paper. He opened it out as he passed it over, and Sir Neville saw the name at the top of the page. Sir Michael Hammond. The press baron read the page quickly, then again, slowly, taking in the detail. In spite of himself, he could feel his eyes widen. What he was reading was unbelievable, but it made perfect sense.

The other man went on. "I can assure you that much of the rest of the material is even more explicit. There are copies of documents with his signature, and photographs of what you in the press call incriminating circumstances. These are genuine, and while you have the first half of the file you may authenticate the documents in any way you wish, just as long as their existence does not become public knowledge."

Sir Neville sat here for a long moment, shoulders hunched and eyes focussed in the distance, like a man trying to discern some distant foe. The tall man with the green eyes did not rush him. Sir Neville slowly made eye contact, and without a flicker of a smile, said, "I believe we have an understanding."

Three hours later, the tall man with green eyes was seated in a board room. It was the headquarters of Readybuild Ltd, one of the biggest and most aggressive construction companies in the country. The man opposite him was John Webster, chief executive and founder of the company. He had all the trappings of the good life, an expensive grey Italian suit, a Jerome and Jerome shirt from which opulent gold cuff links hung, and expensive crocodile skin shoes. However the tall man was not fooled by outward appearances. He knew that John Webster was tough. In twenty years he had built the company up from nothing. He had cut a few corners, but no more than anyone else in a cut throat business. The board room itself spoke of his success. It's location in central London, the expensive furnishings, the crystal glasses and the thick pile carpet left no room for doubt. This was a company with a healthy financial balance.

The tall man started, "Firstly, Mr Webster, let me congratulate you on your success. Building up a company like this must have been difficult, especially in the early years. But you know this, and this is not the purpose of my visit. I know that you are still ambitious for your company. You are aware that there are two massive government contracts to be decided in the next three months, the biggest contracts ever, as the government tries to stimulate the economy. The new motorway network proposed to link four major cities will provide the successful tenderer with significant income for the next six years. The project to create a new university campus to combine three London Universities is even bigger. Again, Mr Webster, you know all this. Just as you know that Readybuild are on a short list with two other companies to bid for this work.

"Let me get to the point. I am in a position to help you ensure that both of these contracts go to Readybuild. I can arrange that you see details of your competitors' bid before you submit your own. That would give you an advantage that you could not fail to realise. I want no money."

John Webster stood up, and held up a hand for silence. "I have no idea who you are. You lied to my secretary to get an appointment with me. Now you are trying to involve me in illegal activities. Leave now, before I call the police."

The tall man remained seated, the emerald eyes never wavering from Webster's. "If you must call the police, then do so. I will wait here until they come. I assure you, however, that there will be no action for the police to take. I would not take a chance on coming here as I have done if it were simply going to get me arrested. I am here with the full knowledge of people who can deliver what I have described. You can imagine the power that such people hold. They have decided that Readybuild should win these two contracts, and only want to help you with some information. They want no financial reward, and afterwards, you will never hear from me, or my people again."

The tall man's obvious confidence unsettled Webster, and in spite of himself, he was impressed. Winning these two contracts would be enormous – their value would make Readybuild one of the top five companies in the UK. He had hoped for one of the contracts, but the prospect of getting them both was something he could only dream about.

"You want no financial reward, you say. That suggests some other form of reward."

"Indeed so, Mr Webster. We ask you to cooperate with us in one small matter. It will be quite easy for you. All that we require of you is that you submit this report." He passed two sheets of paper over, both on Readybuild company notepaper. "The report may not be quite accurate, as you will see, but you can replace it with your own, accurate, version, a couple of weeks later. Blame the discrepancy on a problem with your project management software, and intimate your regret at the error. You will issue the report at your meeting with the Scottish Government ten days before the independence referendum. I know that the date for the meeting is set, and that a progress report is the main item on the agenda for that meeting."

Webster had scan read the report while the tall man was speaking. "To say this is not quite accurate is an understatement. It is widely off the mark. The A9 project is well ahead of schedule, and well under budget. All our previous reports have confirmed that. How can we suddenly turn up and say that it is now running six months behind and projecting a £5 million overspend? That is just not credible."

"Mr Webster, I know that you have not had time to read the document fully. When you do, you will see that it refers to a geological problem that is likely to cause extensive flooding in one of the northern sections of the road. This is true, such a report does exist, and your engineers will have seen it. What we are suggesting is that there will be extensive delays while an alternative plan and route are decided, and that the delay will add to the cost of the project. This geological problem is indeed in your project plan, but it appears as a managed risk for which a solution already exists. All we have done is move it to the unmanaged risk part of the plan. So you can see that it will be easy to blame the mistake on a computer glitch, and then it will be back to business as normal. However, you must not correct the error until after the referendum. I am sure that you will agree this is such a little thing that will harm no one, and yet it will lead to such big rewards. Construction is a tough business, Mr Webster. Sometimes we have to use the rules to suit our needs. Do we have an understanding?"

Webster thought for a moment. It did seem harmless enough, although he could not see who would gain from publishing the false report. These were two huge contracts and would set the company up for years to come.

"We might have an understanding. How do I know that I can trust you?"

"You don't. I can give you proof that I can do what I say. Consider this file." He went into his brief case and pulled out a thin green folder, marked "Top Secret", and spread it on the desk in front of John Webster. Webster could see at a glance that it contained details of four large government procurement contracts. The details should have been strictly confidential, containing many commercially sensitive items. There they were, and one of them referred to information from his own company, so he immediately recognised that this was genuine.

The tall man gathered the file together and replaced it in his brief case. "I take it that this is satisfactory evidence that we can provide you with all that we say we can."

Webster was satisfied. The tall man could not get this kind of information unless he had access to the most secret documents. That meant he had to be working for the government in some capacity. Most of Readybuild's work came in the shape of government contracts. Webster quickly worked out that it would be a bad plan not to cooperate. "We have an understanding," he said simply.

The tall man was happy as he left, and permitted himself a smile. Today had been the more difficult of the meetings. Tomorrow would be much simpler.

At ten o'clock next morning, the tall man was shown into the office of the editor of the magazine, Economics Review, a weekly publication made up from articles written mainly by independent economists, with a few stories added by staff reporters. This mix gave the magazine its reputation for impartiality and for articles from the best economists across the world. As he sat down, he was pleased to see opposite him the magazine's proprietor, Sidney Stevens, easily recognised in his habitual open neck shirt and brightly coloured cravat, and the renowned feisty editor, Janet Cole. Cole on her own just might have been difficult. He ignored the offer of coffee.

Janet Cole started the meeting. "I don't think we got your name?"

The tall man took a neatly printed article from his brief case. "No, you didn't, Miss Cole. However, I have an article here that you will print in your edition the week before the Scottish Referendum. Please do not protest. Your magazine provides a valuable service, allowing the most recent thinking to be shared and providing some of the most accurate and up to date forecasts. In your enthusiasm to get up to date data for your forecasts, sometimes you use unconventional means. This is entirely understandable, but some others might not take such a generous view of your methods. If some of this came to light, life would become very difficult for the magazine, and, dare I say it, for the senior staff. For example, the Chinese government would be displeased to know that you have details of their diamond mining operations in the Ningxia Provence, or the Russians, should they discover that you have access to their plans to relaunch their stock market next spring." He did not say that, unknown to the other two people in the room, these reports had been passed on to them by MI5 agents. He could see that Stevens and Cole were shaken. He would have been surprised had they not been. He smiled, but the smile did not touch his green eyes. "I can ensure that does not happen. Just agree that you will publish this article, and all your anxieties will disappear."

Janet Cole was first to react. "Let me read the article first."

The tall man indicated that she should. It took her four minutes. As she read it, her colour heightened. "As an article, our editorial board would never pass this. It is old stuff, thinking from more than thirty years ago. The arguments do not stack up, and any second year economics student would know all the counter arguments."

Unruffled, the man said softly, "No doubt you are right. I shall just call my friends at the Russian and Chinese embassies, in that case." He pulled his mobile phone from his pocket and started to dial. It was Sidney Stevens who cut him short, his voice half an octave higher then normal. "Miss Cole never said that we couldn't make an exception. I am sure that we could." There was obvious panic in his eyes as he looked to Janet Cole. She was biting her bottom lip, furiously trying to think of some strategy, but finding none. Eventually she gave a slight incline of the head.

The tall man stood up. "I am so glad that you have decided to be sensible. This way we can avoid all sorts of unpleasantries. I look forward to publication, one week before the independence referendum. Run whatever articles to counter this one, or anything you like by way of response but not until after the referendum. As long as you keep your part of the bargain, we will not be seeing each other again." With that, he was gone. There was just one more thing to set up, and that should be the easiest of all. Stevens and Cole sat for a long time in stunned silence, before the editor reflected what hung between them. "Whoever he was, I think, we do what he asks. We have no option."

It was afternoon now, and rain had started to fall, a soft grey drizzle, making the day unpleasant. The tall man seemed not to notice as he went into the coffee house. The two men he had come to see were already there. They were seated at a table by the window, and both wore navy pin striped suits, one balding and in his fifties, the other perhaps twenty five. The tall man knew the older of them. He indicated that they should not get up as he approached, and held his hand out to one of the men. "Good afternoon Freddie. It is good to see you again." If either man thought that it was good see the other, nothing in their manner showed that. The handshake was short and perfunctory. The younger man detected cold hostility.

The tall man sat down, without acknowledging the younger man. "You are familiar with the report that your department has produced on taxation in inner cities." It was a statement, not a question. "On page 18, in the second paragraph the sum of £1470 is mentioned. When you circulate it, by e-mail as you normally do, this will be changed to read £1740. When you send it out you will include on the distribution list this person." He passed over a small piece of folded paper with an e-mail address on it. "Then, a few minutes later you will send out an e-mail drawing everyone's attention to the error. However, this person will not be on the second list. I take this is all quite clear."

As the man called Freddie indicated that he understood, the tall man rose, and left the coffee house. He was content with how things had gone over the previous two days.

Freddie turned to his younger colleague. "That is our brigade. Not easy to refuse them anything. Try to have nothing to do with them, if you know what is good for you. Goodness knows what they are up to now. As usual they ask you for something that seems of no significance, but it will be important in one of their little games."

Chapter Five

Polling Nerves

Christine Milne was confident. She was well on top of her subject. The funding of Scotland. She also knew that in the studio debate her opposition would be Edith Bannon. Christine knew that Edith was no expert on finance, and that her English accent grated with many Scots, not because she had an English accent, but because she kept insisting that she was Scottish. People just did not like the idea of someone who had left Scotland as a child, and made no effort to maintain links with Scotland, or to move back, insisting that they knew what was best for Scotland. The two women had worked together on a couple of projects and had met a few times at other events. Although they were political opponents they had got on reasonably well together, and Christine knew that Edith's preferred way of doing business was to build on consensus rather than to drive confrontation. However, given Edith's lack of detailed expertise on financial matters, Christine had been surprised when she had been nominated for the debate.

Donald Barrie had spent some time that afternoon going over the likely issues for the debate, and he, too, was confident. He knew that Christine was a strong performer, and that she had that rare ability of being able to explain complex financial matters in layman's terms. She had been well briefed with all the latest information. There was just over two weeks to go until the referendum, and the polls were still very much in their favour. There had been some damage done by the Glenturrach debacle, and the unionists never missed a chance to refer to them as a bunch of extremists, but the polls still showed a decent lead. Over the last couple of weeks, the unionists had upped their game. They seemed much better prepared to respond to press releases and statements. Barrie had to admit they were beginning to get their act together, and that it was probably inevitable. They had been so bad until a few weeks ago. They had even managed to wrong-foot him a couple of times recently by making unexpected announcements. Still, he reckoned that the polls showed an eight point lead for independence, and at the beginning of the campaign, they would have settled for that. Besides, it had always been the case that the big push was to come in the last two weeks, probably starting with the live debate tonight. Donald was sure that Christine Milne would be able to land some knock out blows on the economy, and he knew that she was experienced enough to do so in a way that avoided any hint of arrogance, or overconfidence. When he thought about it, he was very lucky – there were a good number of strong performers, people who were good under the spotlight that he could forward for debates. This meant that members of his team were fresh, and the public did not see the same faces every day. The next two weeks were going to be hectic. He had organised seven television appearances and fourteen radio appearances for the three women, which should go a long way to persuading other women to vote for independence, he hoped. Three of these appearances weren't even on news or current affairs programmes. There were debates and phone–in programmes to be covered, news programmes looking for sound bites, and press conferences to attend. The media interest, as expected was intense, and increasingly, foreign journalists were making demands on his time. He had not lost sight, either, of the big debate, two nights before the referendum, when Alistair Morrison would go head to head with Richard Hume. It might all come down to how that debate played out.

That night's studio debate was hosted by Sue Farquhar, one of the channel's heavyweights in the field of current affairs. She had the knack of lulling unsuspecting politicians into a false sense of security, with her friendly, low key questioning, and yet getting them to say more than they had ever intended. The debate got underway with some general questions about the benefits or drawbacks to Scotland of being in the Union. Christine Milne made the usual points about oil income going to London and about investment in national institutions always being based in London – the National Art Gallery, the National Museum, and so on. Edith Bannon had replied by highlighting some areas where expenditure in Scotland was higher than in England, mentioning coastguard and life boat services, rural airstrips and welfare benefits. Then a member of the studio audience asked for some clarity. "So, to pull all that together, is there more spent per head on people in Scotland than in England?"

Sue Farquhar invited Edith Bannon to respond first. "Well it is quite a complex calculation, and it's not very easy always to know from UK budgets, how much is spent north of the border. Expenditure is allocated on a needs basis, so in Scotland, there is greater need, more poverty, more unemployment, it is right that Scotland gets more than her share. The rest of the UK does not begrudge this. Scotland needs more than her share, so Scotland gets more than her share. That is the benefit of the Union."

Christine Milne saw an obvious opening at this. "Well, what Edith Bannon says about it being complex is true. We have to remember that there are two sides to the balance sheet, and Scotland sends more to the London Exchequer than comes back. Now let me address this myth that generous London spends more per head in Scotland than it does elsewhere. There is the obvious point that it is not how much you spend, but what you spend it on. In Scotland, we would want to see more expenditure on infrastructure, creating better homes and replacing some of the worst slums in Western Europe. I acknowledge that Edith Bannon is right when she says that in Scotland we get more than our share of welfare benefits. We don't want this kind of investment, which keeps people in poverty. We want investment in projects that will bring work, and the chance to climb out of poverty.

"However, the calculation has been done on who gets most. It is contained in a report released last week by the Westminster Government. We know that the best estimate of monthly per capita spending in Scotland is £1520. The report on Inner City Taxation in England gives a figure for England, not just the inner cities, of £1740 per month capita spending. This is over £200 per month more spent in England for every person."

Edith Bannon was beside herself. She was animated, trying to get Sue Farquhar's attention. "This is fantasy stuff from the separatists. They will say anything to get your vote. Christine Milne for Finance Minister of an independent Scotland? I think not. She can do all the sums she likes, but as long as she just makes up the numbers she will just get fantasy answers. The figure quoted in the Inner Cities Taxation Report isn't £1740, it is £1470, some £50 less per month than is spent on Scots. But Christine Milne isn't interested in that." Her voice got louder as she reached a crescendo. "She just wants to mislead the public. When the figures don't suit her argument, she just changes the figures. I have a copy of the report with me. Anyone is welcome to check it. Like everything else in their argument to destroy the Union, the separatists have got their sums wrong. You can't trust them to tell the truth, you can't trust them with simple numbers, you can't trust them with Scotland's future."

Christine was stunned. She was aware that one of the programme researchers was speaking into Sue Farquhar's ear piece, and from her reaction, she was being told that Christine Milne had made a big mistake. How could this have happened? She had gone over the figures carefully with her own staff since she got the report a few days earlier. That afternoon, she had gone over the figures again with Donald Barrie and agreed that this was a strong point in favour of independence, and that this close to the referendum, there was no point in not using it. Something niggled at the back of her mind. Alex Watson! Given that it was a Westminster report, he had been surprised that she already had it when he offered to copy her into the one he had received. How had she got it? Before she could think, Sue Farquhar was asking her a follow up question. "Well, Edith Bannon has a point, hasn't she? The figures are set out plainly in the report. You can't just invent them to suit yourself and hope that nobody will notice."

Although Christine Milne was a seasoned performer, nothing had prepared her for this. Her mouth was dry, her pulse racing. She felt a knot in her stomach and was aware that she was sweating profusely. Furiously, she tried to think of how to limit the damage. Should she be contrite, or go on the attack? If she had been wrong, and there seemed no doubt that she had, perhaps contrition was the best route. "I did not mean to suggest that people in England were getting more than they deserve, and I'm sorry if I gave that impression. The income gap clearly varies between rural settings and inner city settings and that is what last week's report was trying to highlight. This was not a report that compared Scotland with England, but inner cities with rural areas." She ploughed on, but was aware that she was waffling, desperately trying to find a way of moving to another point. Sue Farquhar interjected, "You tried to use it as a comparison between Scotland and England, though, didn't you?"

"I didn't mean it in that way. Look, you have to take account of income as well as expenditure. We know that Scotland contributes more to the Treasury than we get back. Scotland has done for many years. In Scotland we have what you describe as a chronic surplus. Yet we don't see the benefit."

It was a valiant effort, but the damage was well and truly done. Throughout the remainder of the debate she was on the receiving end of taunts from Edith Bannon, and to some extent, Sue Farquhar. Even some members of the studio audience joined in with comments like, "Are you sure now?" and much to everyone else's amusement, "so is that one of Hans Christian Andersen's facts then?" By the end of the debate,

Christine Milne felt like a wet rag. She could not wait to get off the set. She shook hands as quickly as possible with Sue Farquhar and a smirking Edith Bannon, who made some comment about being surprised that Christine did not know her brief. She got out fast to where a waiting Donald Barrie hurried her into his car.

"It's not your fault, Christine. Listen to me. It's not your fault. I've had Alex on my mobile, and he confirms that his copy of the report tallies with the Bannon woman's version. My people have just confirmed that the version we have back at the office is wrong. There must be two versions in circulation. How can that be, because our copy came from the cabinet office? It went out on the same e-mail distribution as Alex's copy. I don't get it." He looked at the Finance Minister, and was aware that this was the first time he had seen a minister sobbing. He doubted if she had heard a word he had said. He stopped the car, and gently put an arm round her shoulder. Was he really doing this?

"Christine, it's alright. It will work out. I was going to take you to see Ally, but you'd rather go home? You can see Eddie and the kids will still be up. That might be better for you. I'll sort things with the boss. Don't worry. It will all look better in the morning. I promise." He didn't believe a word of it.

Christine dried her eyes. Between sobs, she said, "Thanks Donnie, take me home. I just want to go home."

Two hours later, Donald Barrie was sitting with the First Minister and Mary Ford in the office of Bute House. Each of them was staring at a full glass of malt whisky that Alistair Morrison had poured for them. He had poured it for something to do to keep busy. None of them felt like drinking it. None of them was sure what to say. They all felt something needed to be discussed. The campaign had just received a huge blow, and nothing could hide that fact. It was now almost midnight, and the three of them had gathered to discuss how they should respond to the beating Christine Milne had taken in the debate. Alex Watson had spoken with Alistair Morrison at length on the phone, and was on his way north on the overnight sleeper from London. The silence lay between them like a dark impenetrable sheet. They had no plan, and were beginning to think that there was nothing to be done until the morning, when Alex could join them.

It was the ring tone on Donald Barrie's mobile that brought them back to reality. He moved to one side of the room, and spoke quietly into the mouthpiece, but it became clear quickly that the person at the other end of the phone was doing most of the talking. Mary Ford and Alistair Morrison were watching him closely, and were aware that he was becoming agitated. This was completely alien to his normal docile and calm Highland manner. Suddenly, he held his hand up. "Is your fax on, boss?" There was no mistaking the urgency in his voice. Morrison confirmed that it was, and heard Barrie say something into the phone before ending the call.

The other two looked at him expectantly. Donald Barrie took a sip of his whisky. "That was Susan from my office. She has started to go through the early editions of tomorrow's papers. There is nothing in the early editions about the debate: that might catch later editions. She is sending through to your fax a copy of an article in the Daily Review. It is a two page spread. This is an interview with Hank Warren. In it, he says that international oil companies would be likely to leave an independent Scotland. He says the creation of a new nation with an untested government and with no track record on dealing with oil companies for setting taxation levels, granting licenses and so on would be too volatile, and would frighten most companies off."

At that, the fax machine kicked into life, and seconds later, the three of them were reading the article with mounting disbelief. Donald Barrie's summary had been accurate, but the article went much further. It suggested that newly independent nations were susceptible to take over by politicians with extremist views, and that even if well run, a new nation would be subjected to speculation on its currency, while the money markets assessed how it would perform. Finally, the article discussed the lack of infrastructure in Scotland to support a booming oil industry, claiming that rail, road and air links were poor, and that Scotland's position on the edge of Europe was a hindrance to getting the oil to the market. The three exchanged puzzled looks. It was Mary Ford who spoke first. "Hank Warren is a legend. Having him lined up against us is a problem. How do we find out what is going on and why he has said this? I thought that I heard he was in hospital close to death."

"He is, Mary," Morrison replied. "He has been in hospital for about two months. I last met him about a year ago, before his health gave in. His views then were completely different. He was clear that as an oilman, he had no role in the democratic processes of another country, other than to represent the views of his industry and in particular, his company. He refused to get drawn into expressing a political opinion. He was privately of the opinion that a post independence Scotland would be an ideal place to do business. His view was that we would be rich enough with oil and gas revenues coming directly to us that we would be able to give the companies tax breaks for research and development and for exploration of more difficult remote and smaller fields. So I don't know what has happened with him. Obviously, the timing of this article is not a coincidence. I wonder when they got the interview, given how ill Hank is."

"Boss, as you say, this is at odds with all that we know about Hank Warren. Given how ill he is, we can't just contact him and ask him what is going on. I can get in touch with his press office in Texas and see if they can cast any light on this. It might be worth contacting the other oil companies to see if they know anything, but I doubt it. We keep in pretty regular touch with their press office staff anyway. Like you said, the oil companies try to steer clear of expressing political views."

The mood was no better next morning when the Referendum Team met in the First Minister's office in Holyrood. All were present, although only the civil servant, Reginald Small, looked like he had slept the night before. Christine Milne was in a bad way. Her eyes were bloodshot, and she looked close to tears. Unusually for her, she was dressed casually, in jeans and a T-shirt, as she settled into a chair between Alex Watson and Donald Barrie. Before Alistair Morrison could start the meeting, she spoke, clearly something she had made up her mind about overnight. She looked down at the table in front of her, as though in a trance. "I am so sorry. Last night I may just have blown independence out of the water. Everything we have all worked so hard for. I was taken for a fool and made to look ridiculous. I am sorry, I have let you all down, and I believe I have let Scotland down. Alistair, I'm only here this morning to resign. Anything you can do to salvage things will be easier without me."

There were astonished looks round the table. Nobody had expected this, but without hesitation, Morrison responded. "I am afraid, Christine, accepting your resignation is completely out of the question. Politically, it would be the wrong thing to do. Imagine what the unionists would make of a senior member of our government resigning this close to the referendum. However, that is not the reason that I am not going to accept your resignation. I will not lose the best Finance Minister in the country. That would weaken the government, not strengthen it. What happened last night was certainly not your fault. I checked my copy of the report, and I had the same version as you. So did Donald. We all did, except Alex, who got his copy through the cabinet office at Westminster. So there are clearly two versions of the report in circulation. That might be an accident, but it might also be a deliberate attempt to set us up."

Reginald Small coughed, and at Morrison's invitation, went on. "First Minister, I would just caution that trying to implicate the cabinet office in a deception without any evidence will lead to a host of undesirable outcomes, breaches of Parliamentary privileges and so on."

"Yes, Reginald, of course you are right, and I appreciate your advice. I would advise everybody here to heed that advice. We mustn't go off making what will be seen as wild accusations. What I am suggesting is that we be on our guard, that we double check data, that we use Donald's office to triangulate information. I know it will be time consuming. But I do not want anything remotely like what happened to Christine last night happening to anybody else. Christine, your resignation should be withdrawn immediately." There were "Hear, hears!" round the table. She forced a smile, and gave an imperceptible nod.

Morrison went on, "However, there is no denying that last night was disastrous. The later editions of the papers are full of it, and much makes for unpleasant reading. Christine, some of it, inevitably is quite personal. Do not read it, or if you do, please realise that it is only aimed at you because it was you in that studio last night. It could have been any one of us. However, the story in the Daily Review with the Hank Warren interview is potentially more damaging. There seems to be no obvious way to refute it. Donald, I believe that you have a bit of an update?"

Donald Barrie still contrived to look bright and attentive, although Morrison knew that he had worked through the night. "I've spoken with Hank Warren's press people. Mr Warren slipped into a coma two days ago, and is not expected to regain consciousness. He has been in hospital for nine weeks, during which time he has not spoken with the press. As far as I know, he did not speak to the press before going into hospital. They admit that in the month or so before he was admitted, he was behaving a bit erratically, and just may have spoken to someone without their knowledge, but they think that is pretty unlikely. His press people will be contacting the Daily Review next week to try to clear this up, but it is not a priority for them at the moment. Apart from handling the publicity in the USA round Mr Warren's impending death, they are also dealing with a delicate situation regarding the company's explorations in the Gulf of Mexico, and that is taking up a lot of their resources.

"I've also spoken with the other oil companies. I dragged a few people out of bed. They are all as surprised as us at the story. They say there is a general agreement not to get involved in local politics, that they disagree with the views attributed to Hank Warren. However, none of them will come out and say this publicly. Their concern, as you know is that if they did, it might be construed as supporting independence, and if we lose the referendum, they will be dealing with a government in London that will not forgive them for taking sides.

"I've also received a request, boss, for you to appear on tomorrow's lunchtime Politics Show to discuss the Warren interview. I think you have to accept, otherwise you will be accused of ducking out."

Chapter Six

Shifting Support

Alistair Morrison had given his usual polished performance on the Politics Show. It had been difficult, and the presenter, Colin Griffiths had certainly not made it any easier. He had known from the outset that Morrison would have to fight a rearguard action, that he could have no response to offer, as to why Hank Warren should issue such a strong warning about the dangers of independence from the oil industry perspective. Morrison felt that his hands were tied behind his back, he could not betray the confidences of the other oil companies and hint that they would actually welcome independence. He was left making a theoretical case for a Scottish government creating conditions that oil companies would welcome. It was then that Griffiths had produced the killer response. "What you are saying sounds all very plausible, First Minister, but it is all predicated on your sums and assumptions. As we found out the other night from your Finance Minister, some of your figures are just wrong. How can anybody be sure that your figures here are right? Why are you to be trusted on this when your government have got other things so wrong?" Morrison had given the usual answers, quoting independent researchers, and publicly available statistics. For all his skill, it still sounded hollow when placed against the mighty figure of Hank Warren, a colossus of the oil industry for half a century. The final nail in the coffin came at the end of the programme, when relaying a message from his producer, Colin Griffiths told the viewers in his gravest and most sincere voice "Within the last half hour, Hank Warren's death has been announced in Dallas, Texas, after a long illness. His three children were at his bedside when he passed away." Any sympathy that Morrison had managed to raise during the programme was immediately transferred to the legendary oilman.

It had been a bad couple of days for Alistair Morrison and his supporters. He had called an emergency meeting with his most trusted staff, Alex Watson, Mary Ford, and Donald Barrie. He had decided against inviting Christine Milne, who was still understandably fragile, and feeling it difficult to handle the barrage of criticism she was receiving from political opponents, the press, and some of her own colleagues, who were holding her responsible for handing the debate to the unionists. Morrison got everyone comfortably seated, then started. "We need some time to think about what is going on. A few weeks back we were leading the polls by a large margin. It seemed that we could do no wrong. It seemed that the unionists could do nothing right. I remember us thinking it was all too easy. I don't believe that we got complacent. We have continued to work hard. Somehow, though, things are slipping away from us. The opposition are ready for us at every turn. They have suddenly got well briefed speakers. Now we are being hit with unexpected problems. Christine's debate was an example, and Hank Warren's interview, too. Is there any way we could have seen them coming? Are there any more on the horizon? If so, what can we do about it? We have about ten days to turn this around, otherwise we will lose the referendum. It is as simple as that. Your thoughts, please?"

"You know," said Mary Ford, "things seemed to start to change just about the time of the anti-royalist story from Glenturrach. Things have never felt quite the same since."

Alex Watson let out a sigh. "For once I might have an advantage over you. Being an MP at Westminster I'm just that bit removed from the day to day campaigning that you are all involved in, so maybe I've had a bit more time to think about things. Here, on the ground you have had to react, and you have not always had the luxury of thinking time. What I'm offering is a theory. I

49

lave no evidence. I'm suggesting that our unionist friends have been playing a dangerous game. They let us build up a lead in the polls, because the task would be to criticise us. If they were ahead in the polls they would have to defend their position, and the arguments against the Union are easier to make than the arguments for. I am saying, by letting us build a lead, they have ensured that the debate is about reasons to avoid independence, and not on reasons to abandon the Union. Equally, the arguments have shifted. Nobody is having to make a case for the Union. Nobody is talking about the Union at all. The entire debate is now centred on reasons why people should not vote for independence. Even we are getting drawn away from the basics, instead of promoting the case for independence, we are spending too much time responding to attacks. These attacks have become increasingly well coordinated, and that is what makes me think that this was the plan all along. I just can't see how they could go from being so inept two months ago to being on top of everything now, unless they were being deliberately inept."

Morrison looked thoughtful. "That sounds plausible, Alex, but where does it leave us? In effect you are saying that we have an opponent that has better thought out their tactics than we have. If that is right, how do we turn that round?"

Mary Ford shook her head. "There is more to it than that. We all know Christine, and we know Edith Bannon. No disrespect to her, but Christine is in a different class. She should have won that debate by a mile. Donald and I watched a recording. It was painful, but we did. Edith Bannon was prepared. She knew that Christine had the wrong figures. You can see her getting excited before Christine quoted the figures. I agree, Alex, they have upped their game, but I think they are getting inside information that is helping them prepare. You know, I had a bit of an alarm bell going off when I couldn't get to the bottom of the Glenturrach incident, but I got caught up in other things. When you start to think about it, that must have been one of the branch members who made the recording and then sent it to the press. One of our members. I'm talking about an inside job."

Morrison looked at Donald Barrie. "Is this true?"

"Yes, boss, certainly as far as the debate goes. Mary and I played it back half a dozen times. The camera is on Christine, but you can see Edith in the background. She knew that the mistake was going to come. You can see her body tense, and her hands clench as soon as Christine started the sentence. When Christine mentioned the report by name, she nearly fell off the podium in excitement. This was before Christine had quoted any figures. Christine gave the figures at the end of the sentence, but Edith was already reacting at the beginning of the sentence."

"Alright then," said Morrison, "let us assume there is an insider feeding information over. There may be more than one. Who is it? How do we find out? How do we know who we can trust, if we don't know who we can't trust? How do we find out what else has been leaked to the unionists?"

Alex Watson interjected. "I'm not saying that we don't have a mole, or moles in our midst. We may well have. It doesn't explain the Hank Warren story though, does it?"

Morrison was about to speak when his phone rang. He listened for a minute then put the phone down. "This is urgent, and it may just give us the answer to where the next surprise is coming from. That was Tom Thomson. He'll be with us in a minute."

Tom Thomson was the Transport Secretary. A small, good natured Aberdonian, Thomson had been a marine engineer before going into politics. By his own admission, he was not the greatest public orator ever to stand for election, and that would hold him back should he ever seek a higher profile job. He was, however, highly respected by all those who knew him. He was tough and competent and thoroughly reliable. It took him less than half a minute to join the others. His eyes were devoid of their usual twinkle. "We have just had this through, and it has gone out through the Holyrood press office as normal. The whole world can see this, and it is wrong." He waved a piece of paper in the air. "This is the monthly update on the A9 from the contractors Readybuild. It says that the project is in trouble. It says that we are running six months behind and projecting a £5 million overspend. That is nonsense, but it has circulated to the press. As you know we circulate these reports as a matter of practice, hiding nothing. It is part of our public accountability. We're actually well ahead of schedule and under budget. I got in touch with the guys at Readybuild and they say they stand by their report, quoting a geological problem that would lead to flooding. Sheer nonsense! We knew about the fault before we let the contract, and we've taken all the necessary steps to deal with it. This is an outrage!"

Tom Thomson indeed looked outraged. Morrison made him sit down. "Tom, I am not going to ask silly questions. If you say this report is nonsense, I believe you. This is the latest in a series of events showing things to be going wrong, or questioning facts. This is in some way related to the referendum, not to the A9 project. The question is, what are we going to do about it?"

It was Donald Barrie who cut in. "This has been nicely set up. You have to admire them, whoever they are. Given the events of the last few days, if we simply issue a statement saying that the contractor has got it wrong, we will get it thrown back at us. We will get it represented as another occasion where we say one thing but the experts say something else. This is an attack on the perception of our competence. It is not an attack on our competence as a government, it is an attack on the public perception of our competence. We have got to go beyond issuing a statement that puts us at odds with the contractor. Remember that their information is out there first, so we are going to be on the back foot again. Tom, you said that the flooding problem had been addressed. Presumably there is some evidence of that, or at least we can get some independent expert to confirm that all necessary steps have been taken. You see what I'm driving at? Instead of pitting politician against expert, deploy expert witness against the contractor."

Tom's face was set in grim determination "I see what you mean, Donald. There is a report, but it is rather long, and very technical. It would take a fair bit of work to get it into the right language. The other problem is that most of the work was done by an engineering firm that is now one of Readybuild's main subcontractors. They use them on work all over the country, so they will not want to be set up as being in opposition to Readybuild. How about this as a compromise? I spend the next few hours with my technical staff summarising the technical report, then do a press conference at which I wave the report about, and offer to make it publicly available."

Mary Ford nodded. "That might be the best we can do. I'd be sure that the unionists were anticipating this, just like they have known about everything else before it happened. They will have their reaction ready, and this is us just learning about the problem."

Donald Barrie added, "Tom, you go off and prepare. Be ready for hostile questions. Try just to stick to facts, and avoid getting into an argument. I'll organise a press conference for 3 p.m. Does that give you enough time?"

Tom Thomson looked at watch. "Four hours. I'll be ready." With that he was on his way.

An hour later, Morrison, Barrie and Alex Watson were huddled round the TV. It was the noon news bulletin, and Edith Bannon was being interviewed. "Well, things just keep getting worse for the separatist government. On top of all the things they have been getting wrong, we now hear that their flagship infrastructure project is in tatters. The A9 project, it turns out is overspent and running late, not as they would have us believe, going on smoothly ahead of schedule and within budget. Their much vaunted claim that they can manage the finances of Scotland is once more called into question. I take no pleasure in this morning's revelation that this project is in such a mess, but we must wonder if there is anything they can be trusted with. Simply, they kept insisting that everything was under control, and if it were not for the contractor coming out and telling us the truth, no doubt this illusion would be maintained. It is typical of the separatists that they try to use the information for their own ends, and that the information is manipulated to help their arguments. What we have seen over the last few weeks, as they come under closer scrutiny is that many of their claims don't stand up. This, I'm afraid, is another. No doubt they will be rushing off to produce a press release saying that the contractor has got it wrong, or there are other interpretations you can put on their report. I ask them just to come clean and admit that there is a problem. Would you trust this lot or a major contractor who has to work with government agencies on many projects to give out accurate information?"

The interview drifted on for another couple of minutes, before they cut to another story about a footballer seeking clearance to play for Scotland. Morrison looked at his colleagues. "I'd guess she was briefed more than an hour ago. Clever, how she has set us up against the contractor, his word against ours, but implied we have reason to misrepresent the facts while the contractor doesn't. She has even been briefed on how we are likely to respond. I don't think she worked that out since the report went public. It was almost as if she were telling the media what questions to ask at Tom's press conference."

Donald Barrie stood up, his face dark with worry as he walked to the door. "I'm going to see how Tom is getting on. I wonder if he saw that. I'll warn him what he is getting into."

Alex Watson looked at Morrison. "I wonder if any of us know what we have got into," he said slowly.

Tom Thomson's press conference was packed. Newspaper journalists, TV cameras, radio mikes and photographers were all jostling for position. Thomson was not a natural performer in front of the media, and would normally have felt intimidated by such a gathering. Instead, he felt a cold fury. A fury against whoever was setting him up, against what he now understood was a concerted campaign against the referendum, against those who would malign the excellent work that his staff had undertaken to ensure the project was going well. Yet he kept himself under control, and knew that he would resist the urge to tell that the contractor was deliberately misleading the world.

He started. "Ladies and gentlemen, thank you for attending at such short notice. I have an announcement to make on the A9 upgrade project. I am in receipt of the report issued earlier this morning by Readybuild Ltd, the main contractor on the project. As you no doubt all know by now, that report indicates that the project is projected to run six months behind schedule and to overspend the budget by £5.1 million. Readybuild's report attributes this to a small geological fault on the northern section of the route. There is a danger highlighted, that by blasting the rock in this vicinity, as we will have to do as part of the construction, we may cause an area of land around the fault line to flood, and so create a small lake or loch. Should this occur, it would affect some farm land, and would require the rerouting of that section of the A9. This would not, however, cause a six month delay and cost £5.1 million. Those figures are taken from a feasibility report carried out three years before the project started. It would in fact delay the project by over one year, perhaps as much as two years, because we would have to acquire the land for the alternative route. It would have been a six month delay had we taken out a preliminary purchase agreement on the land required for the alternative route. It would not cost us £5.1 million, but a sum rather closer to £12 million. This is because the figures Readybuild have used relate only to the contract price and takes no account of the land purchase costs or the compensation to farmers whose land was flooded. So Readybuild have underestimated the scale of the problem. Their report is not factually correct."

Thomson stopped, and slowly looked round the room. Cameras were clicking, microphones were buzzing, but he had everybody's attention. He gave it time to sink in. Things were actually much worse than the Readybuild report. Then he continued. "Because we knew all this as a consequence of the feasibility study carried out well before the route was selected, we knew about this problem. Our engineers were confident that some engineering works could be carried out in advance of the work starting on the project, and that this work would eliminate the possibility of flooding. That work involved creating underground drainage for the water lying in subterranean pools near the fault. Five such pools were identified, and three were found to contain significant volumes of water. The other two were relatively minor. All five have been drained, and permanent drainage infrastructure put in place so that they cannot refill. Remember, ladies and gentlemen, that this was a theoretical problem. It was by no means certain that rock blasting would create the flooding. Yet we have taken every precaution.

"Clearly, someone has misinformed Readybuild, who seem to be unaware of this drainage work. I have here a copy of the all the work schedules and completion certificates relating to the works that I have referred to. My officials will be forwarding a copy of the file to Readybuild for their scrutiny. Readybuild have shown themselves to be excellent contractors and I regard them as valued partners in this project. My officials are also reviewing the file to remove any commercially sensitive material and we hope that once that is completed within the next two days to make it available to the public. I am sorry that you have all come along here for what is probably very much a non story, but I thought it was the right thing to do so that the record could be corrected at the earliest possible opportunity.

"Now let me fill you in on some of the details of the drainage work." Tom Thomson spoke for the next ten minutes. An engineer by profession, he went over in great detail the various technical aspects involved in the drainage schemes, and it was clear that few, if any, of the journalists understood much of what he was saying.

At the end of the conference, Thomson was greeted by Barrie, Morrison and Alex Watson. Morrison shook him warmly by the hand. "Tom, I know how difficult that must have been. You were great. I've never seen you perform so well. You had them eating out of your hand. That hit all the right notes. You were factual and not confrontational. You bamboozled them with detail, and you left them in no doubt that you knew exactly what you were talking about. You should be proud."

"Alistair, if I never have to do that again it will be too soon. It was the thought of getting one back on the dirty tricks brigade that kept me going. I'm off back to my department to oversee what we're doing with issuing this report."

Barrie observed, "He did a grand job, did Tom. Better than I could have hoped for. Yet all he could do was kill the story. He has made it a non story. It won't be rerun on the evening bulletins. However, people will have seen the lunchtime nonsense, and Edith Bannon has got her version out there. A lot of people will have seen that. It will stick, and they will think there is no smoke without fire."

Chapter Seven

Dejection

One week to go until the referendum, and Morrison had called an emergency meeting of the Referendum Team. There was a grim atmosphere in the room, like a feeling of impending defeat. The latest opinion polls had just been published, and Donald Barrie prepared to go through them, with the air of a man already beaten.

"The polls don't look good. Support for independence is melting away. In fact it is looking like we are going to take a real pasting. 29% for, 56% against, and the rest are don't knows. That means that people are not just shifting from us to unsure. They are shifting all the way from independence to the Union. We have taken a real hammering over the last few weeks, and the polls reflect it. Indeed, we are still taking a hammering, despite all we've done. I am at my wits end. I don't know what to suggest for the next week. I can't see how we can turn this round. Can anyone?"

After a prolonged silence, Alex Watson asked, "Is there any good news?"

"Well," Barrie went on, "Tom's efforts at the press conference seem to have done a bit of good. A couple of the papers and one TV bulletin reported on how well he seemed to be on top of his brief, and how capably he had handled the problem. But that is about it. The press has become difficult. Even the ones I've got really good relations with are writing editorials warning people away from independence. There is a new sense of hostility towards us. Or maybe I'm imagining some of it, because I just feel so embattled."

Christine Milne, who had been deliberately protected from some of the front line campaigning since her mauling at the hands of Edith Bannon was looking much fresher now, and had clearly restored some of her spirits. "Somebody once said that a week is a long time in politics. We are up against it, no doubt. We are not just going to accept defeat, are we? Everything has changed, but nothing has really changed. The case for independence remains. We know that. There is the unsatisfactory economic performance over the last hundred years, caused by lack of targeted investment, poor housing, and the worst health record in Western Europe that the Union has presided over, and all the arguments that we are familiar with. Let us use the last week, getting out there and pushing these messages."

Alex Watson looked tired. The bags under his eyes hung like deflated balloons. He sounded tired. "A week is indeed a long time in politics. Last week was the longest I've ever experienced. I wondered if it would ever come to an end. Look at us. We have worked ourselves to a standstill. Everyone in this room, and many, many of our supporters across Scotland, and beyond. Donald puts it well. We are taking a hammering. Now, the great Scottish hero, Robert the Bruce knew that when you faced a beating, the thing to do was to leave the field, and live to fight another day. Well, we are facing a beating, but it's not so easy for us to leave the field. If we take much more of a beating, we won't be able to fight another day. If the referendum goes the way the polls suggest, nobody will take Scottish independence claims seriously for the next hundred years. I think we should look at a damage limitation strategy, and maybe we can come back in ten or fifteen years, if we don't lose too badly."

It was the first time anyone had actually mentioned losing, and it reduced the room to momentary silence. Mary Ford smiled weakly. "Always the realist, Alex. To be honest, I don't think we have any cards left to play. I cannot think how we even approach damage limitation. The rate at which support is leaving us suggests we might be lucky to get 20% in favour of independence. There will be no way back from that. Donald, you have set up all these events for the girls, Mary, Lorna and Jo. What are they going to say? Are they just going to be lambs to slaughter? If we have no cards left, we can't give the three of them any material. I fear we are just going to end up with them being outgunned. I know they are good performers and know their stuff, but they have never had to deal with this level of hostility."

Despite his exhaustion, Donald was still thinking clearly. He remembered that they had almost agreed that there might be a mole operating. The conversation had never been finished, and with all the action and breaking stories, they had never revisited the subject, possibly because it was too painful to think of one of their colleagues as the mole. "Maybe you are right, Mary. Let me think about it. None of them deserve to be hung out like that."

"Is there nothing positive we can do?" Christine Milne was distraught. Although she understood that she had been supplied with wrong information prior to the debate with Edith Bannon, she still blamed herself. In her mind, her performance that evening had started the slide, and everything else that had happened was a result of that debate.

"It is really not my place to say this." Suddenly, all eyes were on Reginald Small, the meticulous and neatly dressed civil servant. Some of the team had almost forgotten that he was there, so quietly did he perform his role, so unassuming his manner. When he spoke, it was quietly, with every word clearly enunciated. "You said a few minutes ago that you have no cards left to play. That is not correct, I think. You will recall the EXCOL report. That discussed among other things the long term future for oil and gas in Scottish waters. Now, I know that the late Mr Warren's interview casts doubt on whether oil companies would invest in a newly independent Scotland. However, if reserves are going to last for forty or fifty years, Scotland would not be newly independent for most of that time. There would come a time when you could no longer regard Scotland as a newly independent nation."

They all looked at him, considering what he had just said, and working out the implications. It was the beginning of a strategy, but could it be developed into something workable for the last week of the campaign?

None of them could think clearly enough to see how this could be used. Exhaustion, lack of sleep compounded with the dread of impending defeat had drained them of all powers of clarity of thought. They were going through the motions of running a campaign, but there was no impetus left. They were playing for the highest stakes and were losing. Yet a few short weeks ago, it had all seemed so different.

Alistair Morrison had kept deliberately silent during the meeting. He was trying to weigh up the mood in his team, to judge who was still ready for battle, and who, understandably, had had enough. He knew now that his team were through, they had nothing left to give. They had given all that they could. For all her spirit, Christine Milne was still too fragile to be used in the front line over the next week. The disastrous debate had taken more out of her than anybody realised, and she was being too hard on herself. It was as though she had assigned responsibility for everything that had gone wrong with the campaign to that one event, and she alone was liable for that. Donald too, who had been a rock throughout the long campaign and a constant source of support and sound advice, was just about finished. He could detect the odd flash of resilience, but Donald Barrie had given his all. He had worked himself to standstill. No one had given more, had dedicated more hours than the young Invernesian. Alex Watson, steady, sensible Alex, had never looked so broken. He was the oldest of them all. He was taking what looked like inevitable defeat harder than any of them. Morrison could only guess at what it had cost him psychologically to discuss the possibility, or rather the probability, of defeat. He had given thirty five years of his adult life to the struggle for independence, and if it didn't happen now, it never would for Alex. Mary Ford, he thought looked lost, almost as if she had no more interest in what was happening. Morrison was slightly surprised at this, for he had always considered her to be indestructible, despite her tiny stature. In the past, no fight had been too big for her, she backed down from nothing. Now she was there, but her eyes were devoid of expression, her shoulders sunken. These were people Morrison had come to know as friends as well as colleagues. People he held in high regard. They were his hand-picked team for the most important campaign he would ever fight. He had no doubt about their calibre. How, he wondered, had it come to this? He was their leader, and not only was their cause looking to be lost, but his friends were lost too. It was his fault. No, not his fault, but his responsibility. What could he do in this last week? Had Reginald Small given him the one piece of information that could start a fightback?

At length, he addressed them all with firm resolution. His mind was set. His tone brooked no argument. "I have lead this campaign. You have, all of you, given more support than I could have thought possible. None of you have anything to reproach yourselves for. I want you all to go home, switch off your TVs and switch off your phones. Spend the next twenty four hours away from all of this. Watch a movie, play with your kids or just stay in bed. I will see you all in two days time, and the world will be a different place, one way or another. Donald, before you go, and you are going home to your wife and young daughter, I need you for half an hour to set up a media conference for me. I am going to tell the people of Scotland why they should vote for independence next week, and it is, as Reginald has reminded us, all to do with oil."

There were some token protests, but in reality, they were all relieved to be given the opportunity to take some time off.

After the others had left, Morrison spoke with Barrie. "Thanks for staying behind, Donnie. I just need to go over a couple of things with you, and then you are going home to rest. I will need you bright, rested and fresh later in the week. First, can you get me a slot on a prime current affairs programme tomorrow? I will be making an announcement about the future of oil revenues after independence. Second, I noticed how coy you were when Mary, Lorna and Jo were mentioned. What gives?"

"Well, boss, I was just thinking about the conversation we had about the possibility of a mole. I didn't want to be drawn on what I would go over with them in case the mole got to know. It would be bad if they went to events only to be mugged by opponents who have been tipped off about what they are going to say. It is horrible to think that there is a leak coming from one of us, but I think we have to face up to that possibility."

"Fair, enough, Donnie. I can't bring myself to believe that we have a mole, but there is no denying that our every move seems to be anticipated. You are wise to take precautions. Let us keep it that way. What were you thinking of them to discuss?"

"I am meant to be meeting with them in about an hour. I am going to tell them to stay on safe ground, Scotland's heritage, our contribution to science and the arts, and to use safe comparisons of similar sized independent countries like Denmark who do not dream of giving up their independence."

"That seems sound. You go home, Donnie, and I'll meet with them and give them your briefing."

Even as Donald Barrie was closing the door, Morrison was reaching for a copy of the EXCOL report from a shelf behind his desk.

That night, Alistair Morrison looked over the third draft of his presentation. He was finally happy with it. He had worked at it for a long time, and he realised that this was because he, like his colleagues, was too tired, and sick at heart. This was his final shot. He was like a boxer who had been on the ropes for most of the fight, and has agreed with his corner that he would have one more round before they threw in the towel. His presentation was, of course based on the EXCOL report, and drew heavily on their figures. The key points were obvious. Oil and gas revenues would give a balance of payments surplus of around £12 billion, rising in times of higher production to £17 billion, and this was a situation that would last for at least forty five years, before reserves began to dwindle. Even then, revenues would run at significant levels for another twenty years. Using the lower figure, this represented £2400 for every man, woman and child living in Scotland. He had a case to put to the Scottish people. Yet through his exhaustion, for the first time in his life, having a positive message to deliver, curiously failed to buoy him up as he went to bed, hoping for his first good sleep in weeks.

Next morning Morrison was having his usual light breakfast of toast and coffee. He was aware that the broadcast he would be doing in a couple of hours should have him excited. It was one of the activities he enjoyed most, normally. He knew, without conceit, that he was a good television performer, and as always, was well prepared. Somehow, that morning, he had no feeling of excitement, and no anticipation that things would go well. He just felt flat, and without expectation. As he drank his coffee, he watched the early morning news bulletin on the small TV set in the kitchen at Bute House, only half concentrating. The early morning sun that had streamed through the window when he had risen had now given way to a grey sheet of drizzle that looked as though it would last for hours, and seemed to reflect his mood. He caught himself allowing his mind to wander to what he might say the morning after the referendum to mitigate the defeat. As he forced himself back to the present, he was aware that on the television, Tom Albright, the Chancellor of the Exchequer was being interviewed. He was a smooth operator, always sounding plausible, but Morrison knew him to be inflexible in his approach to economics. Relatively young for such high office, he was well built, and liked to portray himself as a bit of a sports fan, and was often seen at rugby and tennis matches. Morrison was aware suddenly that Albright was talking about Scotland.

"The report in today's Economics Review exposes the separatists' case for economic independence for the sham that it is. What this argues, quite coherently, is that if the Scottish economy went massively into surplus, because of excessive income from oil, it would present real difficulties for their economy. Remember, though, there is no certainty that it would have these revenues, as Hank Warren explained in his last ever interview that international companies would desert Scotland as a new and potentially extremist nation. But let us assume that does not happen, and all these oil revenues flow into the Scottish economy. You might think that would be good for Scotland, but this article explains that it would actually be detrimental. Put in simple terms the problems are these. Such a surplus would make the Scottish currency strong, but so strong that it would affect their balance of payments in other ways. Imports would be cheap, and goods manufactured in Scotland would become expensive for overseas markets. That would mean a long term decline in Scottish industrial growth and unemployment would follow. In effect, the income from oil would be spent on cheap imports, while Scottish industry went to the wall. Scottish goods would be too expensive to export, and even in the home market, would lose out to cheaper imported goods. While Scotland was cash rich, it would be losing all its industrial base, and creating mass unemployment.

"In effect, if Hank Warren is right they will be unable to develop with a manageable economy because the oil companies will leave. If Hank Warren turns out to be wrong, they will have too big a surplus, and become industrially bereft."

The interviewer asked what effect this would have on the referendum debate and vote. Albright continued. "Well, the Scots are a sensible lot. We can see in the polls of the last few weeks that they can see through the wild claims and extremism of the separatists. This article in the Economics Review just exposes one more flaw in the separatists' case. Most Scots know that the best way forward for them is to stick with the Union and to remove all this uncertainty. We can face the challenges that the future brings together. Together, we are stronger. I am sure that will be reflected in the vote."

Morrison switched the TV off. He could hardly believe what he had just heard. This was an old argument, and there was no doubt that an over strong currency presented problems, but economists had long ago worked out strategies for dealing with those problems. However, he thought about the presentation he was about to give, which was based on how a strong surplus was a good thing. He realised, with a growing sense of frustration that the article that Tom Albright had been referring to actually argued the opposite. The article had been published in what was probably the most respected economics journal in Europe, and people who did not understand the details of economic policy would give that more credence than a politician arguing the opposite. How had Tom Albright been on to this so quickly? The journal was only published and distributed overnight. Even the on line version would not have become available before midnight. With a shrug of resignation, he booted up his laptop, and searched for the article. Wearily, he poured himself another coffee. It was going to be a long morning.

By midday, the First Minister was seated in the Edinburgh studio, feeling hot and uncomfortable under the camera lighting. He had spent two hours reworking his material, and had not had the opportunity to go over it as thoroughly as he would have wished. He felt rushed, having arrived later than intended, and the make-up people and sound engineer had fussed over him since he arrived. He hardly felt settled. Opposite him was the programme anchor man, Eric Dalton, all slick hair and nasal voice, armed with his clipboard full of notes, supplied by an army of researchers. As the titles ran, he started. "Today we are pleased to welcome Alistair Morrison, the First Minister of Scotland. Viewers will know that it is six days until the referendum on Scottish independence takes place, and I am sure that the First Minister will wish to take the opportunity of promoting the case for independence. His party have, after all, made it clear all along that they wish Scotland to break away from the rest of the United Kingdom, and it is his party that have called the referendum. Given the latest opinion polls, however, it looks as though the voters will not support that. Commentators know that much of the case for independence has been based on the Scottish economy being shored up by oil and gas revenues. However, this morning's edition of the influential journal Economics Review made it quite clear that the oil revenues would be a mixed blessing, or maybe a sheep in wolf's clothing. Here is what the Chancellor, Tom Albright had to say earlier."

The programme cut to a clip of the breakfast interview with the Chancellor, before returning to Eric Dalton, smiling, almost leering at Alistair Morrison. "Well First Minister, they say there is a problem. What do you say?"

"Of course there is a problem. There is a problem with independence. The problem is that it isn't easy. If it were easy, we would have been independent long ago. But just because it's not easy doesn't mean it's not worth having. Independence is not an end in itself. It is the vehicle to enable us to create a better society, more just, and more responsible. It is the vehicle to enable us to take our full place in the society of nations, to not be separatists, but to be joiners. We want Scotland to join the international community. Now, let us look at the specific problem raised in the article in the Economics Review. Let me be quite clear. They are right when they say that there is a potential danger. However, there is also a potential opportunity, and I am rather surprised that the article did not balance the two. It is how we grasp the opportunity that removes the risk. If we were simply to gather in all the revenue then the problems the authors describe would surely follow. What we must do is have a strategy for managing the surplus. Economists have been well aware of this danger for some decades, and have devised a number of possible strategies which can be adopted. Also, they make it clear that you can use a mixture of strategies or change strategies as circumstances change. My government is well aware of the options, and from the clip you showed of the Chancellor, he appears not to be."

Dalton interrupted. "First Minister, over the last few weeks we have seen a series of instances where you and your colleagues have been at odds with independent assessments, where your figures have been wrong. Why are you right and the Economics Review journal wrong?"

Morrison had been expecting this line of questioning, "Eric, perhaps you should ask their editorial team why they allowed such an unbalanced article to be published. I don't know why they did that. Look, the unionists tell us that we would have too much money, yet the surplus would be less than they gave to the banks to bail them out of their debt crisis. On the one hand we would be too poor to prosper, on the other they tell us we would be too rich to prosper. How can that be correct? I say that a properly managed surplus will provide us with a tremendous opportunity. Let me get to specific strategy options for managing a surplus. The simplest one is to slow down the exploration rates in the North Sea, that would mean the revenues would come at a slower, more manageable rate. Or there are infrastructure schemes we could invest in, which would actually make Scotland more competitive, not less competitive. Improving transport links and high speed broadband would help, for example. A programme of slum replacement is long overdue, and there is no prospect of that happening while the purse strings are controlled from London. Or we could follow the Norwegian model and create a futures fund, where the excess revenue gets set aside for future generations, or used for large one off capital projects. We might have funded the new Forth Bridge this way. Or we could lend our surplus at reasonable rates to less fortunate countries, the third world or places where natural disasters have occurred. My government would have no intention of just letting the revenues accumulate. We will use them sensibly and wisely for Scotland."

The slot was just about up, and Eric Dalton was wrapping the interview up. His closing lines came up on the autocue. "Thank you, First Minister for sharing your ideas with us. It is for viewers to make up their own minds. You have a respected and independent journal and the Chancellor lined up on the one hand and the First Minister on the other, saying things that are complete opposites. Who would you believe?"

When the First Minister got back to his office he was amazed to see Donald Barrie waiting for him. Barrie held up a hand, half in greeting, and half in apology. "I know, boss, you said take the day off. I'm OK, really. Yesterday afternoon, last night and this morning were enough. You were right, though, I didn't realise how much I needed the break."

As Morrison guided him into the room, Barrie continued. "In the circumstances, what with the Economics Review article coming out of the blue, you were brilliant. I thought you had it. What is going on though? That report is so obviously biased!"

"Aye, Donnie, I was ahead, right up to Dalton's summation. That was nothing to do with the rights and wrongs of the argument. He was just casting doubt on our trustworthiness. It actually doesn't matter how much my arguments are right if nobody believes them, and our problem is that these days, nobody believes us. On economics, the man in the street probably isn't all that interested in detail, he just wants to know that the economy is in good hands. I think that when the dust settles, today will be marked down as another bad one for us. We can win all the arguments, but unless we win the trust, we lose the vote. That is what we have got to do over the next few days. I'm afraid, Donnie, I gave a bit of different advice to Mary, Lorna and Jo. I have told them to concentrate on being sincere, to tell everybody that they are mums, and this is for the future of their children, a future they would not take chances with."

Donald Barrie nodded in quiet acquiescence.

In London, in an office in 10 Downing Street, the Prime Minister poured two pale sherries from a crystal decanter, and handed one to Penny Carson. He permitted himself a satisfied smile. "Let us toast victory. You can almost admire Morrison, you know, the way he came out fighting in that interview, but he has nowhere to go."

Penny smiled back, enjoying the moment, "I know what you mean. Sir David thinks of everything. One of his men was called in as a late replacement technician. The usual one developed a mysterious stomach bug. He was working Dalton's autocue at the end. I will have the briefing for the live debate ready in good time for Richard Hume. Sir David and I have been working on it over the last week. Even Sir Michael Hammond could not go wrong with this brief. Richard will enjoy taking Morrison to pieces in front of a live audience. It will be the final nail in their coffin."

Chapter Eight

The Hacker

Shona Murray felt angry and degraded. She always felt this way after a visit from Mr Wylie, her probation officer. It wasn't him particularly. In fact, over the last year, she had come to acknowledge that he probably was on her side, and had helped with a number of things. It was the whole set up. Every second week he called at her flat. They had agreed this at the beginning of her probation. It was easier than going to his office, and he could always report that he had looked round the flat. That let him report on one of her release conditions. She was not allowed to own a computer, or have access to one at work. Wylie had managed to get her a part time job at the local supermarket, where she did not come into contact even with the stock control computer. Who could live in the twenty-first century without access to a computer? He had just left, and she was in her kitchen, making a pot of tea. Her one bed roomed flat looked out over the North Sea, and she could just catch views of the harbour at Montrose as she went to close the curtains. There she saw her reflection staring back at her from the window pane. She was not yet twenty eight but her life was a mess. Her skin was colourless, grey from four years in prison. Her hair was straight and featureless. It still had the blond appearance, and maybe something could be done with it. Her figure was still good, so there was some hope there. Her eyes were permanently sad. Her clothes were cheap, many of them second hand, bought at charity shops. She lived alone, and had no real friends. Would this be her lot for the rest of her life? The girls in the supermarket were nice enough, but they didn't really mix. They all had their own lives. It had all been so different before the trial. She had just finished University, where she got a good degree, she had a nice boyfriend, foreign holidays, and lots of parties, and cinema trips and so on. She was looking forward to a good career. The world had been her oyster.

Her reverie was disturbed as the door bell rang. She didn't get visitors. It would be kids, or somebody collecting for charity. She closed the curtains and went to open the door. She instantly recognised the man there. He was greyer than she remembered; he looked older, in his sixties, perhaps. Casual dress, different glasses, heavier ones, from the last time she saw him. He seemed smaller than she remembered, and he had put on a lot of weight, though certainly he wasn't fat. Her voice was a whisper, barely audible, "Mr Chisholm." It wasn't a greeting, and it wasn't a question, just an observation.

"Hello, Shona. I know I'm not the most welcome visitor, but I come bearing gifts. A Chinese Take Away and a bottle of wine. Sweet and sour, and chicken with green ginger. Can I come in, please? I have a proposition which I think will interest you."

"The last time I saw you, you didn't ask. You have some nerve, coming here. I thought I would see you at the trial, coming to gloat, but then I realised you were too important to come to that. So, why are you here now? I've done nothing wrong, my probation officer has just left, and he'll confirm that I'm being a good girl these days. So say what you've come to say, then go. You are the last person I'd invite in."

"I know that you have no reason to help me, but nevertheless I'm here to ask for your help. You see, I have a little problem, and you are the one person I know that has the skills to help me. Let me in Shona, before the food gets cold. Hear me out, and if you want me to go after that, I will. You'll never see me again, I promise."

Shona thought about it for a moment, and decided she owed this man nothing. "You ruined my life. You have no idea what the last five years have been like for me. If you did, you wouldn't have the nerve to ask me for help. Just go away and leave me in peace." Shona was vaguely aware that she was shouting loudly, but she didn't care. Her anger at the sheer effrontery of Chisholm's approach had fired up her temper. He was the man in charge of the security services investigation that had lead to her imprisonment, and now here he was, turning up on her doorstep like a long lost friend.

"Please, Shona, call me David. I know our history is that we were on the opposite sides of the law, but I mean you no harm. I couldn't come to your trial, because it would have blown my cover in other operations that I was involved in. I followed it closely, though. Something you said in your defence always stuck with me. You said that you had been trapped by people who were trying to protect the state from individuals, but that all you were guilty of was trying to protect individuals from the state. I thought about that for a long time. I guess that is why I'm here, in part.

"Let me explain. Hear me out for a minute or two and if you want me to go, then I will, but I think you might be interested in helping, because this time I'm on the side of the citizen, against the state. I'm retired now, I have been for three years. Just after your arrest I was promoted to one of the Deputy posts within MI5, but it just wasn't me. I was a field agent, not a desk man, so as soon as I hit sixty, I retired. After thirty two years. So let me make it quite clear. I am not here on official business. Do you know what I believed I was doing all of these years with MI5? I was fighting for democracy. It is as simple as that. I believed that I was protecting the state from attack. I was helping to secure our future. I still believe that, Shona. That was the case most of the time. I'll admit we made our share of mistakes, but that sort of goes with the nature of the job. Maybe your case was one of them. For me it was always about protecting democracy. People higher up than me decided that what you were doing was a threat. Listening to you at your trial was the first time I wondered who democracy was for. For what it is worth, I thought your sentence was too severe."

Shona responded angrily. "The nuclear agencies were withholding important information about leaks of radiation from the public. They had decided that the people who lived and worked near these leaks should be kept in the dark. All I did was get the information, and make it public."

"That is your interpretation, Shona. Others saw it differently. You hacked into the databanks of a government agency and stole information. Information that had been judged to have the potential to cause needless panic in the public. That is why it had not been released."

Shona Murray's eyes flashed. It was the first time in a long time that she had felt a stirring of such emotion. "I suppose public safety didn't come into it. The fact that the government were trying to get support for plans to build new nuclear power stations would have had nothing to do with the decision to hush up the problems. Yet I go to jail and have my life ruined, while they all go on as usual." Every word dripped with contempt.

Chisholm raised a hand "OK, Shona, as I say, that is your interpretation. Maybe you are right, who knows. What I do know is that it is not as black and white as I once thought. I am not going to argue with you, that's not why I am here. Before I get into that, let me ask what you make of the referendum campaign. I take it you have been following it?"

This abrupt change of subject threw Shona, and she couldn't think where this was heading, but she knew that this would not be a random question. It was being asked for a purpose. She was on her guard, and chose her response carefully. "It's not a case of following the referendum. You can't escape it. The TV, radio and newspapers are full of it. What do I make of it?" She shook her head. "It does seem like the independence lot have lost the plot. The last while they've gone from looking good to looking like clowns. That is a bit of a surprise, just how badly they have let it all slip away."

The man opposite nodded. "What if they are getting help to mess up? Help they don't know about. I know enough about how my old colleagues at MI5 work to detect their involvement here. Look, I am no supporter of Scottish Independence, but if there is to be a democratic vote, it should be a fair vote without dirty tricks. That is the opposite of what I spent my working life doing - protecting democracy, not interfering with it."

Chisholm continued his narrative. "However, I have no proof of MI5's involvement. But there will be files. Sir David Lee, the head of the service, is too careful to get involved in something like this without keeping a record. I believe that we have a major attempt to prevent a democratic referendum from taking place fairly. My interest lies in protecting democracy, but in order to do that I need to get evidence."

The girl opposite was laughing, as though genuinely amused. "Mr Chisholm, surely you do not want me to hack into the MI5 electronic files for you? You don't want me to breach my probation conditions, do you?" There was no mistaking the mockery in her manner.

"I'd prefer it if you called me David. I said if you want nothing to do with this, I'll walk away. Please, just hear me out. I know that I'm asking a lot. You are the only person I know with the ability to do this. I think that your observation at the trial about protecting individuals from the state was never more relevant than here. If I'm right, we have the British Government setting out with the help of one of its intelligence agencies to ensure that the democratic process is not allowed to operate. That is the opposite of what I worked for. I have come to the conclusion that our principles are maybe not that different, you and me. We are wanting the same thing, but have come at it from completely different directions. I do not want to let anyone away with defeating democracy, whether they are individual citizens or governments. I think that was your motivation too, when you exposed the nuclear leaks. That is why I want to expose what is going on now. As for you, Shona, it will be your decision. Think though, of the life you are currently leading. What prospects do you have? Where will you be in five years –

the same flat, the same job? What would you give for some excitement, in a just cause? I will not pretend that it will be easy, and we would potentially be exposing some very powerful people. The alternative is to turn a blind eye, and let them get away with it. I know that before your trial, you wouldn't have thought twice about this. Your sense of outrage would have driven you. I'm asking you to be that person again."

Shona thought about what Chisholm had said, and despite herself, she was intrigued. She realised that this was not the kind of conversation to have outside her door, so she gestured to Chisholm to come into her flat. She found two plates and served up the food, pouring the wine into two glasses. They both started eating.

Shona was quiet for a long time, occasionally sipping her wine. He had touched a raw nerve. There was no excitement in her life, no direction, and no purpose. Was that not exactly what she was thinking before he arrived? Yet if she got caught up in this, wouldn't she just end up back in prison? Any additional sentence could see her locked up for a very long time. She weighed up the options, and as she did so noted with some surprise, that Chisholm was making no further effort to influence her decision. Finally, she said, "If I do this, I get a few days of interesting things to work on. Then, if we succeed, we presumably have to go public with what we have found. At that point I'll be back in jail for breaching my probation conditions, and facing charges that will get me locked up for the next ten years. That does not sound like a good trade."

Chisholm nodded. "I knew that I was asking a lot. I know that there is a danger in this for you. I will try to minimise that risk for you. It is not my intention to have you returned to prison. Read this." He took a single sheet of paper from his pocket, and slipped it across the table.

It was a signed statement by Chisholm declaring that he was previously known to Shona Murray as an MI5 agent, and that he had approached her, leading her to believe that he still worked for MI5, that he had recruited her to work on a project that required her computer hacking skills, and that she believed she was working for MI5. The statement was on MI5 headed notepaper. She looked from the paper to him. "If you decide you can help me, keep that somewhere safe in case you do need to use it. Otherwise, obviously, I will need it returned."

Neither of them spoke for a few moments. Finally, Shona stirred from her thoughts and said, "You are really serious about this, aren't you? If we do this, how do we make things public? What happens to you at the end of it? I presume you have thought about that."

"Indeed I am serious. First, don't worry about me. I have decided that for my part, whatever comes my way is a price I'm prepared to pay. Anyway, I can look after myself. It is about being true to myself, and to my belief in democracy. I think there is less chance that I will end up in jail if we succeed, because of what I could bring out in a trial. As for going public, we have to do that before the referendum is held, so we don't have much time, just six days. How we release it, depends on the nature and extent of what we find, and the timescale. No press agency will touch any of this without time to verify everything, and you can be sure that the government will take out restraining orders and injunctions to try to stop publication, I have a couple of alternatives, but let's see where we are when we get the evidence."

Shona gave a deep sigh. "What do you do if I refuse to help, Mr Chisholm?"

"I really have no back-up plan. You have unique skills, and without your help, I cannot see how I can get hold of any evidence. I know where to look, and I know some of the people I would want to interrogate, but even if I were still working for MI5, it would take months of work to piece together. There are people involved in this that I couldn't get near. I guess I would do what I could, but that would be little enough."

Shona drained the last of the wine from her glass. "Very well, then. Count me in. We need to start right away, for we have so little time. You will know that it is part of my parole conditions that I have no computer equipment, so I have no tools to work with. What do you have?"

Chisholm stood up, and started pacing round the bare room. He was caught up in her sudden mood of urgency. He had not been sure that he would be able to persuade Shona Murray to help him, that had always been a potential weakness in the plan, but he had imagined what the next steps would be if she did agree.

"I have rented a cottage a few miles north of here. We will work from there. I took a chance that you would say yes, and have bought the equipment I think you will need. The cottage has a high speed internet connection. Anything more that you need, let me know, and I'll get it first thing in the morning. You should pack enough clothes for the next few days. Also pack your passport, for I might have to get you out of the country when we release the information to the public. Just until the heat dies down, and I get a chance to convince everybody that you were not at fault. Phone in now to your work, and tell them you need a few days off. Make whatever excuse you think best. You go and pack but first, lead me to the sink, and I'll wash up these dishes."

Within the hour, they were in Chisholm's powerful black Audi Avant Estate, driving north. The journey took no more than fifteen minutes, and they were in a secluded glen when he pulled off the road and parked on a gravel driveway beside a small whitewashed cottage. Chisholm lifted the suitcase from the boot of the car and lead Shona into the cottage. From the inside the cottage appeared bigger. They came to a sitting room which was large, and fitted out with two large comfortable sofas and a coffee table between them. A wide screen TV and CD player filled one corner of the room. Chisholm indicated ahead, and took the suitcase with him "This is your bedroom. Mine is just across the hall. The third bedroom is next door, and that is where I've stored all the kit. Why don't you unpack your things? I'll make us a coffee, and then you can inspect my purchases."

Shona was unpacked before the coffee was ready. She found Chisholm in the kitchen, busy with the cups. The kitchen was certainly well equipped with a fridge, freezer, double oven, microwave, four ringed hob, large electronic toaster, and she noticed, a fully stocked wine rack. She saw that the cups Chisholm was pouring the coffee into from the percolator were high quality porcelain, and she wondered how much he was paying for the cottage. Well, she reasoned, that was his problem.

As they drank their coffee she quizzed him on his knowledge of the MI5 information technology system. She had no difficulty in believing him when he told her that he was no expert for he seemed at sea whenever she mentioned a vaguely technical term, and even though any information he could offer would be out of date, she thought that it could be useful. In particular she spent a long time asking him to describe the file and folder structure. She tried hard not to become impatient with his lack of technical knowledge. Then they moved through to the third bedroom.

There was a single bed, piled high with boxes. There was a dressing table with a chair, the obvious place to set things up. Shona started to inspect the boxes. As far as she could see, Chisholm had bought more than she needed. Many of the items were over specified, and he had bought expensive gear. She thought that this probably betrayed his lack of knowledge, and rather than come up short, he had gone over the top. "Well, this lot must have set you back a bit!"

"That is why it was all still in the packaging. If you had turned me down, I'd be taking it back for a refund. It was all bought using a false name to make it harder for MI5 to track it to me. It will delay them, rather than stop them. Same with the cottage, I booked that using a false name. Is every thing OK with the equipment? Do you have all that you need?"

"False names won't put them off the trail for long, and once I log on to their site, the clock will start. As for the equipment, there is more than enough here. Leave me to get on with assembling it and getting connected to the internet. How did you know that I would need all of this?"

"I didn't know what you would need, but half an hour on the internet helped. Then a salesman who knew what he was talking about, but obviously thought he could make his month's bonus from one customer finished the job. Don't worry, the shop was at the other end of the country. Are you sure you want to start that tonight, Shona? It is already almost 10 o'clock."

"It won't take that long, Mr Chisholm. My shift at the supermarket started at half past seven this morning, so I am a bit tired. If I can get this set up tonight, though, we can get a flying start in the morning."

Ninety minutes later, Shona was tucked up in bed, confident that all of Chisholm's expensive material was set up and ready to go. For all her physical tiredness, though, she could not sleep. For the first time in years, she felt excited, too excited to sleep. Her mind was concentrated on possible strategies for accessing the MI5 materials. It was long after midnight that exhaustion turned to sleep.

Across the hall, David Chisholm could not sleep immediately either. He was still uneasy at the thought of involving the girl. He could be exposing her to all sorts of dangers. He knew that he was in danger himself. What he had said earlier about him not facing a trial or going to jail was true, but what he had not said, was that there were other, far more serious consequences that could occur for him. The one thing in his favour was that he knew how the minds of his former colleagues worked, what their tactics would be. Now the die was cast, there was no turning back.

Chapter Nine

Steal

When David Chisholm poked his unwashed, unshaven face round the bedroom door at eight o'clock, Shona Murray had showered and dressed and already put in an hour's work on the laptop computer she had unpacked the previous night. She looked up enquiringly from the screen. Chisholm, she thought, looked slightly comical without his glasses, and with his greying hair unruly and uncombed. He had obviously just pulled a jumper and a pair of jeans on. He still looked as though he was asleep. Indeed, instead of speaking, he let out an extended yawn.

"I'm just going to get washed. Then I'll make us both some breakfast. What do fancy?"

"Something hearty please. I'm hungry. Can it be ready in about half an hour, because I think I'll have some progress to report by then. I never thought it was going to be easy, but these guys are paranoid. They have all sorts of firewalls and cut outs, but I might be onto something. Mr Chisholm," she added as he withdrew, "grilled, not fried. It is much healthier."

Shona worked at the keyboard for just over an hour before Chisholm announced that breakfast was ready. They sat together over a mug of steaming hot coffee, and a plate of sausages, tomato, bacon, and mushrooms, all grilled and accompanied by scrambled eggs. Shona had to admit that Chisholm certainly seemed to know how to work in a kitchen. The sun was streaming in through the window, and they could hear through the open window, blackbirds chirruping. She could not remember the last time she had felt this alive. She knew that the feeling came from her attachment to a computer after a long absence. However, there was more than that. This cottage, secluded and sheltered, with the sounds of the birds, just seemed so clean and fresh compared to her run down flat. Things here were new and functional. Back home, everything was dreary. Her life and her surroundings were dull and uninspiring. Now, she was working on something that was maintaining her interest, not just in the technical issues associated with trying to break into the MI5 system, but the purpose behind it. Preventing the authorities from lying to or misleading the public excited her. This was why she had hacked into the nuclear agency's systems these years earlier. How strange that it was Chisholm, the man who put her behind bars then, who had lead her back to this, had brought her back to life. She felt comfortable in jeans and a T-shirt, just the kind of thing she would have worn before she was sent to prison.

Chisholm was now washed and shaved. His glasses were in place, but he still looked like a man set to relax for the day. He sat back comfortably, finishing his sausage. If he was worried, he concealed it well. Although they hardly exchanged a dozen words he had noticed a change in the girl, and hoped that it would last. Something was different about her this morning, and she looked happier, more alert, altogether better. Even when he was gathering evidence against her and arranging her arrest, he had never quite managed to see her as a criminal. Certainly, she had broken the law, but not for personal gain. He had always sensed a sort of moral outrage in her, like an over developed sense of fair play. At her trial, she had been vulnerable, deserted by everyone, her friends, even her boyfriend had been warned about continuing to associate with her. Her parents had disowned her, and he knew that they had since emigrated to New Zealand. She had been impressive in the witness box, never giving an inch to the prosecutor, but she was on her own. Even her legal team had only mounted a half hearted defence. He promised himself that he would not let more trouble into her life. He had already brought too much. There was a sudden realisation that he had admired her, and perhaps always had. Maybe not her, but what she stood for. He wondered if it amounted to the same thing. They had not discussed progress, and he judged that she was waiting for the right moment to tell him something important. From her demeanour and general cheerfulness, he thought it might be something positive, but he could not allow himself to build up his hopes. If she had good news, might not she have just blurted it out? Slowly, he became aware that she was watching him, a mischievous grin spreading across her face.

"Mr Chisholm, I believe I can do it. I think I've found a way in. It will not be easy, and they will be able to detect that I've been into their files. Their files are really well protected. They have firewalls, scanning systems and encryptions. I will not be able to get at their files directly. One of their systems is version 8.3 of ASS. That stands for Advanced Security System. It is really good at detecting any attempt to enter the system illegally. MI5 run it four times a day, every six hours. It is a full diagnostic check on every file and folder on the system. They have so much material that it takes it an hour to complete the check. Well, it takes fifty seven minutes to be precise. When they built ASS, they were concentrating on protecting and detecting violations of the system they are monitoring. They weren't thinking about anyone hacking into ASS itself. Now, I can hack into ASS, and while it is running its check on the system, it has access to all the folders. If I am in ASS while it has access to the MI5 folders, then, in theory I have access to them. Do you follow me so far?"

Chisholm nodded. Any technical details would be lost on him, but he could handle the straightforward version that the girl was offering. He drained his coffee, and indicated that she should continue.

"OK, then, this is our chance, but it is also our problem. What I have to do is get into ASS when it is running. The next time it is due is at noon. That is about two and a half hours from now. Once we are in, we have to find the right folder, and then copy it. We have to do this during the fifty seven minutes that ASS is scanning the files. Once ASS stops scanning the files,

I lose access. There is one more issue. Once we have identified the file, we have to wait until it has been checked by ASS. That means two things. Most importantly, it means that it won't be detected until the next scan, in six hours time. It also means that we will not run the risk of being detected when we are online, which would enable them to pinpoint exactly where we are. Are you still with me?"

Chisholm nodded. He was trying to take in all the implications of this. "So we have fifty seven minutes, but we can't start copying until we find the right file, and then we have to wait until that file has been scanned. Does that present us with a problem, Shona?"

"Potentially, it does, Mr Chisholm. First, we have to recognise the right files. They will probably be in a folder, so it is a question of spotting that folder. From what you told me, they tend to use generic names, so it might be easy enough to spot. But I need you to read down the list of files until you spot it. Your knowledge of what they are likely to call the file means that you will be better than me at spotting it. The second problem is that if it doesn't get scanned until the end of the run, we might not have time to copy it. I won't know until the run starts what order it will scan the files. There are two likely possible orders. Either they will do them alphabetically, or they will do them in date order, scanning the newest to the oldest or the oldest to the newest. We just have to hope they don't scan alphabetically and have called the folder something that starts with Z."

She gave a shrug to indicate that this was out with her control, then turned to look out of the window. Chisholm had been perfectly pleasant towards her, and had tried to be helpful a few times, offering to do this or that, but she could not bring herself to regard him with any degree of warmth. She sat there for some minutes. Aware that behind her Chisholm had started to clear away the breakfast things. She had already decided that she would not offer to help him with that chore.

"Shona, you said that they would be able to find us if they scanned the file while we were on line, but if they missed that, it would be six hours later before they knew we'd been into their system. Would they still be able to find us?"

"No, they wouldn't if we just copied the file. Not without a good deal of work. Because we wouldn't change anything in their system, all they will see initially is that the system has been accessed. Then they would have to start another process to try to track down where the copy has gone. Eventually, they will find that it came to this laptop, but that will take more time. I don't know how long. Maybe twelve hours, maybe a bit less, but I'd go for eight as a safe estimate. Add those hours to the six before they know that there has been a violation, gives you fourteen hours. I would suggest that we are miles away from the cottage twelve hours after we get the evidence."

There was nothing much for them to do as they waited for the twelve o'clock ASS scan to start. They had initially busied themselves with gathering clothes and putting their cases in the boot of the Audi. After that, Shona ran over the drill a couple of times to make sure that Chisholm knew exactly what he had to do when the scan started. Then they waited. Time moved slowly. Tension mounted. Having come to this point, both of them were impatient for action. Outside, the sun shone brightly. There seemed to be no traffic in the glen, and every noise in the cottage seemed amplified. As the time drew towards noon, their nerves became taut, like violin strings. They could not look at each other, far less speak, in case they broke the concentration. They both knew exactly what they had to achieve within fifty seven minutes.

At last, Shona stood up. It was eight minutes before the scan started. "Time to go," she said as she headed to the bedroom, Chisholm following her. She booted up the system, and everything connected first time. Chisholm pulled up a stool and sat beside her, careful not to get in her way. Suddenly, she was working the keyboard at speed, typing in instructions and lines of code. The screen changed quickly, time and again. Chisholm caught a glance of a page heading that said, "Advanced Security System version 8.3", but had he blinked at the wrong time he would have missed it. Without stopping her work at the keyboard, Shona said, "That is us into ASS." It was three minutes after twelve. There were more rapid screen changes before she said "Right, that's us into the MI5 system. Over to you Mr Chisholm." It was seven minutes after twelve. As she spoke, the screen changed, and brought up a list of files. They were clearly in alphabetical order, and on the screen, the bottom entry was the letter A. It was clear that the highlighter that moved down the page, from file to file was indicating where the scan was. Shona had been right – it was scanning alphabetically. Chisholm started reading the files and scrolling down the list.

He worked through the As. Nothing. The same with the Bs, and the Cs. He was beginning to panic in spite of himself. He knew he had to read slowly enough to consider each file name properly, but there were so many files, and so little time. It was almost as if Shona knew what he was thinking. "You're doing fine, we still have plenty of time."

Chisholm glanced at the clock at the bottom of the screen. It was thirty one minutes after noon. He was starting on the files with the initial letter N.

Momentarily, his mind strayed. Had he missed it? What if he was wrong, and it wasn't there at all? He was acutely aware of the girl sitting silently beside him. Nothing in under N, nor P. Q was a small grouping of files. It was twelve thirty-nine. Suddenly he was pointing at the screen, too excited to speak. There it was! Referendum. That had to be it. Shona had seen it too. The scan was working through the files with M. She gave a silent prayer that there would be a lot of files with names towards the end of the alphabet. Brusquely, she grabbed the mouse from Chisholm and scrolled down. There weren't as many as she had hoped. It would be a couple of minutes yet before the scan had passed over the referendum folder. Quickly, she estimated that it would leave them with about ten minutes to copy the folder. It would be close, and she looked at the folder profile. It was a big folder, with fourteen separate files.

It was twelve forty-six when the scan on Referendum was complete. Eleven minutes before the whole scan would be finished. Her fingers flew across the keyboard for what seemed like an eternity as she navigated her way through the system to the folder called Referendum. Chisholm looked from the screen to the girl. Her eyes shone brightly with concentration, never leaving the screen. All at once the screen changed. A text box appeared at the top, with "Copying Files –Time to Completion." The time was blank, as the computer worked out how long the operation would take. Shona looked at the on screen clock. Twelve fifty. Time to complete was now showing. Seven minutes! Chisholm and Murray looked at each other, their eyes locking.

Shona's voice was a whisper. "Let it run. I'll close it off before the scan ends. We may not get it all, but we will have nearly everything." Chisholm nodded, too tense to speak. They watched both clocks in silence. The clock indicating how long until the copy was complete moved slowly, while the clock that indicated how much time was left on the scan seemed to go so fast. Now it was twelve fifty-six. Time to complete the copy was showing in seconds. Forty five, forty four, forty three. Shona's finger hovered over the escape button. Chisholm whispered to her "Do it!", the urgency in his voice clear. She held off. The clock went to twelve fifty-seven. Still she held off. The countdown continued. Nine, eight, seven. As it reached zero, Shona's finger hit escape, and the screen reverted to the ASS scan, on a file called Zuckonit, which Shona recognised as a term connected with cyber bullying. Three seconds later, the legend came up "Scan Successfully Completed – No Violations Detected."

Chisholm gave out a long slow whistle. "We've done it! That was too close for comfort!" Shona, too, was relieved. Without realising what she was doing, she turned to Chisholm and hugged him for a long minute. Then she said, "Let's see what we've got." She turned back to the screen, and worked the keyboard. "We have one folder called Referendum, and it contains fourteen files. Here is the bad news. All the files are encrypted, which means we can't open them. The good news is that no encryption cannot be broken if you know how, and I know how. It will take a bit of time, though. Mr Chisholm, why don't you busy yourself making lunch? I'm starving. Make something special, because we are celebrating, and while you are doing that, I'll get on with opening these files."

"How long will it take?" Chisholm was anxious to see what the files contained, and could scarcely conceal his elation that they actually had the files.

"I really don't know. If they have used the same form of encryption on all the files, as would seem likely, that would help. Give me an hour, and no interruptions."

It was two fifteen when Chisholm stuck his head round the bedroom door and announced that lunch was ready. It said much for his self control and for his regard for the girl that he had managed to stop himself from asking how she was getting on every five minutes. As he was making lunch, he had paced the floor, watching the clock move slowly, and willing the bedroom door to open to reveal a triumphant Shona Murray telling him that she had opened the files. That had not happened, and he managed not to intrude. Shona followed him to the kitchen, without comment. She took a forkful of the colourful vegetable risotto that Chisholm had prepared. It was, she acknowledged, delicious. Chisholm had opened a bottle of perfectly chilled fruity wine made from the Grenache grape in the south west of France "This is good, just what I need. Mr, Chisholm, the files are open. That wasn't too difficult. The problem is what is in the files. It is unintelligible. That is to say it is in code. Every document in the file has been put into code. I tried a few common code breaking bits of software, but got nowhere. I'm firing in the dark. Code breaking is not one of my tricks. However, it does suggest that the files contain something they really don't want us to see, otherwise why bother to put them into code?"

Chisholm had suddenly lost his appetite. "So what do we do now? I remember all the stories from the Second World War about the Enigma code, and how long it took the mathematicians at Bletchley Park to crack that. We don't have that sort of time." There was a hint of desperation in his voice. "We can't just turn up at some University and ask to speak to the mathematics professor. Are you sure that there isn't suitable software we could use?"

"No, we can't, and no, there isn't any software I know that we could use without a lot of help from an expert," Shona replied between mouthfuls of risotto. Her manner was quite matter-of-fact. "I realised that. So I have been looking at an alternative. I knew that we needed a mathematician, so I accessed the SQA's database. That sheet that I've printed off is the results for the candidates from the schools across Scotland from the last set of Advanced Highers. Have a look."

Chisholm appeared to be taken aback. "You have hacked into the SQA site! I should be angry." Angry or not, he picked up the paper. It was a print out showing the details of all the candidates and their marks. He started to read down the list of names. He was on page seven when he stopped, and looked at Shona as she finished the last of her risotto. "What am I looking for? Give me a clue."

Shona, said, "The risotto is great. Do you have any more?" As she went to refill her plate, she asked "What name are you at?"

"Farmer."

"Have you been looking at the marks?"

"Yes."

"What do you see?"

"I see a lot of kids who pass this get somewhere between 70% and 85%. Mainly low seventies. I've come across four, I think, who have made it into the 90s, with the top score being 92%."

"OK, Mr Chisholm, go to the Ls and tell me what you see."

Chisholm rearranged his papers until he had the Ls in front of him. He scanned the paper for a few minutes. Then he looked up slowly. "There is one kid here that it says got 100%! Rory Lawson. Is that what I'm supposed to find?" He couldn't keep the impatience out of his voice.

Shona finished her next mouthful of risotto. She was enjoying herself. "Look at his date of birth."

Chisholm did. "He's only fifteen," he said dully. Shona put down her fork. She moved in her chair so that she was looking directly at Chisholm. "He was only fourteen when he took the exam. I used Google to find out more about young Rory. His 100% was no fluke. Six months ago he won a European award as young mathematician of the year. Open to all of Europe for people under the age of twenty five. There is a string of other awards and recognition going back to when he was seven. The lad is a mathematical genius. Just when we need a genius, up he pops."

Chisholm looked at her incredulously. For a moment, he was lost for words. Then they all came out in a torrent. "We can't approach him. We can't risk getting him into trouble. He is just a kid; he won't know what he is getting into. What if he doesn't want to get involved? Shona, we can't do this. What about his family?"

The girl had been ready for this reaction. "Too risky for the boy, but you didn't hesitate to involve me, did you, Mr Chisholm? You said you were motivated by protecting democracy, and I almost believed you. So, you will not take that final step. As for Rory Lawson's involvement, I think that is up to the Lawson family. They don't sound to me like a family that sits on the fence. The father, Hugh, had refused to pay the tolls on the Skye Bridge and has five convictions to show for it. His older brother, Angus, is at University, where he is one of the leaders of the Students for Independence organisation. I think it is worth asking them. Look, Mr Chisholm, we are going to have to leave here in a few hours, before they come looking for us. It is a long way to the Lawson address, which sounds like a farm near Plockton, up in the West Highlands. If we don't break this code, there is no point in having the files, and all of this has been a waste of time. You will have got me back into prison for nothing. I'd suggest that you think about what you are going to say to Hugh Lawson, about how much you need his son's help. Or do you want me to do that too?"

Chisholm relented; an unexpected tinge of guilt touched him about involving the girl. "Alright, but if we get there and find that they are not interested, we don't push it."

It took them a further two hours to clear the cottage, and fill the car with various items. Shona, for the first time saw how much food Chisholm had piled in the cupboards, as he packed it into bags and then into the car. He had prepared a picnic hamper with food for them both to have on the long journey north. Once the girl was in the car, Chisholm went back into the cottage and spent another half hour ensuring that there were no finger prints left behind, nor any material that could provide genetic information about the recent occupants. The cottage smelt of bleach before he was finished. It was seven o'clock on Saturday night when he set the Satnav for an address some six miles east of the picturesque little town of Plockton. As the Audi left the glen, it occurred to him that his former colleagues would by now, be aware that someone had been interfering with their internal files.

Chapter Ten

Search

Sir David Lee was happy. He was content with the ways things were going. Just last week, his agents had successfully uncovered a plot to mass produce very good fake United Kingdom passports, and in doing so, they had uncovered and arrested a ruthless gang who were involved in people trafficking. The work of MI5 had been rightly praised for bringing this nasty group of people to justice. He had been congratulated by the Home Secretary and the Prime Minister, and the press had been very complementary.

He had met with Penny Carson, and she had conveyed the Prime Minister's satisfaction at how the campaign against Scottish independence was progressing. He had worked with her to produce a briefing paper for Richard Hume, the Deputy Prime Minister to use in the televised debate on Tuesday night. That would kill off calls for independence, and Thursday's referendum would be a formality. That would secure his department's funding. Penny Carson, whom he could not bring himself to like in any way, would brief Hume the next day, Sunday. The brief was explicit, and would drive home all the points where the independence debate had been turned towards the unionist case. The strongest elements were the cross examination of Alistair Morrison which Hume would use to break any arguments that the First Minister might use. Hume was one of England's best known barristers before being elected to the House of Commons, and his reputation for cross examination was fearsome. Sir David respected that. Indeed, he had used Hume as a prosecutor in the past because of his ability to break down witnesses. Hume could not fail. He had the ability, MI5 had provided the evidence against Morrison's government and its claims, and

Carson would ensure that Hume knew all the right points to drive home.

He had spent the afternoon watching his football team, Chelsea, score three times in a good victory over Aston Villa. Now he was home, getting ready to go out for the evening with his wife, Emily. They were going to dine at his club, where the food was always excellent, and the wine list extensive and eclectic. They would be joined by his wife's sister, Jenny, a Head Teacher at a Primary School in one of the better suburbs of London, and her husband, Tony, who was a neurosurgeon. Sir David liked them both, although they did not get the chance to meet up as often as he would have liked. Sir David was looking forward to the evening. Emily had bought him a new tie and he liked the way it matched his dark Italian suit. He had just started to adjust his cuff links when his mobile phone rang. Sir David saw on the display that it was Danvers calling him. Eddie Danvers was Head of Communications, which meant he was responsible for a range of things that involved technology. His section handled all work connected with mobile phones, from monitoring suspects' calls to interrogating confiscated phones. They also handled issues concerning computers, often finding long since deleted evidence buried deep within the hard drive of someone's laptop. One of their functions was the security of MI5's own computer system. Danvers would not normally have been at work over the weekend. Sir David identified himself to Danvers.

"Sorry for contacting you at half past seven on a Saturday night, but I thought you would want to know about this. Our routine security check has revealed that someone has been trying to get into our files. The check shows that that no files were accessed, no files were corrupted. That means there are three possibilities. They may have accessed the system, but been unable to get into any of the files, so they just gave up. Secondly, they may have had a good look round the system with a view to working out how to access the files, and they intend coming back when they have developed a plan. The last possibility, the least likely, but still possible, is that they have managed to copy a file or files without opening them. As you know, we run these checks every six hours, and there was no hint of this in the previous check. So it has happened during this afternoon. As I see it, Sir David, there are two things I must do immediately. We have to work out how they got in, and plug that gap. At the same time, we need to check to see if any files have been copied. We can do both of these things, but they will take some time. Given the amount of material we hold, it could take twelve or fifteen hours to check every file to see if it has been copied. If anything has been copied, we will be able to discover where it went. That will take more time, but we can do it."

Sir David had taken in all this information, and was calculating the next moves, even as Danvers spoke. Clearly, the next steps lay with the Communications Section, and Danvers, competence personified as always, seemed to be on top of things. "OK, Danvers. Let me know the minute there are any developments. I know it is Saturday night, but pull in as many people as you need. I want you to get to the bottom of this quickly."

"The team are already here, Sir David, with reinforcements on their way in."

There was nothing more to be done. It was worrying, certainly, that someone had been trying to hack into their files. Why now? However, there was nothing specific to go on. It could be anybody from a journalist trying to follow up a story to a crank trying to access information for the sake of it. It might also be a terrorist group trying to discover what MI5 held on them. They might be interested in an old case, or a recent case. It was less likely that they would be after a current case, Sir David knew, because the covert nature of their work meant that few people knew what the current cases were. Nevertheless, as he put his jacket on, he felt certain that he would not relax until he knew what was going on. He hoped that this was something he could deal with. He was determined not to let it spoil his evening.

* * *

Eddie Danvers had fourteen people working throughout Saturday night and into Sunday morning. There were times, of course, when some of them had little to do, when the diagnostic software was running. However, most of them were deployed on finding the security gap, the way the hacker had managed to get into the system. He had sent out to an all night take away for pizzas and coffee, but the team were tired. There was natural disappointment among them at being called in on a Saturday night, but they all knew that was a constant possibility, and they all understood the importance and urgency of the task they faced. Danvers paced the floor like an expectant father. He was forty years of age, but looked more like fifty. He was slightly built, and walked with a hint of a stoop. His brow seemed permanently furrowed, and his nervous hands were never still. Periodically, he spoke with the team searching for the security gap. They were having no success. They had been working flat out now for eleven hours. The diagnostic software would have about another three hours to run, and so far there was nothing to suggest that anything had been copied. Danvers rubbed the stubble that had grown on his chin overnight and decided to visit the gents, to splash his face with water, and generally freshen up. The morning sunlight was streaming in now, and he thought that he should go round his people, taking breakfast orders. He had already contacted a second team, and they would relieve this team in two hours, at nine a.m. They could go home to their beds for a well earned rest. There would be no rest or sleep for him, though.

He felt better for washing his face in cold water. He was drying off with paper towels when one of the younger members of the team searching for the security gap came in. Danvers felt he had to acknowledge his presence, and for lack of something more meaningful, he asked "How are things going, Peters?"

Peters, a gangly young man with glasses and a mop of fair hair, replied honestly, "Not well, sir. We've run everything we can think of. Twice. We are running out of places to look. One or two of the guys are beginning to wonder if the detection itself has a glitch – that actually nobody has been in the system at all. Certainly, we can't find any trace of somebody getting in."

Danvers was suddenly excited. "Peters, you said it was like nobody had been into our system! What if they haven't? It means we are looking in the wrong place! We have systems that enable us to access the system to run all these checks. What if they managed to access one of our diagnostic systems – they would be able to access the system the same way as we do. Come on!"

He more or less dragged Peters with him, despite the younger man's insistence that he needed to visit the toilet. Danvers quickly gathered the team round him, renewed urgency in his every action. He asked a few questions and got responses that confirmed what Peters had told him. They were running out of options. Everything had been checked and double checked. They were becoming convinced that there was nothing to find. Danvers explained his theory, that the hacker had gained access through the diagnostic software, and immediately he could see some nodding of the heads as the team considered this possibility. They made hasty arrangements to go back and investigate the various diagnostic systems for breaches. They had just left, and he was sitting on his own when Holly Adams, who had been keeping an eye on the diagnostic scan burst in. "They have copied a folder! The folder is called Referendum. The scan has a bit to go yet, so they might have copied something else as well."

Danvers was disappointed. He knew the scan was over 90% complete, and he had been beginning to hope that with no copies detected, the last part of the scan would also reveal nothing had been copied. He was too much of a professional to let the disappointment show when he replied. "Very well. How long has the scan still to run?"

"It will be completed within the hour, sir."

It was exactly 8 a.m. when Danvers phoned Sir David. Sir David was normally awake and dressed by this time, but he and Emily had been rather late back from the club the previous night, and he not slept particularly well, partly because he had eaten rather a lot, and had done so later than normal, and partly because he was concerned about things after Danvers' call. He slipped out of bed, where Emily was still asleep, pulled his multi coloured Langley Dressing gown over his navy blue Modena pyjamas, and moved into the next room before answering the phone. The call was not unexpected, but nevertheless it felt like an intrusion.

When Danvers spoke, it was purely to give the facts. His voice betrayed no emotion. "Two things to report, Sir David. First is that we haven't yet worked out how they were able to access the system. We are still working on it, and we will find it. Whoever did this is extremely good. Our systems are highly sophisticated, but they got in and out with barely a trace. The second thing is that they have copied one folder, without breaking the encryption. I would think anybody with enough knowledge to get into our system will not have too much difficulty breaking the encryption. The folder they copied was called Referendum."

Sir David's heart skipped a beat. "Did you say Referendum?"

"That's right. Does that mean anything to you? Does it provide any clues as to who might be responsible?"

Sir David thought quickly. Only four people knew of the existence of this folder, and there was danger in widening that group. However, the perpetrator had to be tracked down, and with maximum effort, so Danvers would need to know something of the contents to point him in the right direction. He would need to tell Danvers, much as he might have his reasons for not doing so. "It is a file on surveillance activities of a group who were threatening to disrupt the Scottish independence referendum. It had some highly confidential material in there, so it was coded. They won't break the code easily, but we need to get it back quickly. I suggest that you start looking in Scotland, Danvers."

"Sir, if it is Scotland, there is only one hacker capable of doing this. I doubt if there are a dozen people in the world who could have broken into our system. The Scot is a girl whose name you might recall from the nuclear scandal a few years back. Murray."

"I remember the case well. That makes perfect sense. I'll get Williams to come in and take over field operations to track her down."

Six hours later, Williams phoned Sir David from his office in Thames House. "Sir David, I think you will want to see this for yourself. I'm sorry to disturb your Sunday afternoon, but I think you should come over here now." Williams was not given to exaggeration, Sir David knew, so he readily accepted that he should go.

When he arrived at Thames House some thirty minutes later, having made his apologies to Emily, he went immediately to Williams' office. Williams stood to greet his Head of Service, rising to his full height of six feet and four inches. His piercing green eyes suggested trouble. Danvers was also present. A projector had been set up, with a screen at the far end of the room. Danvers had not slept for thirty two hours and it looked like it, with his eyes sagging and his brow more furrowed that ever. However, he sat in front of his laptop, and was clearly in charge of the visual images that would form part of the presentation. Williams started.

"It looks like it was a good call to start with the girl Murray. She is out of prison, on probation." He signalled to Danvers and an image appeared on the screen. "This is her. It was taken the week before she was released. She has been living in a one bedroom flat in Montrose, on the east coast of Scotland. She has been meeting regularly with her probation officer, Mr

George Wylie. I spoke with him this afternoon and he was none too pleased about being contacted on a Sunday. He says that she complies with her probation conditions, and seems to have settled down well. He says she is no trouble. However, it gets interesting. She works at the local supermarket, and she phoned in sick on Friday. She has not been seen since. One of our men went round to her place and couldn't get an answer. He tried the neighbours. One of them said she saw a man at her door on Friday. The woman gave us a description – not great but something. In his sixties, wearing glasses, below average height. Now, Murray lives in a flat with a common front door. There is CCTV at the entrance to the building. Here is a picture of the man arriving." Danvers started changing the image. "And here is him leaving some time later with Murray. Now he is carrying a suitcase. He didn't have one when he went in, so we can assume that it is Murray's. Notice how he keeps his face turned away from the camera. We don't have a clear picture of him, but as far as anybody could tell, it is the same man that the neighbour described. Then they move out into the street. We are lucky here again. There is more CCTV. You can see them gong to this black Audi Avant, and the man puts the suitcase in the boot while the girl gets in the passenger seat. The man is still carefully keeping his face away from the cameras, but you can see from this frame that the registration number on the vehicle is visible. Danvers will show you it magnified. We tracked this vehicle to a car rental company in Manchester. When we contacted them, they told us it had been taken on a two week rental. It had been paid for by credit card. The name on the card was David Lee."

Sir David turned puce and spluttered with righteous indignation. They were using his name! "That will not be a coincidence. Go on." He couldn't conceal the fury that he felt.

Williams continued. "We got details of the card, and so far we have found two other transactions. The first one was for a whole load of computer gear from a store in Bristol, and the second for the rental of a cottage, just north of Montrose. Then someone here had the bright idea of doing more checks on the CCTV footage from Montrose. In particular we looked to see if there was a clear view of the man when he parked the car, since there was nothing we could get when he and Murray left. This is what we came up with."

Danvers flashed a photograph on the screen. The man's face could be seen. It was some distance away, and the quality of the picture was not good, but the grainy face he saw made Sir David bang the table in rage. "That's David Chisholm! What is he doing there?"

It was Danvers who answered. "Chisholm ran the operation that caught Murray, so there is a connection."

Williams carried on. "Chisholm is not a fool. I think he is trying to tell us something. I think he is trying to tell us that this, whatever it is, is his operation. That is why he is using your name. He is not making it too easy for us, but he is indicating that he is running the show and the girl is doing what she is told. He might even be telling her that he is still with us. Sir David, two things. I have a helicopter waiting, and with your agreement, I'll head off to this cottage that he has rented, although I'd bet they are gone by now. I'll meet up with some of the team from Glasgow, who are making their way there now. Second, why would Chisholm start working against us? It doesn't make any sense."

Sir David rubbed his nose thoughtfully. He was back in control of his thoughts. He didn't let his anger interfere with the task in hand. "Maybe it does, maybe it does. I had asked him to take over the project we were running on the homeless protesters, and he asked me whether we were perhaps interfering with their democratic rights. Three days later, he resigned. He was old enough, and had all the service he needed, so I thought no more about it. Just maybe, he was beginning to question our methods. Danvers, you need some sleep. You are out on your feet. Get home, and pass the investigation to someone else in the meantime."

When they were alone, Sir David turned to Williams. "You know this must never get out. Do whatever it takes. It will take them ages to break the code, so that gives us some time, but the quicker it is brought to a conclusion, the better. Leave no loose ends. That includes the girl, innocent or not. Do you understand? Keep in touch."

Williams nodded gravely, and headed for the helicopter, with one of Danvers' experts in tow, an experienced man called Simpson. Sir David was looking more worried than at any time since he took the job. He knew better than most that Chisholm had been a great field agent, and he had considered him to be trustworthy beyond question. Would Williams be a match for him? Whatever he was up to, Chisholm might prove difficult to stop. He had some hours start on them already, and it would take Williams some time to get to Montrose.

Chapter Eleven

The Mathematician

Chisholm and Shona had made good time, despite the road works and contraflows on the A9 as part of the upgrading project. The traffic had been relatively light, travelling at that time of night. They had travelled west from Montrose to join the A9 at Pitlochry, then headed north before turning off the A9 south of Newtonmore, and branching off towards the west. They had stopped by a loch to eat the picnic that Chisholm had prepared. The food had disappeared quickly, and Chisholm was surprised at the girl's appetite. He had prepared chicken skewers, salad sandwiches and ham sandwiches set off with English mustard, a raspberry cake, and lemonade to wash it all down. The picnic stop was a welcome break, for they had not exchanged two words since they had left the cottage, each deep in their own thoughts, and each unsure how to start a conversation with the other. The nearest they came to a conversation was when Chisholm had told Shona that she would find some CDs in the glove compartment in the car and she should choose one to play. She had looked at them and was unimpressed with his classical music taste. Mozart, Beethoven and Verdi were not her taste. She had asked him if he had nothing from this century, and they had finally agreed on silence. Despite making good time and not having many stops, it was well after midnight before the black Audi made it into Plockton. Chisholm was tired. The drive had been difficult. Apart from the tension between him and Shona in the car, the roads were narrow and full of twists and bends and had required full concentration. Shona Murray had not slept, but was clearly not tired. On the contrary, she was eager to press on, and suggested that despite the late hour they continue out to the Lawson place. Chisholm argued that it was too late. Hugh Lawson would not open the door to anyone at that time of night, and that they should try to find a bed for the night and go out to see the Lawsons first thing in the morning. Shona countered that there were already no lights on in Plockton, so they would not be able to find a room there. She had no intention of sleeping in the car. They argued for a couple of minutes, neither giving in, but it was clearly getting them nowhere. In the end, Chisholm was forced to agree that there was no obvious sign of life or anywhere that looked as though it would offer a bed. It was 2 a.m. They reached a compromise. They would go out to the Lawson place, and if there was a light on, they would knock on the door. Otherwise, they would return to Plockton, and try to find a hotel that would let them in.

Although it was a clear sky with a full moon it was difficult to find the Lawson home. The road was badly lit, and there were various tracks leading off from the road. They had taken one such track and had driven about a quarter of a mile before realising it was the wrong one. In the dark, and surrounded by pine trees it was difficult to turn round, and twice Chisholm thought the car had become stuck in a rut. At last they returned to the road, and eventually found the right track. Fifty yards on, they could see a light. It was very difficult to make anything out, and Chisholm turned off the headlights as the Audi approached the house. There was no mistaking it, there was at least one room still lit up. It was almost 2:30 a.m. now, and Chisholm was reluctant to approach the house. However, urged on by Shona, he went to the door, as she watched from the car.

In the still of the night, he could hear the sound of a television as he approached the door, and knocked. There was the sound of furniture moving, and the door opened. The man standing there was perhaps five foot six tall, but had the broadest shoulders Chisholm had ever seen. Even in this light it was clear that he had the ruddy complexion that accompanies an outdoor life, and a bushy beard. He wore a brightly checked shirt, jeans and slippers. If he were surprised to see a stranger at his door in the middle of the night, he didn't let it show. He studied Chisholm slowly, and looked over his shoulder towards the Audi parked in front of his house. When he spoke, it was with a slow deep voice that seemed to fill the night air. "And what can I do for you, mister?"

Chisholm wasn't really sure where to start. "Are you Hugh Lawson?"

"Aye, that's me."

"My name is Chisholm, David Chisholm. I'd like to speak to you and your wife. I'm sorry about the hour, but it is quite important."

"It is nothing to do with Angus, is it? Is he alright?" It was a natural reaction to someone calling in the middle of the night.

"Angus?" Chisholm fought through his tiredness to remember that Shona had told him about the older brother who was at University. "No. No, it is nothing to do with him. I do need to speak to you and your wife, though. Urgently."

"Well, Mr Chisholm, what can be so urgent that it couldn't wait until the morning? You won't be speaking to my wife, though. Mrs Lawson is away in Nairn, visiting her aunt. It's just me and my younger son here, so we'll have to do. You're lucky we're both up, watching late films. Have you got somebody in that car, there?"

Shona was waved over to join them, and they went indoors. Lawson called out to his son. "We have visitors, Rory. Will you make a pot of tea?" Turning to Chisholm, he added, "Unless you would prefer something stronger? Maybe a dram?"

Chisholm indicated that tea would be fine. He wondered how many households would extend such a welcome in the middle of the night to a couple of strangers. As they came into the sitting room, they saw the son disappear into the kitchen. From the view they got, he was clearly taller than his father, and slimly built. Lawson invited them to sit down, and they took seats opposite each other. Lawson turned off the television, but not before they saw enough of the film to realise that they had been watching some martial arts movie. The room was comfortable, and looked lived in. The chairs and sofa were big, the kind you fell into. On the wall were a couple of fading pictures of highland scenes, wild craggy mountains and moody skies. On the Welsh dresser sat a wedding photo of a younger, but unmistakable, Hugh Lawson and a very pretty bride. Either side of this sat a photograph of a boy, or perhaps more accurately, a young man. These photos revealed a striking resemblance, and must have been Angus and Rory. Shona took all this in quickly, but her main interest was Rory. If she was going to work closely with him she wanted to know what he was like. Before she got comfortable in the seat, she excused herself and went to the kitchen to help Rory with the tea and the cups. Left alone with Chisholm, Lawson asked "So Mr Chisholm, what is this all about?"

Chisholm was still rather unsure how to proceed, so in order to give some thinking time, he replied "Let's wait until the others come in so I don't have to repeat things."

Meanwhile, in the kitchen, Shona had introduced herself to Rory and under his instruction was finding four mugs and putting some shortbread on a plate. She had thought Rory might have been a quiet, bookish sort of boy, but that did not appear to be the case. He had the look of someone who had spent his life on a farm. His upper body was strong, his face open, with a ready smile, and was dressed trendily in a pink T-shirt that bore the legend Abercrombie & Fitch. When she said to him, "So you are Rory, the maths genius?" He looked rather embarrassed, and replied "How do you know about that?" He was, she decided with some relief, a normal teenager who just happened to be an exceptional mathematician.

Rather than explain, she picked up the tray with the full mugs now on it and said with an encouraging smile, "You'll find out in a moment."

As they drank tea and nibbled at shortbread and chocolate biscuits, Chisholm started the story. He left out no detail, and Shona nodded in agreement and added confirmation here and there. She expanded on his rather weak description of how he knew her, but Hugh Lawson remembered the court case well. It had been fully covered in the press. He had looked at Shona appraisingly, and seemed satisfied that this was indeed the girl whose picture had been in every news bulletin during the two weeks of her trial. Shona also took over the narrative when describing how they had obtained the MI5 folder. It was Chisholm, however, who explained that they were here in the hope that Rory, the mathematician, could break the code. "I remember the court case," Lawson said to her. "You may have been on the wrong side of the law, but you were certainly morally justified."

"It was a bit like your stance on the tolls on the Skye Bridge," Shona replied.

"Aye, but I didn't go to prison for my beliefs, whilst you did. The government were covering things up, and you took your right to know straight to them. I admire you for that," Lawson told her.

"Well, Mr Chisholm -"

"David!" Chisholm interjected.

"Sorry. David here was the one who put me behind bars in the first place, but he has convinced me that he is on the right side of morality this time around," Shona told Lawson. "It seems MI5 is doing the politicians' dirty work by fixing the referendum. The fact that the file is coded shows that they have something to hide, and it is something we certainly have the right to know about. We need Rory's help. This is no joke. This is a matter of simple democracy. The government may go parading around the Middle East with the armed forces waving the flag of democracy, but surely it is utterly hypocritical if they let this happen, or even command that it happens on their own doorstep?"

"What do you need my Rory to do? Is there any danger involved? I don't want my son being taken away by the security services," Lawson pointed out.

"We need him to look at the files and try to decode them. As soon as he's cracked it we'll leave you in peace, or at the first sign of MI5 closing in we'll leave you in peace," Chisholm said. "I know MI5. I used to work for them. MI5 are ruthless. They do not care if there are children involved. They will get what they want and then leave again, never to return. They live under a permanent veil of secrecy enforced by the government."

At this point, Rory was looking at Shona with increasing wonder since he had heard the description of her background, and saw her smile and give a reassuring wink. Chisholm concluded, "As Shona says, MI5 will know by now that somebody has copied the folder. They will be trying to retrieve it. So helping us is not without its risks. If Rory can crack the code before they find us, we'll be gone, and you simply deny that we have ever been here. Otherwise I'll tell them that you were coerced into helping. What do you say?"

Father and son had become more incredulous during the forty minutes it had taken for the story to unfold, interrupting only occasionally for clarification on some point of detail or other, and were by now fully engaged with the situation. Hugh Lawson turned to his son. "Well, Rory, what do think? Can you do it? Crack the code, I mean."

Rory was on the edge of his seat. He was aware that all eyes were on him, and he was conscious of Shona's gaze. He thought for a long moment, and when he answered, he spoke to his father. "I don't know if I can break the code. Shona has the right software, so that will help. Obviously we don't have much time. If I had a few weeks, I'd say that I had a good chance, but at best I would have a couple of days. I think I'd like to give it a go, though. You know that I'm too young to vote in the referendum, and you and Angus keep going on about it being the most important vote in Scotland for generations, something that could really change the future. Well, maybe I can help change the future by breaking the code. That might change the whole nature of the vote on Thursday. This is my chance to contribute, Dad. I really want to try."

Hugh Lawson simply nodded to his son, as though he had expected no other response, and turned to Chisholm. "That is your answer. Look after him well."

There was general elation in the room, and for the moment lifted the veil of tiredness from Chisholm and Shona. Rory's warning about the chances of him actually breaking the code were temporarily forgotten. At last Hugh Lawson brought them back to a sense of reality. "It is almost four o'clock. You are not going to start now. We all need some sleep and an early start is called for. Shona, you can have Angus's room, but you will have to make do with the sofa, Mr Chisholm. Don't worry about alarms, I'll get you up in the morning."

Ten minutes later Chisholm was snoring loudly on the couch. He was so tired that he had fallen asleep, even before Hugh Lawson had put the light out. Along the corridor, Shona had fallen asleep on the top of Angus's bed. She had not realised quite how much the previous day had taken out of her, and had lapsed immediately into a deep sleep. She had not moved a muscle when something woke her. Deep in her brain her senses were telling her to waken up. Slowly, she surfaced. What had woken her? It was light, and she looked about her. How long had she slept? She looked at her watch. 7:30. She struggled with her wakening senses to remember what had woken her. There it was again! The smell of cooked food, of breakfast being fried. She made her way to the kitchen via the bathroom, passing a slowly stirring David Chisholm on the way. In the kitchen, Hugh Lawson was working over two hot pans. Rory was tucking into a plate with egg, bacon, sausage, beans, black pudding and potato scone. Beside him sat a steaming hot mug of coffee and a round of toast and marmalade. He stopped eating long enough to say, "Hi."

Hugh Lawson handed over a full plate. "Same for you, young lady." It wasn't a question, rather it was a statement of fact. She nodded, and sat beside Rory. Lawson was chattering on about his croft having sheep, but he had a couple of cows and he had to be up early to milk them. Shona was amazed at how fresh both the Lawsons looked. They must have had even less sleep than she had. Eventually, Chisholm joined them, rubbing his eyes. He noted that for all her protestations about preferring grilled to fried food, she was making short work of the plateful in front of her. Lawson served a similar plate to Chisholm and said, "Rory and I have been thinking. We have a small game lodge about a mile from here, into the forest. The three of you should go there. You will get peace to work. It may need swept and dusted, but there is a bed, and a stove. You will have electricity. There is no internet connection there, so that might be a problem. I'll give you food away so you can stay there as long as you need. You can take some bedding and towels. If anybody shows up here asking for you, I'll put them off."

Shona answered for them both, "That sounds just perfect. But we won't need supplied with food. Mr Chisholm is carrying enough food in his car to feed an army." Her smile robbed her words of any offence.

Chisholm interrupted. "That is a good idea, I'll give you a phone to keep in touch with us, one they won't be able to hack into. Rory will have the other. We should leave his phone here. If they get this far, they are likely to start monitoring your calls, so this will be the secure way to keep in touch. The phones are in the car, and I'll get them for you before we go."

By nine o'clock, the three of them were busy in the lodge. Chisholm was sweeping and dusting. Nobody had used the lodge for some months, and while it was clean, a good dusting was obviously needed. Shona was setting up the computer equipment, and Rory was studying the hastily erected screen showing the first page of coded text, paper at his side, and pencil in his hand. Outside, it was one of those glorious but too infrequent West Highland mornings when the sun shone from a clear blue cloudless sky. The lodge itself was of wooden construction, situated in a clearing, surrounded by tall fir trees. It was about half a mile along a dirt track. There was one bedroom with two single beds, a small kitchen with an old stove, which was still in apparently good working order, and a sitting room. It was here that Shona and Rory were getting down to work. Half an hour later, with all the equipment set up and working, Shona and Rory had instructed Chisholm to take a walk in the forest, and come back just in time to prepare lunch. They needed to be able to concentrate, and Chisholm's presence, no matter how unobtrusive he tried to be, was a distraction. By now, all the equipment was in place and working. Rory had given Shona a couple of formulae to try, but when she ran them over the first page of the first file, they were obviously not correct, and the printout looked like a random jumble of letters. Undaunted, Rory worked on, scribbling notes on his paper, occasionally stopping, and biting the end of his pencil, lost in thought. Chisholm knew there was nothing he could do, and as he remembered Rory's earlier expression of doubt, he wondered if there was any chance at all for them. Even if, against the odds, he cracked the code, what then? He realised that his mood was becoming morose, and he suspected that was due to tiredness. He decided that after lunch, instead of taking another walk, he would stay in the lodge, and sleep in one of the beds. Another thought struck him. If his former colleagues were to show up, his place was with Rory and Shona, to ensure that they came to no harm.

It was 2 p.m. when Chisholm announced that lunch was ready. Somewhat reluctantly, Shona and Rory came through, Rory carrying his pencil and some paper with him. They started on the soup that Chisholm had prepared, Rory working as he ate. Shona answered Chisholm's unspoken question. "Nothing yet. It is early days, though." She nodded in Rory's direction. "I've never seen anything like this. I thought I could get wrapped up in computer problems, but he is incredible. He just keeps producing formulas for me to feed into the software to test. Fantastic!"

Within ten minutes they had finished the salad that had followed the soup. Shona and Rory returned to the computer, while Chisholm cleared up the lunch plates, and then went, as he had promised himself, to sleep on one of the beds. He was asleep within minutes.

Chisholm was vaguely aware of someone shaking him gently, and calling his name. Slowly, he struggled to focus on Shona standing over him. He reached for his glasses. "Is everything all right?"

"Yes, there is nothing to be concerned about. Rory and I are just going out for a walk in the fresh air to clear our heads. We'll be about fifteen minutes, and we'll stay out of sight, in the woods. I would have stopped long ago, but he just keeps on going. Even he is needing a break now. Maybe you could prepare some food. I think we're both hungry."

"What time is it Shona?"

"It's eight o'clock. We let you sleep on because it gave us peace and quiet – well apart from the occasional snoring. But mainly because you looked as though you needed it. There is really not much you can do to help at the moment. I think you might be getting a bit old for all this excitement." She smiled as she spoke, and Chisholm regarded the mild rebuke as the friendliest gesture he had had from her since he knocked on her door in Montrose.

Chisholm rose and looked out into the sitting room. There were sheets of paper everywhere, covered with scribbled formula. He picked one up and examined it. He recognised some of the mathematical symbols, but it meant nothing to him. Alone, he started to prepare the evening meal.

Having had their walk, Rory and Shona returned to work while Chisholm completed the preparation of their evening meal. It was just after nine o'clock when they sat down to a big bowl of pasta, followed by cheesecake and cream. Shona was clearly despondent, but Rory seemed to have boundless enthusiasm. When she suggested that they had done perhaps all that they could do for the day, he replied that he was just getting started. "I can do this. I don't know how quickly, but I can do this. We have not got it yet, but we have eliminated a few possibilities. There is something there, a pattern, but I can't quite see it yet. There is something I'm missing. It is a good puzzle. I can't stop now. When we started I thought it could take weeks. Well, it still might, but the more I work with this, the more I am sure that I can do it, that the code is solvable." He sounded as though he was enjoying himself, relishing the challenge, and was not ready to stop. There was also something infectious about his enthusiasm that got to the others. Shona agreed that she would work on with him. Chisholm wished them luck and went to wash up. He had agreed with their conclusion that he was not much help to them at this stage. He felt useless. This was all his doing, and here he was, dependent on two people that he had no business involving in this dangerous escapade. When he went to bed at midnight, his mood gloomy again, they were still working, Rory now bent over his paper furiously scoring out letters. His eyes were alight with eager anticipation, but there was no sign of success. Shona was trying to keep up with him, feeding formulae into the software, and running pages of one of the files through each formula. Time and again, what came out looked like nonsense. Rory would pour over each of the print outs, as though he could discern some meaning from them. Occasionally he would spend a long time over one print out or another. He kept on insisting that they were making progress, but she couldn't see any.

By three o'clock on Monday morning Shona had fallen asleep by the laptop, her head cradled in a crooked arm. Rory nudged her, and half carried her, half lead her to the second bed in the bedroom. Chisholm was still fast asleep, snoring gently. He laid the exhausted girl on top of the bed and covered her with the bedclothes. Then he headed back to the sitting room, and his notes.

Chapter Twelve

The Net Closes

It was almost eight o'clock on Monday morning, and Williams looked like he hadn't slept. In fact he had slept, but only for about three hours, and very uncomfortably at that, in the back seat of a silver Jaguar XFR. The back seats of cars were not designed for people of his height to lie down on. At least the car had not been moving. It was parked alongside another silver Jaguar XFR, outside the cottage recently vacated by Chisholm and Murray. He was awake now, rubbing sleep from his eyes and stretching his long limbs, trying to get some feeling back into them. The morning was dry, but overcast, and there was a chill wind blowing up the glen from the North Sea. Hardie had just returned from an expedition into Montrose, and was a welcome sight, carrying bacon rolls and coffee. He would be reporting to Sir David shortly, and he had little to tell him. He had not expected to find any leads at the cottage. Chisholm was far too clever for that. He had to go through the motions, though, because you could never be certain. It had been a long night, and he was not in the best of moods. Lack of sleep always affected him that way. He knew they would find Chisholm. It was only a matter of time. He had no doubt. Equally, he had no concern about the folder – that it was coded would make it useless to anyone who didn't have the key. Chisholm might have the folder, but without the code, neither he nor anyone else could make any use of it.

Last night had met his expectations. The helicopter had landed at a location about 15 miles south of Montrose. He had been met there as arranged by three of the Glasgow team. They were headed by Roger Roberts, and this pleased Williams. He had worked with Roberts before, and held him in high regard. Roberts was a big, heavily built, bearded Yorkshire man, almost as tall as Williams. He was experienced, resourceful, and could work on his own initiative. It had been his idea to bring two cars, in case they had to split up. Roberts had been accompanied by two younger men, neither of whom Williams recognised. They were introduced as Johnston and Hardie, and by their accents Williams judged them both to be Scots, probably Glaswegians. They both looked tough and competent, and both sported close cropped hairstyles. Johnston had a thistle tattoo on the back of his left hand. To his satisfaction, Williams discovered that they both knew when they were expected to speak, and when they were expected to keep quiet. That would not be a surprise if Roberts had trained them. The two cars had proceeded to the cottage, arriving late and after darkness had settled. The cottage had been locked. After checking the outside of the cottage, they affected entry in moments, using tools and some skills that many burglars would like to add to their repertoire. They were unconcerned about their cars being visible from the road – it was a quiet glen, and this was a holiday cottage, with different people renting it. A different car outside would attract no attention whatsoever. For the same reason, they had no anxieties about the lights in the cottage. Following a quick cursory search of the premises, which revealed nothing, the four of them started on a meticulous search, looking for anything that might help them prove that Chisholm and Murray had been there or that might indicate where they had gone. Simpson, the IT specialist, remained outside in the car. They had gone through each room, inch by inch, drawer by drawer, but found nothing. Even in the kitchen, there was no hint that anyone had eaten there, or that food had been prepared there. Chisholm's cleaning up had been thorough indeed. Apart from a faint smell of cheap perfume in one of the bedrooms – presumably, the bedroom used by Murray, the only sign that anyone had been near the cottage in weeks was outside, where there were tyre marks on the gravel driveway. When, by three a.m. the four of them were satisfied that there was nothing to be found, Simpson was allowed in. He connected up his gadgetry to the internet connection in the cottage, and spent the next three hours or so proving that there was no detectable trace of internet activity from the cottage over the previous forty eight hours. This was exactly as expected, but they had to try. While Simpson worked, Williams had slept, uncomfortably, in the car.

Williams picked at a piece of bacon that was lodged in his teeth, took a drink of the brown coffee that in other circumstances he would have regarded undrinkable, and headed into the cottage, with his phone in his hand. The others were under strict instructions to stay outside. He wanted to be sure that nobody overheard any of his conversation with Sir David. He looked out the kitchen window, and could see the others standing by the two cars, their breath visible in the morning air, as they drank their coffee and ate their rolls. Only when he was satisfied that he was alone, did Williams start to punch in the numbers for Sir David's secure phone line. The Head of MI5 answered on the second ring. Sir David, it transpired, had been at his desk since 6:30, called in early by an excited Danvers. Williams quickly and succinctly relayed the night's events without a hint of disappointment. Sir David, had expected nothing more, and let Williams finish his account without comment. Williams continued "So Chisholm has the folder, we are agreed on that. Because it is coded, it is of no use to him. He would not have expected it to be coded, because he knows that hardly any of our internal files are. The fact that it is coded will convince him that it contains material that we are determined will not leak out. All he can do is print off something that looks like a set of monkeys have randomly worked at a keyboard. To be able to do anything with it he has either to decode it, which he won't be able to do without help, or give it to some organisation that can decode it. He won't do that, because nobody, certainly not any of the news

116

agencies, is going to be interested in something that looks like rubbish. He has nothing to show them. Some of the international terrorist groups would have the expertise, but they wouldn't be interested in a referendum in Scotland, and besides, Chisholm will not have a means of contacting them. Remember, all his service was working on internal threats, not international ones. So he will seek help to decode the folder. There are not that many options open to him. Maths Departments of universities are the obvious places that might have the expertise, but they won't want to get mixed in something like this. When he seeks help, though, it will leave a trail, and we'll get him."

Sir David had been waiting patiently. He had important news to relay, but he wanted Williams to clear his mind of all that he had to say first. When Sir David eventually spoke, he carried all the conviction of a man who was certain that he had the right answer. He spoke slowly, every word carrying equal emphasis, inviting no interruption and no disagreement. "Our analysis is similar. Chisholm will have to find a way of breaking the code before he can do anything. I'm told that no code is unbreakable, but the ones we use on these ultra secret files are about as close as you can get. Let me come back to that in moment. First, I must tell you that I sent a team to Chisholm's address in Gloucester. He lives alone. There was no one at home. His car was in the garage. It looks like he has packed some clothes, but left no clues as to where he might be headed. Neighbours say that they haven't seen him for about a week. It is confirmation, if we needed it, that it is indeed Chisholm we are dealing with.

"Working on the basis that he will need to get help to break the code, and that he is operating somewhere in Scotland, we started last night running a special surveillance of Scottish agency IT systems. As you know, Danvers' lot keep an eye out for any attempts to hack into any government agency, so it was easy for us to bring that forward. I had to bring Danvers into my confidence, at least up to a point, so that he would have some idea what to look for. Frankly, I thought it would be like looking for a needle in a haystack, but it looks very like Danvers' people have hit the jackpot. It seems that such attacks are rare, and so when they do happen, they are easily spotted. There have been two such attacks, and they occurred within fifteen minutes of each other, not long after the point where Chisholm or the girl would have got the files open and realised that they were coded. Somebody hacked into the Scottish Criminal Justice System, and accessed the records of one Hugh Lawson, convicted on a number of occasions for failing to pay bridge tolls. He will not be of interest to Chisholm. The Scottish Qualifications Authority has also been hacked into, and the records accessed are of one Rory Lawson, son of Hugh. The son, it seems is a mathematical genius, a phenomenon with numbers. He will be very much of interest to Chisholm. Danvers got me here earlier this morning to tell me about the connection. I am sure he is right; that these events are not coincidence and I have no doubt that Chisholm has gone to try to get the boy to help. Goodness knows what sort of story he will give him to get his cooperation. I will give you the address of the Lawson family, and I want you to get there with all haste. Do whatever is necessary. You have my full authority. Do you understand?"

Thirty minutes later, having deposited Simpson at the train station in Montrose to find his own way back to London, the two silver XFRs were heading towards Plockton, Roberts warning bleakly about delays due to road works on the A9. Roberts and Williams travelled in the back of the lead car driven by Hardie, while Johnston followed closely behind. The route was identical to that taken by Chisholm and Murray some thirty six hours earlier. They drove hard, making up time through the morning traffic, until they joined the A9. After that, for long stretches, there were speed restrictions set at forty miles per hour, and occasional traffic lights to stop progress all together. The volume of traffic was high with cars, vans, lorries and coaches stretched out in single file, bumper to bumper, as far as the eye could see. There were no overtaking opportunities. Williams sat in the back seat, and fumed helplessly.

* * *

As the two cars joined the A9, Sir David Lee was meeting Penny Carson, in a very secluded lobby of a very exclusive hotel in central London. As usual, she was immaculate in her customary grey trouser suit and white blouse. Sir David had lost all the terseness of his discussion with Williams, and was now the essence of affability. He did not like the woman he was meeting, and he could sense that she did not like him. Relations between them would never be cordial, and while there had been something of a thaw over the last few weeks, the behaviour between them at best could be described as polite. He had to admit, however, that their meetings had been very businesslike and productive, and she had delivered efficiently on all that he had asked of her. He could admire her professionalism, but found her to be cold and cynical. Certainly there was nothing to cast any doubt on her reputation for fanatical loyalty to Nigel Braithwaite. They got themselves organised with a pot of coffee and some biscuits. When the waiter had disappeared, Sir David invited Penny Carson to report on activity since their last meeting. She sipped her coffee, considering for a moment how much information Sir David needed to know. She made full eye contact, and smiled, but it was a smile that did not touch her eyes.

"I spent two hours with the Deputy Prime Minister yesterday afternoon. Before we met he had the brief we had prepared for him. He clearly had a good grasp of the brief, as you would expect. He is travelling up to Edinburgh tomorrow afternoon to be ready for tomorrow night's debate. He was rather surprised at the depth of the briefing, and wondered how I could be so sure of what Morrison's weak points would be. Without giving anything away, I was able to reassure him of what we know, and he was quickly able to relate that to various events in the campaign. Then I went over with him the specific points to attack Morrison on, and he is confident on all of these points. He understands the tactic he is to use, and sees no difficulty. Morrison is a good performer and debater, but there are too many points of attack for him to come through unscathed. He has his lines of cross examination clear, and we rehearsed them. I think he is looking forward to the debate, and he is relishing the thought of scuppering Morrison and his band of followers.

"We also rehearsed the presentation that he will give after cross examining Morrison. Although we fully expect Morrison to be dead in the water by then, the presentation which your people have prepared will drive home the dangers and uncertainties of independence, including some of the uncertainties we have planted. It will all be very plausible. Certainly we can expect Morrison to retaliate that these uncertainties are faced by all countries at some time or other, which is true, but by that time he will be looking defeated and desperate."

"The PM is pleased with how things have gone. The latest opinion polls show things going very much our way. In a sense, then we only have to hold our own during the debate to win the vote. However, with the preparation we have, we expect to hold the advantage and to win the debate hands down. Then the referendum will be a formality and a humiliation for the separatists. Morrison and his lot will be finished."

Sir David nodded in satisfaction. "I understand that Morrison is meeting with his team this afternoon to discuss the outline of his presentation and tactics for the debate. I have reason to believe them to be in some disarray. In any event, I will be able to forward details of their plans to you by six tonight. Not his presentation, but an outline of what he intends to say. You will have it minutes later. You can brief the Deputy PM as you see fit, but I'd suggest that you tell him that it is intelligence led information, so as not to compromise our source. Agreed?"

Penny Carson was enjoying the meeting, for everything was working out as expected, maybe even better than expected. "Yes, Sir David, that is agreed. He will not enquire too deeply anyway. He knows that there are certain things that are better for him not to know. I take it everything is going well and there are no little problems that we need to worry about?"

It was a routine enquiry, and Sir David was expecting it. He was certain that Penny Carson would have no inclination that an electronic folder had been copied. He had decided much earlier in the morning that he would not tell her about the incident. There was every chance that Williams would catch up with Chisholm and bring the matter to a swift conclusion before any damage was done. It was possible, too, that Chisholm would not be able to break the code, even if he had managed to enlist the help of the boy genius, Rory Lawson. Sir David was also aware that he had been specifically instructed by the Prime Minister to record nothing of their conversations or activities. The whole event might yet be blown open and the copied file become public, but there was nothing to be gained at this stage by mentioning the matter to Penny Carson, and by association, the Prime Minister. That would not help his plan in any way. He simply smiled back at her and said, "What could possibly go wrong? I think we have covered all the bases, don't you?"

* * *

Over a light lunch of cucumber sandwiches and Earl Grey tea in his office, Nigel Braithwaite was being updated by Penny Carson. Braithwaite, although outwardly bright and cheerful, was looking beleaguered. The media were incessantly hounding him, and he and Tom Albright were getting an increasingly tough time in Parliament about the state of the economy. The latest figures showed the economy slipping into recession, unemployment increasing slightly, and inflation nudging upwards. Some commentators were beginning to highlight the situation with the UK's credit rating, and the effect that was having with the increase in the cost of borrowing working through to hit the man in the street. There were also increasing anxieties about rising crime rates in inner cities and increasing speculation about strike action in the public sector, which had borne massive cuts as his government had tried to get borrowing under control. He was reported to be considering a cabinet reshuffle to help address the problems, but he knew that any such move would be interpreted as a panic measure by the financial markets, and that might make the situation worse. It was true that he wanted to change some of his senior colleagues. Although they had all been appointed by him, some of them were not up to the job. He knew this, or suspected it before he had appointed them. Their appointments had been necessary, however, to maintain party unity, to make it seem that all wings of the party were represented in the cabinet, and to accommodate one or two individuals who had strong individual support from the public, and were seen as populist appointments. There were at least two appointments that had been made to appease major donors to party funds. He badly needed some good news, and hoped that Penny would be providing that in relation to the Scottish independence referendum. Certainly, the opinion polls over the last weeks had been very encouraging, and the latest information he had, suggested a landslide vote against independence. He listened intently while Penny briefly summarised recent events with which he was already familiar, and he could tell from her relaxed manner that there were no nasty surprises about to come. Finally, she brought him up to date with her session the previous day with Richard Hume, and that morning's meeting with Sir David Lee, missing no details of significance from her account.

"So, Penny, it is all set. You have done well, as has Sir David. The referendum vote has been turned round, and Richard will be well capable of ensuring it stays that way after tomorrow night's debate. I think Sir David has earned his elevation to the peerage. Lord Lee of wherever."

Penny looked at him quizzically. Brathwaite explained, reasoning that she was his most trusted and loyal confidante. "Tomorrow is the last day for nominations for the Honours List. Sir David will be nominated for and will receive a peerage. He will accept this as a sign of my gratitude. However, as a member of the House of Lords, he will have to resign as Head of MI5. Once he has gone, and a new Head is in place, we will negotiate the 15% budget cut that I need from MI5. Lord Lee, as he will be then will be in no position to refer to any informal agreement not to impose cuts on his service."

He could see Penny shifting in her seat, and she broke into a broad grin. "That, sir, is what they call a master stroke!"

Chapter Thirteen

Deception

Hugh Lawson cursed silently to himself. He had been in the barn working at the stripped down engine for three hours now. He had thought it was going to be a straightforward task, but it was proving to be quite difficult. He wiped his forehead with a big, grease covered hand, and looked at his watch. It told him that it was just after noon. Five more minutes, he told himself, then I'll stop and prepare some lunch. All morning he had kept the phone near, hoping to hear from his son that he had broken the code and was coming home. He was still waiting. Hugh Lawson was a man of high principle, brought up by strict parents, on the croft that he now worked. He had made the place productive, and been able to give his sons opportunities that he never had. Not that he was in any way bitter, he had loved his childhood on the croft and as his parents' only son, he had never anticipated anything other than one day he would inherit the croft. It had happened earlier than he expected, and earlier than he had wanted, when his father suffered a stroke almost twenty years earlier. He had only been fifty-five, and while he had made a decent recovery, he never regained enough strength for the heavy work involved on the croft. He had died some twelve years later, and his mother had moved out, despite his protestations, to live with an unmarried sister in Fort William, where she still lived. He was proud of the boys' achievements. Angus was doing well at University, doing a course on agriculture that involved a lot of work on livestock management. There was an unspoken expectation on all sides that Angus would one day return to take over the croft. Rory was rather different. He was a good lad, and liked nothing better than helping out round the croft, especially with the sheep. But Hugh couldn't quite understand what the boy could do with numbers and equations. He and his wife had first become aware of something unusual when Rory was about seven. They had known that he could do the sums he got as homework from the local primary school, and then one day while he was playing quietly in the same room as them, an astonishing thing happened. They had been working on the accounts for the croft for the year. They stopped and made themselves a cup of tea, dreading the hours of counting and squaring all the figures that they had spent most of the day transposing into their ledger. They couldn't have been out the room more than ten minutes, but when they came back, everything was squared off, and Rory was grinning contentedly. Amazed, they had checked his workings, and found no mistakes. Now the maths he did was well beyond their understanding, and Mr McNeil, head of the maths department at his secondary school had admitted that some of the things Rory took on were beyond even him. For that reason, the school had, to their credit, fixed up a weekly internet session for Rory, with the Professor of Applied Mathematics, Jacques de Villiers, at the University of Cape Town. The two of them discussed topics and worked on projects that nobody else seemed to understand. Rory seemed to have great powers of concentration, and would spend hour after hour working on these projects. That was why Hugh had almost expected his son to look at the code, then take an hour or so to work it out. Nothing had ever defeated Rory. Hugh's concern for Rory's future was simple. It was all outwith his experience. He had no reference point. Try as he might, he could not see what the future might hold for Rory. Just what were the career opportunities for a mathematician?

It was unusual for Hugh to be alone on the croft. His wife was away in Nairn, nursing an aunt who had just come out of hospital after a hip replacement, and she would probably be away for another four or five days. Angus was at University, and it was a long journey back home, so he didn't get back very often. Rory was good company, and this week the school was on holiday, so he had anticipated that he would have had Rory's company most of the time while his wife was away. For the first time in his life, he realised how isolated and remote the croft was, his nearest neighbours' house being almost half a mile away. Then he heard the sound of a car engine. Briefly he allowed himself to hope that this was the man Chisholm bringing Rory home, but he could see through the jamb of the barn door that the car was a Jaguar, not a black Audi Avant. He went back to working on the engine, while keeping an eye on the car. He heard the car door slam, and footsteps on the muddy forecourt. He could see two men making for the front door of his house. They looked big, and very official. He had no doubt that these men were connected with Chisholm's story. He watched as they knocked at his front door, and waited. When no answer came, one of them shouted in a loud deep Yorkshire accent "Anybody there?"

Taking his time, Hugh picked up a cloth, and emerged from the barn, wiping his hands. He called over to the men, who had not yet spotted him. "Hello! Over here! What can I do for you?"

The men came towards him, scattering a group of hens as they did so. "Are you Hugh Lawson?" asked the taller one, with the green eyes. Lawson noted that it was a home counties accent, not the Yorkshire accent.

"Aye, that's me," he conceded.

"You have a son Rory?"

"What now? Who wants to know?"

The man with the green eyes flashed an ID card from his pocket, and replaced it in his jacket pocket before Lawson could examine it properly. "D.I. Duckham of the Serious Crime Squad," he said by way of introduction. "This is my colleague, Inspector Pullar. Don't worry, your son isn't in any bother. We just need to ask him a few questions, that's all. Is he here, or in school?"

"No, neither. The schools in these parts are on holiday this week. So he is taking the chance to enjoy himself. What is all this about? It must be important for you two gentlemen to have come up here."

The man who called himself Duckham was doing all the talking. "Your son is something of a genius with numbers, I understand?"

"Aye, Rory does well at the maths."

"Well, we have information that a gambling syndicate are trying to recruit him, probably by deception, to work on some gambling formulae for them to use in casinos. This is organised crime we're talking about, Mr Lawson, dangerous people. We want to protect Rory. Can you tell us where he is, please?"

Hugh Lawson had spent the last day deciding what he would do if someone did call trying to track down Rory and Chisholm. He had decided the most successful lie would be the one that was closest to the truth. He still had to make it sound believable. He looked from one to the other, as though in disbelief. He wrung his hands on the oily cloth, then raised his head in what appeared to be a slow dawning. "Mr Duckham, I think you might be too late. This morning, they came this morning about nine. A man and a woman. They said that Rory had won some national maths competition, and they wanted to discuss the prize with him. He wins loads of things like this, so I thought nothing of it. When I think about it, he usually gets notification by letter or by e-mail, sometimes a phone call." He was letting just the right amount of panic creep into his voice.

Duckham continued, "So did they see Rory?"

"No. He was gone by then. But I told them where he was! They will be looking for him." By now the cloth was twisted round his wrist, almost stopping the flow of blood, and he was actually hopping from foot to foot.

Duckham tried to calm him. "What did you tell them, Mr Lawson? Where did you say Rory was?"

"I told them he had gone to Portree for the day."

"What was he doing there, who was he going to meet?"

"I don't know, I'm not sure who he was meeting up with. Look, he's a teenager. He doesn't tell me anything. If you have kids yourself you will know what like it is.

There are a couple of lads I hear him talk about. Norman Macleod, and Alistair Macleod. I don't think that they are related. You will find that there are a lot of families in Skye that are called MacLeod. Maybe he was meeting up with a girl – I don't think he would tell me if he was." All this came tumbling out, forcing the green eyed man to raise a hand for silence. It was partly true. Rory had been intending to meet with some friends that morning.

"OK, Mr Lawson, I can see that we have upset you. I'm sorry. We thought we were ahead of them. A man and a woman, you say. Can you describe them?"

"Aye, of course. The man, he was older, sixty something. Kind of grey hair, specs, about my height, but thinner. He did all the talking. He's not from around these parts. The lassie, I didn't pay much attention to her, she was younger, fair hair. That's all. Oh and they were in a big black Audi."

"The man asked me when Rory was due back, and I told him he'd be on the bus at five in Portree, so he'd get home here about six."

"Did they ask you to describe Rory?"

"Describe him? No, they did not."

"What happened next, Mr Lawson?" The tall man was controlling the urge to rush on in pursuit of was were surely Chisholm and Murray, and to conduct the conversation in what would be regarded as a professional manner. Besides, there might be something more he could find out.

"Well, they just said that they would spend the day sightseeing - they made some crack about the scenery - and come back in the evening. But they will have gone straight to Portree, won't they? Can you do something?" The despair in Hugh Lawson's voice sounded so genuine that it might have won him an Oscar.

"You say it was about nine that they came? About three hours ago?"

"That's right."

"When did Rory leave?"

"I took him into Plockton for the bus at half past eight."

"Just one more thing, Mr Lawson to help us. Can you tell us what Rory was wearing, and do you have a photograph of him?"

"Aye, just a minute." Hugh Lawson ran for the house as though his life depended on it and returned in less than a minute with a school photo in a frame.

"That was taken about three months ago. I think he was wearing jeans and a navy blue hoodie."

"Thanks, Mr Lawson. While you were in the house, I thought of something else that might help. Has he got his mobile phone with him?"

"No, no he doesn't. It's sitting on the dresser in the house. Sometimes he forgets it. Sometimes he doesn't bother taking it because there are so many spots where there is no reception, what with all the hills. Can I get it for you?"

"Please. It probably has the numbers of his friends on it, so we can start checking with them."

Lawson nodded and ran back to the house. He came out seconds later holding the Sony Ericsson high. He handed it over to the one calling himself Duckham.

"What can I do, Mr Duckham? This is my boy!"

"Leave everything to us, Mr Lawson. Stay here in case he comes home or phones you. Keep the phone lines clear. I'll see about getting someone from the local constabulary to come out and be with you. Is there a Mrs Lawson?"

"Aye. She's away visiting a sick aunt. Wait 'til she hears this. She will ... I don't know."

The tall man tried to sound reassuring. "Perhaps it is best not to worry her just yet. We don't know that they have got him, and you haven't given them his description. I'm off to start a search immediately. Portree can't be that big a town, is it?"

"It's big enough for these parts, but nothing like London or Glasgow."

The two men headed to their car, telling Lawson to try not to worry. They turned the Jaguar round, and headed back towards the road at speed. Hugh Lawson stood there for a moment, a thoughtful look on his face. Then he started to walk slowly after the car, taking care not to be seen. About 20 yards down the track he stopped. From behind a tree he watched as two identical cars were parked together. After a few minutes, someone got out of one of the cars and climbed in the other one. Then the car he had left drove off. The second car didn't move. Lawson made his way back to his cottage, more thoughtful than ever. By the time he had reached the door of the cottage he had made up his mind about what to do next.

Williams and Roberts had left the cottage and rejoined Johnston and Hardie just before the dirt track met the road. They had left their car and moved to the back seat of the other Jaguar. Williams was calculating their options, while Roberts quickly brought the other two up to date on the conversation they had just had with Lawson. When he finished, he turned to Williams and asked, "Do you believe him?"

Williams thought for a moment, then replied. "I'm inclined to believe him. He was able to give us a passing description of Chisholm, but not Murray. If he had been lying, he would have embellished the descriptions with more detail, thinking that would be more convincing. You could see his reaction going from unconcerned to high anxiety. He appreciated the urgency when I made him get things from the house, he ran, almost in a panic. No, he was trying to speed us on our way rather than delay us. I believe him. Have you any doubts?"

Roberts shook his head, "No, his reaction seemed completely genuine. No argument about handing over the boy's phone, and he was worried about his wife. There is just one little niggle, though. I thought we would be a lot more than three hours behind them."

Williams considered this. "We don't know for certain when they left Montrose. That might have been later than we thought. Certainly if the thoroughness of the clean up Chisholm did in the cottage is anything to go by, they didn't leave in a rush. Let's say they were

130

twelve, even fifteen hours ahead of us, that would have meant that they would have arrived here late last night, Sunday. They couldn't have used their cover story plausibly then, so they would go off for the night in a nearby hotel, and come out first thing this morning. Remember, they don't know that we know they are after the boy, so they have no reason to believe we are so close to them."

Roberts inclined his head slightly to indicate that he accepted the logic of what Williams had said. "That makes sense. Of course they won't need a description of the boy. He will be well known in a place like this, a bit of a celebrity with all these prizes he keeps winning, and they've probably got pictures of him from the internet. What is the plan now?"

Williams had had long enough to work out his next move. When he spoke, he was decisive. "We told Lawson that we would get someone out to sit with him. Hardie, when we leave, you get into the other car. Give it twenty minutes, then get up to the cottage. Remember, you're from the local force. Keep a watch out for anything, and report to me on any activity. I want you to be full of sympathy, make him cups of tea or whatever. Try to get him talking. Anything about the boy that might help us track him down. We are going to head into Portree. I'll phone his pals on his mobile and see what we can establish. Any of you know your way round Portree?"

It was Johnston who answered. "I was there for a week when I was about ten, on a family holiday. The main thing I remember is that it rained a lot. It's not big, the population can't be much more than three thousand. Nice harbour, and I think there were lots of cafés."

"OK, lets go, and Hardie, keep in touch!" With that, Hardie switched to the other car, and with Johnston driving, the others set off in the direction of Portree. Almost as soon as they had set off, Williams was trying to get Rory Lawson's phone to work. There was no signal. He kept trying. Eventually, just as the Skye

Bridge was coming into view, he managed to get a signal. He opened up the address book in the phone, and let out a whistle. "As Lawson said, there seem to be a lot of Macleods," he said to no-one in particular. He started with names on speed dial, first Alistair Macleod. There was no answer. Then Norman Macleod. The call went straight to voicemail. Then he tried Tommy MacNab. On the fifth ring it was answered. "Hi Rory!"

Williams explained, "I'm not Rory. I found this phone, and I was just dialling a number on it to find someone who knows the owner so I can return it. Could you do that for me? Where could I meet you?"

"No problem. There are a few of us at Giovanni's by the harbour. We'll be there for the next while."

Williams replied, "Good, I'll be there shortly," and hung up. He repeated the address to Johnston, and then said to Roberts, "It sounds like he hasn't met up with his mates."

Ten minutes later, Johnston parked the Jaguar by the harbour. Giovanni's was unmistakable, on the other side of the street. It was a coffee house with an Italian flag flying above the door, and the name in bold lettering, alternate letters being green and red. Williams left the others in the car and went in. Inside, the décor looked surprisingly stylish, with leather seats and couches, white walls with framed prints hanging, showing the works of some of the great Italian masters. In one corner, towards the back there was a group of teenagers, maybe a dozen. The group was split roughly equally between boys and girls. As Williams approached the group, he held out Rory's Sony Ericsson, and asked "Tommy MacNab?"

A dark haired boy wearing a green T-shirt made a sign with his hand, "Are you the man who found Rory's phone?" He made no move to rise. Williams confirmed, "Yes, that was me. I take it he's not here?"

"No."

"You are his friends. Do you know where I can find him? To give him back his phone, I mean."

"Have you tried his house? He lives on the mainland, near Plockton." It was only MacNab who was answering, the others were watching the exchange between them.

"Look," Williams went on, "I'm not familiar with these parts. I'm up here on business, and I don't have time to chase round the country. If you are going to see him, can I leave his phone with you?" Williams reckoned that this was one of those places where everyone was known, and certainly his accent didn't fit in. Admitting he was visiting the area would add some credibility to his story.

It was one of the girls in the group who answered rather offhandedly. "We don't know when we'll see him next. Maybe not for a week. He was supposed to be meeting us here, but he hasn't turned up." Williams guessed her annoyance was not at him, but at Rory for not showing up. She must be the girl that his father suspected the boy was seeing.

"OK, thanks anyway. I'll just hand it in at the local police station," said Williams. He turned and left to a loud murmur of comment from the group. When he got back into the car, he told Roberts "It looks like they have got him. He was meant to be meeting up with that bunch in there, but never showed. So they got him somewhere between the bus terminal at Plockton and here. Presumably here, given that he had already left when they called at his home. Where would they take him? Right, let's get back to Lawson's place." Johnston put the Jaguar into gear, and took off.

Chapter Fourteen

Flight

On Monday morning, Chisholm had woken just before eight o'clock, refreshed and alert. He saw Shona asleep on top of the bed opposite him. He had no idea how long she had been there, or how late she and Rory had worked after he had gone to bed. It was an easy decision to leave her undisturbed. He swung his feet out of bed, onto the loose rug that lay between the two beds. His mind was already racing with possibilities and questions. How much progress had they made? Surely if they had succeeded they would have woken him. Had they decided it was impossible? Did Rory still feel so enthusiastic? What were his former colleagues up to?

Chisholm headed to the toilet, and was vaguely aware that he had not seen Rory, but he was unconcerned. The boy was probably asleep in one of the chairs, and obscured from view. Finished in the toilet, and feeling better for having washed and brushed his teeth, he pulled on his socks and shoes. He went quietly from room to room, but there was no sign of Rory. He retraced his footsteps, calling out gently. There was no response. Where had the boy gone? Had they, at some point during the night, decided that solving the code was beyond his powers? Had he gone back to his house? Chisholm could feel the apprehension rising in the pit of his stomach. He had always had reservations about involving such a young boy. Chisholm went outside to the car, and looked about, again calling gently. Once more there was no response. He circumnavigated the lodge. He went a few yards into the wood. There were no footprints visible in the mud, but then, most of the track was hardened, and wouldn't show footprints. It would be easy for the boy to pick his way avoiding the muddier bits of the track. There was no sign of Rory. All of Chisholm's training had taught him to stay calm in situations like this. He stopped, weighing up his options. The first thing he needed to do was check with Shona whether she knew where he had gone.

Shona was in a deep sleep, and he had to shake her none too gently before she roused. She surfaced slowly like someone climbing out of a large, black pit, the light hurting her eyes. She could hear the urgency in Chisholm's voice, but it took long minutes before she could understand what he was saying. "Shona, do you know where Rory is? He's not here."

She heard the words, and detected the urgency, but her head still hadn't cleared enough to respond. Chisholm took her hand, encouraging her to sit up, and to concentrate, still speaking quietly. Suddenly the implications of what Chisholm was saying hit Shona through the fog as she sat bolt upright. There were no silly time-wasting questions like "Are you sure?" Instead Shona said, "He's not here? He didn't say anything to me about leaving. Give me a minute to get ready. We'll have to find him."

It was less than a minute before she was on her feet, and helping Chisholm search the lodge for a note, or any indication of where Rory might have gone. They found nothing. Shona was forcing herself to stay calm, but she could hear her nerves jangling. She had worked closely with Rory all the previous day, and they had got on well, a natural and easy rapport had developed. There was a certain bond forming between them. He seemed like a younger brother to her. Chisholm had confirmed that he had searched the immediate vicinity of the lodge to no effect. They stood by the door, considering their next move, Shona fighting a rising urge to just rush out into the woods and shout his name at the top of her voice. Why had he left, and where had he gone? Where should they look? Chisholm was calmer and more structured. He was trying to think where the boy might have gone. When he had gone for a walk the day before, he had quartered the ground, looking for possible hiding places in case they found themselves cornered, or just other features of interest. Now he was frantically trying to recall the topography thinking of anything that might give a clue as to where Rory might have gone. The woods were full of trees with protruding roots, and it was quite possible, Chisholm thought, that if the boy had gone for a walk to get some air, he could have tripped over a root and damaged an ankle. He feared that Rory might be lying injured somewhere. Slowly they became aware of someone whistling in the distance, and the whistling was becoming louder, drawing nearer. Chisholm opened the door, and there was Rory, totally unconcerned, walking towards them, past the car. He was carrying something. He waved, and shouted a greeting. Chisholm and Shona exchanged looks, mainly of relief, but Chisholm also felt a hint of anger that the boy should have gone off without telling them, leaving them to worry. As Rory approached them, they could see that it was a bowl he was carrying. He grinned at them, "Nice to see you two sleeping beauties up and about. I've been away gathering our breakfast. Duck eggs. Fresh, there's nothing like them!"

Inside the lodge, he explained that he knew where ducks were nesting nearby. These were ducks that had been reared on the croft, but had found a pond in the woodland more to their liking. Besides, as he said, he needed the fresh air, and he could not sleep, his brain wouldn't switch off from the code breaking. He was in his element, and totally in control. He said that having had a break of an hour or so, he was ready to start working again, and that Chisholm should prepare breakfast while Shona came and helped him. They would stop when breakfast was ready. Chisholm didn't argue, but did register some displeasure that Rory hadn't told them he was going out. The boy acknowledged that, but countered that they were both fast asleep when he had gone. Then, with Shona in tow, he headed back to his notes, and she to the computer to await his instruction.

At 9:15 they sat down to a breakfast of duck eggs, sausage, bacon, and mushrooms, all fried, and accompanied by piping hot coffee and fresh orange juice. Apart from the eggs, all of this came from the larder of food that they had brought with them from the cottage. Chisholm noted that Shona was now raising no objection to fried food, and put down her earlier insistence on everything being grilled to her feeling she had to point out to him that he wasn't controlling her. At this point, Chisholm felt that he was being controlled by Rory. He really did not understand what the boy was doing, and suspected that Shona had only the vaguest grasp. However, he had to admit that the duck eggs were indeed delicious, and the breakfast plates were clearing fast. He asked Rory about progress. The boy had long since realised that Chisholm would not understand any of the techniques he was using, and he didn't have time to explain.

"We're getting there, Mr Chisholm. Shona is a great help. She is really good on the keyboard, and follows exactly what I ask her to do. That has speeded things up a lot. I can't say how long it will take to break into their code. We just have to keep working, but every hour I'm getting closer." With that he picked up his mug of tea and headed back to work. Shona exchanged glances with Chisholm, shrugged, and followed Rory. Chisholm sighed to himself, and started clearing up the breakfast dishes.

After clearing the kitchen, Chisholm busied himself between the lodge and the car, finding an old basin and some cloths. Purely in an effort to keep himself occupied, he washed the car. Occasionally, throughout the morning, he looked in on the other two, silently, careful not to disturb them. Mostly, they were oblivious to his presence. He was becoming increasingly agitated, because he knew that he couldn't help, he felt useless. He watched the two of them at work. His team, as he was coming to think of them. Chisholm was beginning to discern a pattern of work that they had fallen into. Rory would work at his notes, making scribbles, then writing a summary that he would pass to Shona. She would ask a couple of questions, and then start to work at the keyboard for some minutes, before printing the results of her efforts. Rory would pour over the printout, taking more notes, before adding it to a growing bundle of discarded sheets. Then the process would start again. Chisholm did not know if they would succeed, but observing their efforts, he was proud of them. He couldn't explain it, but he felt more of a bond with these two than he had ever done with any of his colleagues over the years. Maybe it was their youth, or their enthusiasm. Maybe it was their naivety, their honesty, or their sense of doing what they believed in. Maybe it was that they were vulnerable, or maybe he was just getting soft as he got older.

Just after noon, he announced he was going to prepare some lunch for them, that they could stop for a break in about half an hour. Without looking up, or stopping work, they grunted approval, and he made his way back to the kitchen. He was beginning to wonder whether he should call the whole thing off, admit defeat. Rory seemed to be able to go on for ever. He had hardly slept in the thirty-four hours or so since they met him. That could not be good for him, and he, Chisholm, had a moral duty to look after the boy. Then there was Shona. She was desperately short of sleep, too. More than Rory, she showed it. She had risen from the computer and stretched herself, and splashed her face with cold water frequently throughout the morning. The lines round her eyes were deepening by the hour, or so it seemed. She was trying to work at Rory's pace, and it was breaking her down slowly. He was considering how he would tell them to stop. He knew they would argue, for they had put so much time and effort into this task, but he was becoming more and more certain that for all Rory's enduring optimism, time would beat them. Was it not time to admit that? Absent-mindedly, he was working at the stove, boiling up water for a pasta dish while he grated some parmesan cheese. Suddenly his thoughts were dramatically interrupted by a squeal. Shona! What had happened? He dropped the cheese and opened the door into the sitting room. His eyes widened like saucers at the scene that unfolded.

Rory had picked the girl up by the waist, and was spinning her round and round. She had her arms wrapped round his neck, and was kissing the top of his head. In one hand she was clutching a piece of paper. Chisholm watched incredulously as the scene unfolded. Shona's feet were now on the ground, and the two were hugging each other tightly, like long lost friends reunited. In their excitement, they were jumping, almost dancing as they hugged. It took fully a minute before Rory became aware of Chisholm's presence. Over Shona's shoulder he caught Chisholm's eye, gave him the broadest grin ever, and indicated a thumbs up sign. Eventually, Shona also realised that Chisholm was there. Without speaking, she waved the sheet of paper in his direction. Silently, she invited him over to join in their hug. Chisholm had no doubt what they were telling him, and put his arms round them both, as they embraced in excited silence. Afterwards, he couldn't remember how long the three of them had stayed like that, silent, too filled with emotion to speak.

It was the boiling pan of water that broke the spell. Chisholm rushed off to deal with that, all thoughts of lunch gone. When he came back into the sitting room, they were both seated, Rory with a grin still on his face, and quietly punching the air, while Shona gazed at him in wonder, still holding the sheet of paper. Chisholm went to her, hand extended and asked for the paper. "That's it," she said. "That is the first sheet in the folder. You can see that the formula we typed in has translated it into English! Not just that, but read it! If the rest of the material is anything like this, it will be the scandal of the century! I just can't believe it."

Chisholm took the paper, sat down and slowly and carefully read the A4 sheet forcing himself to take in the significance of every word. He had to agree with Shona's assessment. When he had finished reading it to his satisfaction, he laid it to one side, and asked Rory, "How did you do it?"

The boy was still sporting a huge triumphant grin, but when he spoke, it was with modesty, and he stuck to the facts "Well, it was difficult. I was on a wrong track for most of yesterday, and even when I was on the right track there was something wrong. Then, during the night, I realised what was going on. I was sure of it. They used a double code, which means they changed it from English into one code, then they applied a different code to the version already in code. I think the technical term for using more than one code on the same document is stacking. Once I had worked that out, it was a case of working through various possibilities. First they used a keyboard cipher. So they moved all the letters two spaces back on the keyboard." He picked up the keyboard to demonstrate. "Look. The first five letters are QWERTY. What they have done is change it so that every Y becomes an R, every T becomes an E, and so on. Once they had completed that, they then recoded it, using a space code. That means that they move spaces between words to appear three letters after where the space should actually be, and, for good measure, they removed all the Qs, which were actually Es in the original script."

Despite listening attentively, Chisholm had not really understood Rory's explanation. "Rory, you are wonderful! That is brilliant work."

Rory held up a hand, "Don't forget Shona. Without her, this would have taken much, much longer."

Chisholm turned to address the girl. "Yes. Shona, you've been brilliant from the start. Breaking into the MI5 material, accessing the files, and now this help for Rory, you have done more than I could have hoped for. I can't begin to express my appreciation to both of you, or my admiration at your abilities. Very obviously, I would not have got anywhere having these files in readable order without your efforts. Now that we have them, however, it is time to get you two home safely. Starting with you, Rory."

"Mr Chisholm, that's where you are wrong," Rory replied. "You don't have the files yet, at least not all of them. We have printed off the first page of one file, because it would have been a waste of time printing off more until we knew that we had broken their code. There are a whole lot of files in that folder. It is likely they have used the same code for all the files, but they may not. They may have changed the code for different files. So I need to stay until you have the last file printed."

Chisholm suddenly looked crestfallen. That they might have more than one code to break had never occurred to him. The implications of what the boy had just said hit him, almost like a physical blow. Unseeingly, he found his way to a chair. He needed to think how to respond. What an idiot he had been, not to consider this possibility. How long would it take to break all of the codes, one by one? It had taken almost two days to break one code. Thinking aloud, he said to no-one in particular "How long will that take?"

Rory, in his usual upbeat fashion, responded, "Let's look on the bright side. Maybe they have used the same code throughout. That would be quite logical. They would only put something into code if they believed that would safeguard it. If they believe that they have safeguarded it, then they wouldn't feel that they needed to change the code. If they thought that the code was compromised, they would change it for all the files, not just some of them. On the other hand, if they have changed it, they will almost certainly have used a similar combination of codes. Now that I know what I'm looking for, I'll manage to get them quite quickly. The first thing we should do is print of one page for each file, and see how many of them come out right. Then I can start work on any of the files we still can't get, while Shona prints off the ones we can get. Remember, Mr Chisholm, my bet is that they will be in the same code."

With what seemed like unbelievable speed, the atmosphere had changed from the unbridled euphoria following the initial success in breaking the code to diligent concentration on the task. Shona was suddenly working at her keyboard, isolating one page from each file. Rory was loading the paper into the printer. Chisholm was reading again the single page that had been printed, and beginning to formulate a plan for releasing it to the world - if they got the rest of material printed, and if it turned out to be as devastating as this first page suggested. He had always understood that the contents of the folder would be damning, but now that he had a sample in his hands, he could begin to visualise the various options open to him. News agencies in the UK might shy away from this, but there were international news agencies that would not. Some of these agencies had no reason to feel well disposed towards the British government. Time was the enemy. This was Monday lunchtime, and the referendum would take place on Thursday.

Shona was still working at the keyboard, getting the last pages set up to run with Rory's formula. Rory had loaded up the printer, and was seated opposite her watching expectantly, when the phone rang. It was the phone which Chisholm had given him, so it must, he realised immediately, be his dad. The ring had made them all start, and Shona stopped work. Chisholm indicated with a nod that Rory should answer the call. They all waited, aware that there could be a number of reasons for the call. It might be a general enquiry about progress, or asking if there was anything that they needed. Chisholm had warned Hugh Lawson not to make unnecessary contact, but they had been out of touch for well over a day now, and it would be entirely understandable if he was getting anxious. It might be important domestic news – his mother was away working with a convalescing relative, and something might have happened there. He might have been visited by someone that aroused his suspicions. Rory knew that all three of them needed to know what was going on, and would ask him as soon as the call ended, so he put the phone on "speaker", the way Chisholm had shown him, to let the others hear the conversation. He reckoned that would save him the effort of repeating everything. Chisholm was impressed with the boy's quick thinking, and signalled his approval. Shona moved her chair into a position to better hear the conversation, fully aware of how important it could be.

"Hi, Dad. Everything all right?"

"Yes, I'm OK, but you have not much time. They're on to you." Over the next four minutes he gave an accurate account of his visit from the men claiming to be from the Serious Crime Squad. He spoke without interruption, and left out no significant detail. By the time he stopped his narrative, Chisholm had recognised that Duckham was actually Williams, that there were two cars, both silver Jaguar XFRs, one parked by the road at the end of the track to Lawson's place, that the rest of them had gone on a chase to Portree, and that someone was going to sit with Hugh Lawson. Chisholm quickly realised that this would mean the parked XFR moving up to the house. He had known Williams for some years, and while the two of them had never been friends he was aware that Williams was a very competent, even ruthless agent. He wouldn't waste much time in Portree, but at least Lawson had bought them some time by sending him there. Lawson clarified a couple of points where Chisholm asked for more detail, before finishing the call with a heartfelt plea. "Mr Chisholm, look after yourself, but please, watch out for Rory. Make sure nothing happens to him." There was no panic or desperation in the request, just the natural concern of a father for his son.

"You have my word," said Chisholm solemnly, not feeling at all sure how he could keep his word, as the call ended. The three of them looked at each other for a moment, in disbelief. How had they been tracked down so quickly, they wondered? Chisholm felt an overwhelming responsibility for the safety of the other two. Over the years, he had often had to put field agents into dangerous situations, and he had always felt uneasy about that. They had been trained professionals who understood the risks. Shona and

Rory were different. They were members of the public, mixed up in something they didn't really understand. Rory, at times, almost seemed to treat the whole thing as a game. They certainly were not equipped to deal with anybody like Williams and his colleagues. Could he, Chisholm, justify putting them at further risk? Yet he was so close to getting the evidence that he needed. Was there a way he could do that without them? He saw the uncertainty on the faces of the other two, and knew what he had to do.

"OK, here's what we do. There is no time to argue. We need to get away from here. Rory, you can walk back to your house from here. Give them a story. Say that I approached you in Portree, but you wouldn't get in the car, that you got away from me. You can run faster than the old man, and you know your way round Portree better than me. Say that you decided not to meet up with your friends, and came home instead. Shona, start packing up the computer gear and load it into the car. I'll get you to a train station. Get yourself over to Ireland, and lie low until I clear this up. I'll give you an envelope with enough cash to keep you going for a few weeks, but it won't take that long."

Shona and Rory exchanged meaningful looks, and shook their heads in irrevocable certainty. "No!" they said in unison. Rory carried on. "You need me until you have the last file printed. You already know that. There is no other way. Anyway, I can't go home. They will see through any story I give them, and I'll be in trouble, and you will be given away. So you're stuck with me for a bit longer."

Shona added, "He's right, and you know it. As for me, you don't get rid of me either. Without me, you don't know how operate the software to apply the formula to the files. We are all part of this. For better or worse, we are in it together. We have come too far to stop now. Besides, there is something more I can do for you that I haven't mentioned yet, because we've been too busy with the codes, but I have been thinking about it, and there is one last piece of the jigsaw you need me for. I'll explain later. Give me a hand to clear away the gear and load up the car. We'll need all this gear, but I guess you are right that we should get away from here."

Chisholm made to argue, but was quickly and loudly put down by the other two, who were already switching off the computer and printer. Rory was gathering up his handwritten notes and stuffing them into a box. Shona gave Chisholm instructions about what equipment went into which box, and he started loading boxes into the car. Their clothes were already in the car, they hadn't even paused to take them out when they had arrived at the lodge. Chisholm's mind was already racing ahead, thinking about where they should head for, and the best way to get there. He knew that it was imperative that they find somewhere to set up their equipment, so that they could print out the remaining material. He hoped fervently that Rory would not have to crack any more codes. With Williams on their tail, they might not have time for that. In between carrying boxes to the car, he grabbed some of the food from the little kitchen. They might need that if it took them a long time to find a place where they would be safe and able to work.

It took just over fifteen minutes, working flat out, for them to switch everything off, pack it all up, and load the car. Chisholm went back to the lodge to clean it, and remove traces of their presence. He was nothing like as thorough as he had been at the cottage in the glen, but it would pass a cursory inspection. It was a few minutes after one p.m. when Chisholm, with Shona in the front passenger seat and Rory in the back, put the Audi into gear, and pulled away from the lodge. The Audi was sparkling in the early afternoon sunshine, after being washed that morning.

Chapter Fifteen

Chase

As instructed, Hardie had waited 20 minutes. Nothing had happened during that time. Only one vehicle, a battered old Fiat, of indeterminate colour had passed by, driven by what Hardie took to be an elderly woman, and with no passengers. He made his way up the track to Hugh Lawson's cottage, and parked by the barn, scattering a quartet of ducks in the process. As he made his way across to the cottage he could see Lawson standing by a window, looking out forlornly. Before he could knock on the door, Lawson opened it. The worried eyes, the clenching and unclenching fists, the agitated manner of the walk all added up to the very essence of the distressed parent. Lawson looked appraisingly at the newcomer.

"Are you from the police? Duckham said he would send somebody."

"Yes, sir. May I come in?"

Lawson showed Hardie into the sitting room, and invited him to sit down. He did not ask to see any identification. He did not need to. Hugh Lawson had lived there all his life, and, in a rural community, all the local police officers were well known. The man in front of him was a stranger. It would have taken much longer to get someone that he didn't know to come from further away. Lawson was certain that this man did not belong to the local police force. He had decided that he should play out the role of worried father and build on the encounter with Duckham.

"Have you heard anything, constable?"

"No, sir. Brown, by the way, Constable Brown. Try not to worry. I've been liaising with these guys from the Serious Crime Squad, and believe me, they are good. From what I understand, they know the gang involved, and where they are based. They will get them. And remember, the gang are not after your boy to harm him.

They want him for the help they think he can be to them. Duckham and his colleagues may well find the gang members before they find Rory. Or he might find Rory first. By the way, the description you gave of the man has allowed Duckham to make a likely identification, so that helps, too."

"I wish I could share your confidence, constable."

"I appreciate this is difficult for you, sir. Of course I can't give you any guarantees, but I'd say there is a lot of cause for optimism. Look, Mr Lawson, can I make us both a cup of tea? In the meantime, if there is anything at all that you can remember about the man and woman, however insignificant, please tell me. You never know what might help."

Lawson nodded, and Hardie made his way to the kitchen, without waiting for permission, and filled the kettle, found some cups, tea bags and milk. When he returned to the sitting room with two full cups of tea, conversation was difficult. He went over to the dresser and picked up the picture by Hugh Lawson's wedding photograph. "Is this Rory? A fine looking lad, if I may say so."

"No, that's my other son, Angus. He is away at University. I gave Rory's photo to Mr Duckham." After that the two men drank their tea in a miserable and embarrassed silence, Lawson staring at the floor just in front of his feet.

Johnston ignored speed limits as he pushed the Jaguar XFR back along from Portree to the bridge. He needed no urging from his passengers. There was little traffic to impede his progress. Williams had developed a plan for this eventuality as they had driven up from Montrose that morning, and was now considering the best way to put that plan into action. He knew that even with a couple of hours head start, Chisholm could be anywhere. They had only two cars at their immediate disposal, and could not hope to cover all the possibilities. The search would have to be widened, and more pairs of eyes recruited to watch for Chisholm. That meant making the search public, and it would be very suspicious if he did that without speaking to the boy's family first. Reaching for his phone, he tried to call Hardie, but couldn't get a signal. He cursed out loud, and tried again. It rang out at the third attempt. Hardie answered immediately. "Are you with Lawson? Good. Are you out of earshot?" There was a pause, while Hardie moved into an adjoining room. "OK. They have the boy. I'm heading back to the cottage. I'm going to arrange for this to go public so we can get the police involved in hunting for Chisholm and Murray. I'll also get a real local bobby to relieve you, and then we can head up the search. Lawson needs to be told his son has been kidnapped, and he needs to let his family know. It would look really bad if word got out publicly before the family had been told. Can you put Lawson on now?"

Hardie called out to Lawson and held out his phone. "It's Mr Duckham. He has some news for you."

Lawson took the phone tentatively. "Is it good news?"

"Just listen carefully to what Mr Duckham has to say," Hardie replied encouraging Lawson to hold the phone to his ear. Slowly Lawson did so.

"Hugh Lawson here. What is the news, Mr Duckham?"

"Well, I'm afraid that it is not good. Rory never met up with his friends. It appears that Rory must have been taken by the people who came to your house. We have no alternative but to regard this as a kidnapping. It's not like a usual kidnapping. We know that he hasn't been taken for ransom, but for his ability. So they are not going to contact you. They may make Rory phone you to assure you he is all right, and that you shouldn't report his disappearance, so we would like to put a monitor on your phone so we can trace any such contact. As long as they think Rory can be of some use to them he will be safe. We know a lot about this gang, and they are capable of violence, I won't lie to you, but they don't go in for wanton violence. They don't want to draw attention to themselves. So, Mr Lawson, here's what's going to happen. We know where their headquarters are in England, and we'll put a surveillance team on that. We don't know where they have taken Rory, but they have not had time to get him out of Scotland yet. So we are going to issue a description of Rory and of the two suspects to all the Scottish police forces. The net will close on them pretty quickly, I'm sure. Mr Lawson, you should let your wife and family know what is going on. I will be back with you in ten or fifteen minutes, and I'll answer any questions you have then. Is that all clear?"

"That is a lot to take in. I think I've got the gist of it, though." Lawson was genuinely bewildered at this turn of events, but already thinking of what he would say when contacting his family.

"Good. Have courage, Mr Lawson. Could you put the constable back on please?"

Lawson handed the phone back to Hardie, and returned to the sitting room. He had decided to take a chance, calculating that it wasn't much of a chance, really. He could hear the other man talking into the phone to Duckham, as he picked up the house phone and punched in Angus's mobile number. His luck was in. Angus picked up the call immediately. He must have had the phone in his hand. Hugh spoke quickly and urgently to his son.

As Hardie finished his call with Williams, he was aware that he could hear Lawson speaking in the next room. He hadn't expected Lawson to phone his family until he had rejoined him, but he couldn't have been on the phone much more than a minute. He hurried through, silently. He wanted to hear what was being said on the off chance that something useful would materialise, but he did not want to appear to intrude on the family anxiety, so he stopped in the doorway. It took a moment for him to realise that although he could hear everything, he could not understand what was being said. Gaelic! They were speaking to each other in Gaelic, the ancient Celtic language still spoken mainly in the Hebrides and in pockets of the West Highlands.

Lawson had guessed, correctly, that he was safe – there were only about 60,000 Gaelic speakers, and Lawson was gambling that the man beside him wasn't one of them. Hardie moved into the room, and mouthed to Lawson that he should speak English. That Hardie requested Lawson to speak in English was proof enough that he did not speak Gaelic. Lawson gave a silent sigh of relief.

"Angus, the policeman here wants me to speak in English." Hugh Lawson finished the conversation three minutes later, having told Angus the outline of the alleged kidnap by a gambling syndicate, with the promise that he was going to call his wife, and that he, Angus, should try not to worry, the police seemed to have things under control. Yes, it would be good if Angus could come home immediately, for the family should be all together at a time like this. Finally he suggested that Angus contact his mother, once he had a chance to talk with her. When he put the phone down, Hardie looked at him accusingly. "What is all this speaking Gaelic for?"

"We are Gaelic speakers, and regard it as our first language. We always speak Gaelic within the family. Lots of families around here do. Surely you should know that if you are with the local constabulary. Angus would think it strange if I started a conversation with him in English."

Hardie swallowed the rebuke, for he had to maintain his cover. Besides, he could see that Lawson had enough on his mind. "I'm sorry, sir. I didn't mean to sound, well, aggressive. I don't speak the language, and I'm not really from around here. I transferred up from Strathclyde just about a year ago. It's all quite different here from Glasgow. Go on, phone your wife."

Hardie would never know that in the 90 seconds or so of frantic Gaelic conversation, Hugh Lawson had managed to tell Angus a number of important things. He had told his son that Rory was in good hands, that he knew exactly what Rory was doing and it had his approval, that the man with him was not a policeman, that they should try to ensure that Rory and his two companions stayed at liberty for as long as possible, even though that meant appearing to go along with the kidnap story and that he, Angus, should pass all this on to his mother, because he, Hugh, would not get the chance. It was a mark of the relationship between father and son that Angus accepted all of this unquestioningly. If his father said it, it must be so. By the end of the conversation, Angus understood the reason behind the apparent kidnap, but had realised that the story of the gambling syndicate taking Rory was a rouse to cover up some other set of circumstances. He realised that his father could not discuss things over the phone, but he was eager to know what was really going on, to discover what his younger brother was mixed up in. He wanted to get home as soon as possible and hoped that he would get the chance to discuss things with his father without their conversation being overheard. He was partly reassured that his father, during the Gaelic part of the conversation, had been positive, assertive, even in his manner, and had sounded very sure and confident. Angus would phone his mother as requested, and then head for the croft, making all haste on his Kawasaki D Tracker motorbike. He had chosen the model for economy rather than speed, but it was nippy enough. On a motorbike, he would be able to weave in and out of the slowest traffic on the road works along the A9. The journey home should take him less than four hours.

When Hugh Lawson spoke to his wife, conscious of Hardie's presence, he stuck rigidly to the version of events involving the gambling syndicate, and offered no hint that there might be another explanation. He concluded by telling her that he had already spoken to Angus and that Angus would be in touch with her, she should take comfort in her contact with Angus, and that their older son was on his way home.

Chisholm was driving carefully so as to avoid undue attention. He had decided that he needed to avoid main roads. It was unavoidable that they would have to drive part of the way back, however, and that this would take them past the track leading up to the croft. Hugh Lawson had told them there was a car parked there, keeping lookout. Chisholm had considered this. Perhaps the car would move, and he thought it possible that whoever was in the car would move up to the house. They would want a presence there in case Rory contacted his father. He could see little point in them keeping watch at the end of the track, because they would assume that their prey would be long gone. In any event, he had no alternative but to risk it. He shared his concern with his passengers, both of whom were keeping close watch as they drove past. There was palpable tension in the car as they approached the turn off for the track, matched only by the sense of relief as they passed by undetected. Hardie had moved up to the cottage only five minutes earlier. They had to travel about another half mile on the main road before turning off onto a B class road. Chisholm explained his intentions to Shona and Rory. He was going to make his way south using B roads and back roads. He needed to avoid the A9, where the Audi would be easy to spot, and once spotted, the heavy single file traffic would make any escape impossible. Once in the more densely populated central belt of Scotland, they would find a place to stay, probably a hotel, and then set up the computer and printer in the hotel room and work on printing out the contents of the folder, or give Rory space to work on any more codes that might be needed. Chisholm indicated that he knew some possible hotels that they could use. By now, they had turned onto the B road. It was narrow, with lots of bends and curves. The countryside was hilly, so there were many small rises and falls in the road, making it difficult to see any distance ahead. Chisholm could see a narrow, winding river, little more than a burn on the left side of the road, and realised that the road was following the path of this river.

Williams, seated in the back of the Jaguar XFR, was concentrating on his next move. Johnston was making good time, and they had left the Skye Bridge behind them and were nearing the turn off to Lawson's croft. It was a bright sunny afternoon, and the scenery around them was stunning, but none of them noticed. Williams said to Roberts, "I'm going to have to make a few calls to get things arranged. Given the problems with reception on the mobiles, I'll make them from Lawson's landline. I don't want him to hear what I'm saying or to know exactly what the arrangements are. While I make these calls, you must keep him engaged, and make sure he can't hear what is going on." What he didn't say was that he also didn't want Roberts to hear the details of his calls.

Before Roberts could answer, Johnston interrupted. "Sir, I'm certain I saw a black Audi on that road down there. Just a glimpse, as it disappeared round a bend. I'm sure though, because it was gleaming in the sun."

Williams considered this for all of one second, and then urged Johnston. "Go!" Johnston may be wrong, it might be an Audi. He had said he only caught a glimpse. Even if it was a black Audi, there could be no certainty that it was Chisholm. It was, however, a chance worth taking. Sometimes luck was with you. "How far ahead was it?"

"Maybe half a mile, or a bit more given the bends on the road," Johnston replied. He had already increased his speed further, and had turned off the main road onto the B road. He was taking the bends on the narrow road as fast as he could, accelerating fiercely away from them. The gears were working hard and the tyres were squealing as they pushed on. "There!" he shouted, pointing excitedly. They could briefly see a black car, visible for a moment on a higher stretch of road where the bends construed to momentarily put the two cars in each others' line of vision. Unquestionably, it was an Audi Avant.

In the car ahead, Chisholm was driving at a sensible speed, concentrating on the road. Imperceptibly, he was increasing speed as in a casual voice he said to the others, "There is a silver Jaguar XFR behind us. We can't outrun it."

In a reflex reaction, Rory and Shona turned together to look out of the rear window. They couldn't see anything, but the casual certainty of Chisholm's manner left them in doubt that he had indeed seen the pursuing vehicle. He was also now driving at speed, taking corners at reckless angles and flying over the little summits in the road. "Rory, are there ways to get off this road unseen?"

Rory's heart was in his mouth as Chisholm threw the car round another bend, bouncing off a grassy verge as he fought to keep control and straighten the vehicle. "About a mile ahead there is a fork. Take the left turn. That takes you back into the forest, and there are tracks there we can use." Chisholm nodded, praying he could put some distance between him and the XFR so that when they reached the fork those in the chasing car would not see in which direction they had gone. He raced on, reaching a small summit. There it was, perhaps 100 yards in front of him, on the longest straight stretch of road he had encountered. It was perhaps a shade under two hundred yards before the next bend. A caravan being towed! He swore loudly. Who would bring a caravan over this road?

Behind them, Johnston was working his car to the limit. The gap had closed, but he knew something else. He said to the men in the back seat, "It is Chisholm, and he's seen us. He has put his foot down." His passengers had worked this out for themselves, and were holding on automatically to the seats in front of them despite their own seatbelts. The car slewed round bend after bend, Johnston driving with superb control. Once, twice, they caught a glimpse of the car ahead. The gap was now a little over quarter of a mile.

Chisholm had to make an instant decision. He could see that little river by the road had a small kink in its path. It left the roadside which it had hugged so tightly for a short distance, no more then twenty-five yards.

For this distance there was a grass verge running between road and river, at it's widest about ten feet across. Just maybe, he could judge it so that he could use this area to pass the caravan. His foot pressed hard to the floor, Chisholm urged the car on. There was no time to explain to the others what he intended. Rory held the seat in front of him, terror written all over his face. Shona's eyes were closed tightly. Chisholm was now only yards behind the caravan, and almost level with the start of the grass verge. It was now or never. He was committed – there was no way he could stop the car from hitting the caravan without veering off the road. Suddenly, violently, he swung the car to the left, on to the grass, and in one movement straightened it up. He held it there for as long as he dared, less than a second. The verge was disappearing as the river rejoined the road. He swung the car to the right, back onto the road, praying that he would miss the car that was towing the caravan. He was vaguely aware of the look of astonishment on the other driver's face as he applied the brakes. The Audi bounced as it hit the edge of the verge. Chisholm somehow managed to straighten the car as it landed on the road, escaping contact with the other car by a hair's breadth. Now Chisholm was braking frantically as he fought to slow the car down before the next bend, perhaps twenty yards away. Thankfully, the bend was not as sharp as some of the others, and despite hitting a glancing blow against a rock at the road side, he regained control. A road sign flashed by, indicating the fork Rory had described was just ahead. How far would it be? Could he afford to slow down? One more bend, and there was the fork. As instructed, he took the left fork, barely slowing down.

Johnston hadn't seen the caravan before. It had been too far ahead, but travelling much more slowly that he was. He had just come to the start of the straight where Chisholm had suicidally overtaken the caravan in time to see the caravan disappear round the bend. He realised immediately that this meant that Chisholm had somehow succeeded in putting this slow moving vehicle between the two of them. He knew that the narrow road would make it difficult to pass the caravan, but he had to try. He covered the straight and was taking the bend when he saw a point about three hundred yards ahead where the road widened. That would be his chance. He blasted the horn and flashed his lights to ensure that the caravan driver had seen him, but he had to slow down. The caravan slowed down too, coming to a halt opposite the wider patch of road. Johnston overtook it, but the manoeuvre had cost him valuable seconds. He took off, pressing the XFR to its tolerance level, and leaving behind a very bewildered and shaken caravan driver and his wife. When Johnston came towards the fork in the road, he yelled over his shoulder "Which way, sir?"

Williams tossed a mental coin, and roared back, "Left, go left."

Although they didn't know it, the gap was now almost half a mile and the road was now lined with trees, mainly firs. If anything, the road was now more full of bends and curves, and they were tighter than before. Chisholm could not afford to slow down. He knew that the odds were even on the chasing car making the right choice at the fork. They had passed a couple of tracks leaving the road heading into the wood, and Chisholm was considering whether he should take one, when he became aware that Rory was leaning forward, his head through between the two front seats. Now he was pointing. "There! Take that track, coming up!"

Chisholm wondered what was so special about that particular track, but trusted Rory's local knowledge. He checked his mirror quickly. There was no car in sight. He swung off into a narrow dirt track which wound its way gently through the trees. Chisholm reckoned that after they had gone thirty yards, they would be completely obscured from the road. He slowed the car, and asked Rory "Why this track?"

"Keep going," Rory urged. "My cousin, Iain Beag lives another quarter of a mile along here. That means little

Iain, but he's not little now. He got the name when he was a lad, to distinguish him from his dad, Iain Mor, big Iain. He'll help us and we can hide the car in one of his barns."

Johnston carried on for about three miles, driving at breakneck speed along the narrow, twisting road, meeting no other vehicle, although he was careful not to take any undue risks. Eventually the road opened out into a long straight, cleared of trees on one side, where sheep grazed contentedly in a fenced off field. He and the others in the car could see there was nothing in front of them. If Williams was disappointed, it did not show when he spoke. "OK, they must have taken the other fork. At least we know they are still in this part of the country. Right, Johnston, turn us round and get back to Lawson's cottage. They will be wondering where we are. Try to make it a little less hair raising."

Chisholm, drove slowly towards the clearing. On his right as he approached there was a medium sized stone-built house on two floors, and two wooden barns on his left, one fairly small, but the second barn was a substantial size. The house was surrounded by a bright green fence, and a there was a small pretty flowered garden between the gate and the house. A paved pathway ran from the gate to the front door. A black and white Border Collie that had been sitting at the door leapt up and ran towards them barking loudly. This appeared to Chisholm to be an act of warning rather than one of greeting. Chisholm made to pull up by the gate, but Rory indicated that he should go to the second barn. "There will be room to park the car inside the barn, out of sight."

Chisholm did as instructed. From the inside, the size of the barn became apparent. Strewn down the left hand side was a selection of farm implements, many of which looked as though they were attachments for a tractor. Chisholm recognised a sprayer, a mower and a baler, and by the door, a trailer, but there were more that he could only guess at. Towards the top of the barn were bales of hay or straw, and a ladder leading to a floor above, which extended about half the length of the barn. To their right was a set of six animal pens, all of which appeared to be empty. Rory opened the door, telling the others to wait where they were. Shona saw the dog jump at him. The dog recognised Rory, who met it with a grab, and patted it heavily round the head "Hello, Shep, boy." The dog, obviously excited, and still barking had its front paws on Rory's chest. Rory pushed the dog down, and started towards the barn door with the dog running round his feet. Shona and Chisholm saw him wave to someone, and then he disappeared out of their line of vision, as he left the barn.

They sat in the car for the next fifteen minutes, wondering what was going on, but grateful to be out of sight, and presumably safe for the moment. Shona rummaged amongst the luggage that had been quickly moved from the lodge into the car, and found some chocolate biscuits. She helped herself to one and offered one to Chisholm, which he gratefully accepted. Both of them were conscious of the need to calm down after the adrenalin rush resulting from the chase, and they did not speak much, until Shona asked "Well, what know? Does this change your plans?"

"I don't think so, Shona. We have got to get the rest of the material printed, and we must find a way of making it all public. I think we have more chance of staying at liberty to do that in the central belt, where there are more people to mingle with, more chance to become anonymous in the crowd. I still think that the best way of getting there is by avoiding the main roads."

Shona considered this silently, before simply saying, "Yes."

When Rory reappeared he was carrying a tray with three mugs of steaming tea and a plate of sandwiches, and wearing a broad grin. "It's all fixed. I've explained to Iain what help we need. We need to ditch this car. It is too well known. Iain is going to bring his Volvo round, and we can borrow that. I think he's going to tidy it up a bit first – it's always full of chocolate wrappers and crisp packets. We should leave this car here, in the barn. I've told him not to contact my dad, and that if dad contacts him to say that he hasn't seen us. Iain's a good guy. He won't let us down."

Chisholm was impressed, but worried. "That's really good, Rory, but how much did you tell him? The less he knows the better. That way, if he does get questioned, he can't give anything away."

"I told him just about everything, Mr Chisholm. Don't worry. He is sound. You have got to stop being suspicious of everybody. We don't all behave like spies and criminals. Would you rather I told him nothing and got no help, or that we trust him and get the help that he is offering?"

Chisholm was aware of Shona watching him intensely, awaiting his response. "You're probably right, Rory. I need to learn to trust people a bit more. When you have been in this line of work for as long as I have, you learn not to trust your own shadow. I guess I'm learning to trust you two, and that is a start."

They heard the sound of a car pulling up by the barn, and a car door closing. The dog was barking as it came into view, followed by a giant of a man. Standing well over six feet tall, broad shouldered and with long hair catching in the wind, it was impossible to discern any of Iain Beag's finer features as they looked out from the relative darkness of the barn into the bright sunlight streaming through the entrance where he was silhouetted, striding towards them purposefully. Rory announced by way of introduction, "This is my cousin."

He stopped three feet from them. Shona found herself looking at the blue checked shirt on the man's chest. Slowly, she raised her eyes another fifteen inches to meet his eyes. "You are little Iain." She said with an incredulous shake of the head. At this range, she could see that the man was about her own age, in his late 20s, with a handsome, full face beneath that shock of brown hair. His eyes wrinkled up in friendly smile. "Aye, that's me. I used to be little, when I was about five. Now, Rory has explained that you have a spot of bother, and it would help if you were using a different car. There you go." He handed a set of car keys to Chisholm. "You are welcome to hide up here if you want. Any friend of Rory's is welcome here, but I understand that you might want to be on your way."

Chisholm thanked him profusely. This was more assistance than he could have wished for. "You have done too much already, but there is just one more thing. Can we wait here for another hour, just to be sure that there is no search still going on in the vicinity?"

"No problem. If you are going to be here for an hour, you had better have something proper to eat. You go ahead and transfer your things from this car to the Volvo, and I'll and prepare something."

Rory went to help Iain. It took Chisholm and Shona less than three minutes to transfer everything into the big, dark, blue and extremely battered Volvo. The car was old and Chisholm wondered how it had ever passed its MOT. He had to admit however, that it was exactly what they needed to avoid drawing attention to themselves. Once everything was transferred to the Volvo they sat down on one of the hay bales at the back of the barn. Iain and Rory returned carrying big bowls of vegetable soup and as much bread as they could eat. Shep, the Border Collie, moved between them, looking for scraps of bread. While they ate, Iain Beag announced, "I'm going to take the tractor out. That will give me a chance to poke about and see if the coast is clear before you leave."

They all agreed that this was a good idea, albeit beyond anything they could expect from him. A few minutes after leaving them in the barn with a cheerful wave, they saw him pass by the still open door seated on the tractor which sported the distinctive green livery of John Deere. When he returned some ten minutes later, he was smiling. "There is no sign of anybody out there. You should be safe enough."

Five minutes later, with another round of heartfelt thanks to Iain Beag and in return, his exhortation to be careful, they were on their way, keeping to minor roads.

Chapter Sixteen

Despair

The discussion was taking place at the First Minister's residence at Bute House. Alex Watson could not be present in person as his duties as a Member of Parliament at Westminster required his presence in London. However, a secure teleconference arrangement had been set up to allow him to participate. Donald Barrie was making the final arrangements, fussing over the volume controls as he set up the technology. He had the room to himself. It was ten minutes until the meeting was due to start, and he suspected that the meeting would not take long. People would start arriving shortly, and Alex would be coming into the studio in London at any minute. The purpose of the meeting was to advise Alistair Morrison on the line he should take in the televised debate scheduled for Tuesday, the next day. They already knew that he would face Richard Hume, the Deputy Prime Minister, and that he was an effective cross examiner. Donald thought that the meeting would be short because the situation was hopeless and no-one would have any ideas to contribute. He knew that Alistair Morrison would not prolong the meeting, for he had a fear that things might degenerate into recriminations and self pity. In the end, it was always going to come down to the two of them, Morrison and Hume. Ultimately, Alistair and he would draft out the presentation and rehearse the strategy. This meeting was more about keeping colleagues involved and up to date with their plans than it was about expecting genuine insight and help. The time for that was past. As a strategist, Donald realised that. They had been out gunned and outmanoeuvred. Try as he might, he could not see how that had happened. How, he had asked himself many times in the last couple of weeks, had they slipped from leading the polls to impending disaster? How had they been moved from leading the debate to being caught out, and having to respond? How had they been made to look out of step with the rest of opinion and forced to defend their positions? He knew that even when that defence was watertight, and well presented, as had been the case with the A9 project, there was always a public feeling that there could be no smoke without fire. There had been a persistent erosion of trust and each episode where they appeared to be at odds with some independent expert contributed to that erosion. This had been more than a concerted effort to improve the unionist's performance. He had never experienced anything remotely like this, where, it appeared, every day he and his colleagues were driven back, unable to stem the flow. He could think of nothing that could turn things round in the last couple of days before the referendum, and he was sure that none of the others would have any great suggestions either. He felt sorry for Alistair. He was very much the public face of the campaign, and it was he who would have to face Richard Hume live in front of one of the biggest audiences ever seen in Scotland. More than that, the debate was being shown internationally. Journalists from many countries had been interested in the campaign. It had made news round the world, particularly, he thought with a sense of irony, when it looked likely that they would win. That was when most of the international and foreign TV companies had signed up to take the debate. He wondered if they would have been so keen to sign up to something of a no-contest, the outcome of which was already clear and would lead to no change. After all, it was change that was newsworthy, and no change was not so interesting. It was Alistair that would face the incriminations afterwards. Donald wondered whether Alistair would be able to continue as First Minister. Having been beaten so badly in the referendum as now seemed inevitable, his authority would be questioned at every turn, and he would be fatally damaged. He was worried for the man he called "boss", almost as worried as he was about the outcome of the referendum itself.

On screen, Alex Watson appeared, with a face like thunder. "Hello, Alex, can you hear me?" Donald enquired.

"Loud and clear, Donald," said Alex as he settled into the comfortable chair in front of the camera.

"Are you alright, Alex? You look a bit flustered."

"Bearing up, Donald, bearing up. It is difficult down here. There is somebody waiting at every turn ready with a snide comment or a carping remark. They are gloating already. I know that we have never been popular down here, but now, with a few honourable exceptions, they're behaving like a pack of baying wolves. I know things are bad up there too, but it's unbelievable here. Take just now, coming here to the studio. I passed a group of backbenchers that I hardly know. I doubt if I've exchanged ten words with any of them. As I was going past they started giggling and a couple of them burst into a chorus of "Donald, Where's Your Trousers." They think it's a great joke. I know it's childish, but it's incessant. I wish we could find a way of shutting them up," Alex concluded with feeling.

Donald could hear the hurt in the older man's voice, and felt helpless. "I can only imagine what things are like down there, Alex. I'm not so sure that there is much we can do about it. Just a minute, I think I hear someone coming."

The door opened and in walked two members of the Referendum Group in discussion together. It was Christine Milne and Mary Ford, whispering quietly to each other. They looked haunted, as though they wanted to be somewhere else, anywhere but here. Christine had recovered somewhat from her debate with Edith Bannon, but her confidence level had been low ever since. Mary seemed to have shrunk into herself and looked even smaller than she usually did. She was quiet and withdrawn which was the opposite of her usual demeanour. They managed to exchange greetings rather tersely with Donald and Alex, just as Reginald

Small, the civil servant arrived. They got themselves organised with coffee. Soon everybody was in place, except Alistair Morrison. It was most unusual for Morrison to be late for anything and there was a strained silence as they waited.

At four minutes past two, four minutes after the meeting was due to start, Alistair Morrison came in and apologised for the delay. They were all seated at a table, and had papers with them, although only Donald Barrie had notepaper in front of him. He would take notes that, some time later, would be used by Morrison and him to prepare for the debate. Morrison started without preamble. He was terse and serious. "We have had a really bad time of it. We are all suffering, personally, and as a group. One way or another, it will all be over soon. I have to say that it looks as though things are getting no better. Donald has our latest set of canvassing figures, based on work done over the weekend. It was reading them that made me late. They make grim reading, in the main. Donnie, can you go over the numbers, please."

Donald Barrie took a deep breath. They really were not going to like this, although it was probably what they were expecting to hear. "Ladies and gentlemen, the headline figures are these. Those intending to vote for independence, 19%: Those intending to vote against independence 63%: Undecided 18%. We have been in meltdown for weeks and this is the lowest point. We have tried to ask what has influenced people's voting intentions. It seems that quite a number of those who intend to vote against us are not particularly against Scottish independence as a concept. What concerns them is whether they trust us, or consider us competent to run our own country. Basically, it is their futures and they want them to be in good hands. Right now they don't think that is us. When we break things down further, we can see that the part of our vote which has held up best is among women over forty. That is the group we tried to target with Mary, Lorna and Jo. Admittedly, this was the group where support was weakest in the first place, but the girls have gone out there and based their work on people trusting them as mums, not on policy or debate. Now, women over forty are only one segment of the public, but they are the only segment where our main message has been trust. It is lack of trust and confidence that is losing votes everywhere else. I think that the message is clear. It is the issue of trust that we need to concentrate on, rather than the independence arguments themselves. I don't know how we do that in the time we have left."

Alistair Morrison looked round the table. There was silence. "Has anybody any ideas?" Nobody raised their head. They were all studiously avoiding eye contact. He let the question hang there for a long time, and still there was no response. After a time, the silence became embarrassing. Morrison had to do something. Looking directly at the camera, he prompted, "Alex?"

Alex Watson had never been at a loss for words in his political career before, but realised that he had nothing material to add. "Alistair, I hear what Donald has to say, and I'd guess that his analysis is pretty much right. But you can't go out there tomorrow and just say, 'Trust us because we're a trustworthy group.' You need some message about why people should vote for independence. We all know the arguments and the evidence. I think you have to use them. The issue about trust is more difficult. You have always had a pretty good personal rating on that score. Up until now, that is. I think you should just be yourself. Let your sincerity shine through. I don't see what else you can do."

Following Alex's lead with some relief, the others round the table assented, without adding anything new. Morrison went round the table and asked them one at a time for their views, missing out the civil servant. Without exception, they paraphrased Alex Watson's advice. Morrison had expected nothing else, but he had to try. Showing no sign of disappointment, he moved on, "That is what we will do then; I will reiterate the main points in favour of Scottish independence. For clarity, can we list those arguments that we think it is important that we use, so that Donnie and I can work on that overnight?"

They were pleased to be on more familiar ground now, and anxious to overcome the earlier awkward silence. The next twenty minutes were taken up with each of the politicians proposing particular lines of argument and introducing items of supporting evidence. Morrison recognised that for those round the table this was a cathartic experience, and allowed the discussion to go on beyond the point where he had heard all the views he required. There were occasional minor disagreements on which topics required most stressing, but eventually they had produced a list of subjects on which they were all agreed. Donald Barrie had jotted them all down, and summarised them at the end to everybody's satisfaction. As Alex Watson had said earlier, they all knew the arguments supporting independence, and there were no surprises on Donald's list. Morrison concluded by advising them that he could be accompanied to the debate by three people, and that he intended taking his wife, and Donald Barrie. As for the third person, he was considering asking Tom Thomson, the Transport Secretary. Thomson held only a junior ministerial post, it was true, but he had the appearance of someone that voters trusted. Nobody disagreed, and Barrie was certain that they all felt relieved that they hadn't been asked to attend. Morrison thanked them all for their efforts, and closed the meeting, getting Donald Barrie to stay behind to start working on the presentation. Alex Watson set off from the London studio, stone faced, looking as though he was ready to clobber the next person to make a jibe in his direction. The others shuffled out, looking glad to be going somewhere else. The entire meeting had lasted just thirty five minutes.

Donald was rather surprised to be asked to stay behind, for he had agreed earlier with Morrison that they would work on the presentation that evening, and put the finishing touches together the next morning, incorporating any developments that might occur overnight. He knew, of course, that Morrison would have some good reason for asking him to stay. He excused himself, went into the hall outside the meeting room, and made a quick call to his office, for two reasons. He needed to tell them that he would be back later then expected, if at all, that afternoon, and to see whether there was any more news that would be of interest to them. When he returned he saw Alistair Morrison sitting, apparently doodling on a piece of paper, behaviour Barrie had never seen before. He asked, full of concern, "Look, boss, what is it?"

For a moment, Morrison said nothing, almost as though he was unaware of the other man's presence. He was staring into the middle distance, trying to gather his thoughts, and work out how to start. Then he put his pen in his pocket, and looked squarely at Donald. "This is completely unfair of me, Donnie. I need to sound off. I need to vent my frustrations, my anger and my disappointment. For my own sake, I just need to let it all out, and you are the strongest person I know and I trust you beyond question."

"Boss, that is not being unfair. We all need to let off steam once in while. Look at you, you carry us all. You have done for the four years since I've known you, and you probably did it for years before that. I've often wondered how you did that, helped everyone without ever seeming to need any help yourself. So if you need some help now, that is not unfair. As for me, I'm grateful if I can provide that help, even if it is just a sympathetic ear. Boss, I'm flattered and humbled that it is me you chose to come to. Just get it out. Say what needs to be said. You will feel better for it."

Morrison talked uninterrupted for the next ten minutes, his voice sometimes breaking, his eyes moist. He spoke of how as a boy he had developed a love of Scottish history, and a pride in the role that Scotland and Scots had played in that history; how as a young man he had concluded that Scotland would have a better future as an independent nation; and how heavily he felt the burden of the imminent defeat, for his colleagues and for the nation he sought to lead.

Morrison's voice was breaking with emotion, and Barrie noticed an unashamed tear trickle down his face. Barrie had listened in silence. This man, whom he had come to regard as indestructible and almost infallible was here in despair, struggling to maintain control of himself, far less the campaign. He could only guess at the turmoil Morrison was going through. That he had spoken in this manner was proof enough that Alistair Morrison, the man, not Alistair Morrison the politician, was at the end of his tether. He had nowhere to turn. The difference between the collected appearance that Morrison was still managing to maintain in public and this bleak self analysis was astonishing.

"Boss, what can I say? I'm not going to make stupid comments, like telling you it will be alright, or that everything will work out. We both know that's not true, and you wouldn't believe me anyway. I'd just lose credibility with you. So let's just think about things for a minute. Yes, you are the leader, so of course you have responsibility. You also have a team of people round you, and you are good at delegating. It is an excellent team, one that I'm privileged to be part of. We must all share some of that responsibility. You saw the meeting that we just held. Nobody there had any fresh ideas to offer. Believe me, they have been asking others for suggestions too. There is group accountability. You cannot take it all on your own back. Remember that while we might lose the referendum on Thursday, it was you and your leadership that got so close. You got closer to establishing an independent Scotland that anyone else in three hundred years. So try to stop being so hard on yourself."

"Donald, I know that there is something in what you are saying, but just now, I can't stop blaming myself. I feel that instead of bringing the country to the dawn of a new day with all the possibilities that offers, I've brought it to the brink of a dark abyss where the future offers the same underachievement, the same inequalities and the same lack of investment that we have seen for the past fifty or sixty years. It feels as though I have let everyone down."

"I understand that, boss, but ultimately, the responsibility rests with every man and woman who casts their vote on Thursday. That is what democracy is about. You can put the arguments before them, but you can't dictate how people will vote. You will put the arguments before them, you will present the evidence. There is no more that you can do. For better or worse, it is in the hands of the people. You have to accept that. All you can do now is make your presentation as good and as slick and convincing as possible. So, when do you want to make a start? We can do some work now, or leave it until this evening as we had planned."

Morrison was looking out of the window, absently watching the sun reflecting off the buildings on the opposite side of Charlotte Square. After a while, he seemed to realise that Donald was waiting for an answer. He shrugged his shoulders heavily. "We know the independence arguments. We don't need to rehearse them or prepare how to present them. I could reel them off in my sleep. So could you. It's not as though we're presenting anything we've not discussed many times before. There is not much work to be done. At least Richard Hume can't attack us on the basis of the evidence. Why not just come round here tomorrow morning at ten thirty as arranged and we can go over any last minute developments?"

Donald raised an eyebrow. "Well, if you are sure. I don't like leaving you with the whole burden."

"I'll be fine, Donnie. Thanks for listening, for letting me unburden my feelings in this way. Just getting it out my system helps a little."

As Donald Barrie left Bute House, he felt helpless, dejected and useless. More than that, he felt concerned for the wellbeing of the First Minister.

Chapter Seventeen

Overnight

Chisholm drove the Volvo along back roads and through villages. He avoided townships of any size, and certainly steered clear of main roads. Now Rory was his front seat passenger and Shona was in the back seat. All three of them kept a vigilant outlook for any cars that might be following them. Progress was slow – the roads were difficult, full of bends and curves, always narrow. At one point they had found themselves behind a heavily laden tractor for almost two miles, never getting out of second gear, and finding no overtaking opportunity. On another occasion they spent a mile driving behind a Peugeot 308 being driven very tentatively by an elderly woman. Chisholm was determined to do nothing that would attract attention to them, so he contented himself with driving very conservatively. In some ways it suited him to make leisurely progress. At some point they would have to get into the more populous central belt, and after dark, they would be more difficult to identify. He knew that the blue Volvo gave them some protection: no-one was looking for that. However, just to make them even more unrecognisable, he was wearing a baseball cap, borrowed from Ian Beag, to obscure much of his face. At one point, Rory, in an effort to reduce the obvious tension in the car, rummaged in the glove compartment of the dashboard, and found, as he knew he would, a selection of Country and Western CDs. Chisholm was harsh, telling him to put them back, and insisted instead that they listen to the local radio for any news that concerned them, or of any news of road closures or road works. They drove on, mile after interminable mile, through the late afternoon sunshine, without seeing anything to raise their suspicions. The countryside, for the most part was open with wide views across glens and lochs, and in the distance, big, foreboding mountains that even on a bright sunny day like this loomed black and purple, massive lumps of granite rising to meet the blue of the sky, with tails of silver where a narrow river or waterfall was visible. The road crossed bridges from time to time, over fast flowing streams that came down from the mountains. They passed isolated houses, some apparently belonging to crofts, and small communities, sometimes just twenty or thirty houses huddled round a primary school or a church. Occasionally they saw the ruins of old castles, or derelict towers built in bygone days when there was real power in the old Highland Clan system. They had taken only one major risk. They had already lost a great deal of time, skirting round sea lochs by back roads, and Chisholm had become increasingly concerned about arriving in the central belt late at night. He had decided that instead of finding a way by back roads round Loch Leven, a long narrow loch, which would have added at least an hour to their journey, they would risk crossing the bridge at Ballachulish, at the head of the loch. He had parked the car about quarter of a mile from the bridge, and crept forward to observe activity at the bridge. He found a high vantage point, some distance from the road, and watched intently for twenty minutes, using the binoculars that he had taken from his case. Only when he was absolutely satisfied that there was nothing to worry him, did he make his way back to the car and proceed to cross the bridge.

As they progressed untroubled, their hopes and spirits began to rise. Chisholm had mentioned the name of a hotel that he knew and intended that they should stay at. This, he said was in Livingston, on the road between Glasgow and Edinburgh, but much nearer to Edinburgh. The weather had taken a turn for the worse, and the bright sunshine of the early afternoon had given way to dark rolling clouds, inky black and bearing the promise of rain. They had been on the road for almost six hours, and as they had approached the central belt of Scotland, the villages had turned into small towns, and had started to appear more frequently. They had turned up the volume on the car radio every time there was a news bulletin, but there had been no mention of anything that concerned them. Chisholm had indicated to the others that rain would help them as they came into this populated areas. It would impair visibility and make them harder to spot. In any event, they hoped, no-one was looking for a blue Volvo. However, to make themselves even less obvious, they had agreed that Shona would lie flat along the back seat, to make it appear that there were two, not three, people in the car. Having made their way south, they had then travelled west through the Trossachs, an area of outstanding natural beauty, still sticking to their plan to avoid main roads for as long as possible, and were near the ancient city of Stirling, the one time capital of Scotland, a place of huge relevance in Scottish medieval history. As they approached, the large fortress castle which overlooks the city, dominated the darkening sky line. Chisholm had decided that he had no alternative but to join the motorway. At least it wasn't far, only about twenty five miles to his intended destination for the night.

On cue, as the Volvo joined the motorway, the rain started. It was as though the clouds had been converted into a waterfall. Visibility, even with headlights on and wipers at full speed was poor. Chisholm drove carefully. The early evening traffic was quite light, the peak of the rush hour having passed some twenty minutes earlier. They had gone about fifteen miles when Chisholm announced, "There is a police car with its lights flashing coming up quickly behind us. Shona, stay down, and if they stop us, we say you were asleep. I'll do any talking."

With his heart in his mouth, Chisholm kept driving through the rain, maintaining a safe speed and a safe distance between him and the car in front. The police car was close behind them, then it was level, lights still flashing, as it overtook them, and then it disappeared down a slip road just ahead of them. With a sigh of relief Chisholm said, "It's OK. They weren't interested in us." Just as he did so the seven o'clock news bulletin started on the car radio. The first item was about a murder trial that had been going on for some days at the High Court in Glasgow. Then the newsreader continued "Reports are coming in from the police about an abduction in the West Highlands. They say that a teenage boy has been kidnapped by a woman and an older man, and a nationwide search has been organised and is ongoing. Police forces throughout Scotland have been asked to look out for a black Audi Avant, which the kidnappers are believed to be using. The boy's immediate family are being looked after. Police hope to reveal more details shortly."

After a moment's silence, Chisholm said, "Not to worry. That was bound to happen, sooner or later. It was only a matter of time. At least we know that they are still looking for the Audi. We'll be at the hotel in a couple of minutes. Shona, you stay in the car, out of sight. Rory, you come in with me. A man and his grandson. If they have the registration number of the Audi, they will be able to trace the credit card I used to hire it, and so they will also know by now that it is me that they are looking for. They will have put a trace on that card, so if I use it again, they will know within minutes. I'll pay cash for the room for one night. Rory, we'll register our name as Fletcher. I've used that name staying here before. We'll take in a suitcase and the laptop. That won't look suspicious. Once we're settled in, I'll come out, using the fire escape, and collect you Shona. We'll get the rest of the things in that way."

They turned off the motorway, and Chisholm continued for another half mile before pulling into the parking area of the Stag's Heart Hotel. He parked close to the building, at the back, taking care to ensure that the car was in shadow, and well away from any lighting. The rain had not let up, and he and Rory ran as they grabbed the laptop and a suitcase, and splashed through puddles into the hotel entrance.

Shona lay still, curled up into an uncomfortable ball, in the back of the car for an interminable fifteen minutes. The rain battering off the car roof had not lessened in all that time. It was quite dark outside, and on the couple of occasions she had raised her head to look out, she had been unable to make out anything other than the wall of the hotel. The rainwater on the window virtually obscured everything. She was getting quite stiff. The Volvo was a big car, but there wasn't enough room for her to stretch out in the back seat without making herself visible to any prying eyes. As the minutes passed slowly, she began to wonder where they were. Surely it didn't take this long to book into a hotel? Where were they? Had something gone wrong? She was considering what she should do. Chisholm had said he had used this hotel before. Was there a chance that he had been recognised by the hotel staff as the man involved with the reported kidnap? Given that the news had offered no descriptions, that seemed unlikely. A more likely possibility was that the people at MI5 knew which hotels he had used when working for them and were watching those hotels. After all, she reasoned, he must have submitted expense sheets detailing where he had stayed. With the car engine turned off, there was no heating, and she was cold and miserable. For the first time since Chisholm had appeared at her flat in Montrose, she was on her own, and she felt vulnerable. As the minutes dragged past, the feeling deepened now. She checked her watch for the fifth time in as many minutes. They had been gone twenty minutes. Something must surely be wrong. She considered alternative courses of action open to her, and concluded grimly that she was more or less out of options. No sooner had she thought of something when she thought of reasons why she shouldn't do that. In her anxiety, the desire for flight was almost overwhelming. She could drive away. But where to? Chisholm had taken the car keys. That wouldn't do. She could walk away. She would get soaked, and she had little money. If the authorities were on to Chisholm, surely they would be on to her too. She could march into the hotel and try to assess the situation. After all she didn't know for certain that Chisholm had been taken. She thought about this, and realised that if Chisholm had not been taken, he would come to the car for her, and if she was not there, what then? She tried to force herself to think clearly, to stay calm, but the tide of fear was rising in her stomach.

The sudden noise penetrated her brain like a sharp needle hitting a nerve, cutting through the incessant drumming of the rain on the car roof. It wasn't all that loud, but it was unexpected, and for a moment she didn't know what it was. In a panic, she sat up and saw a face at the window. It was impossible to tell who the face belonged to. The darkness, the torrential rain and water cascading down the car window made it impossible to distinguish. Instinctively, she recoiled curling her knees up to her chest. Then there was a key in the lock and the door opened. Rory, dripping wet, his hair matted and stuck to his head, grinned at her. "Hi, Shona. Sorry it took so long. We've been sorting out some food in the room, and we had hoped the rain might have eased off. Come on, let's get the stuff up to the room. Mr Chisholm is holding the fire escape door open for us."

Shona said something uncomplimentary, which fortunately Rory didn't hear, as she took a moment to regain her composure. Then she was out of the car helping Rory grab their things from the boot of the Volvo. She followed him as he led the way to a metal staircase that ran up the wall of the hotel, taking care to keep the printer she was carrying, dry. Splashing and kicking water, she realised as she climbed that there were only two floors to the hotel. The night was so black, and the rain so heavy that even at this distance she could get no sense of the size of the hotel. The darkness of the night, at least, was something to be grateful for. As they reached the top of the fire escape, a door opened, and there stood Chisholm, silhouetted against the light of the hotel lobby, beckoning them in to a long corridor with bedroom doors off on either side. Swiftly and silently they ran along and entered into the room Rory indicated, Chisholm bringing up the rear. Their room was only three doors away from the fire escape.

Dripping rainwater, Shona looked round the room. There were two single beds with drawers between them. There were duvets on each bed, in lemon and white covers, with matching pillows. Neutrally painted walls in an off-white shade that hinted at yellow and brightly coloured orange and lemon curtains gave the room a bright appearance. There were a couple of Jack Vettriano prints hanging on the wall. By the window was a table, on which she noted a coffee pot and cups, with milk and sugar, and two trays of freshly cut sandwiches. There was a bench style table, which ran the length of the room attached to the wall opposite the beds. At one end was a small TV and at the other end was the usual array of coffee and tea making facilities. In between, someone had laid down the laptop, and that was fine, because there was an electrical socket nearby. At the near end of the bedroom was a door that she realised must lead into the en suite bathroom. She put the printer down beside the laptop and sat on the bed nearest her. Chisholm disappeared into the bathroom, and emerged with fresh white fluffy towels, tossing one each to Rory and Shona. "Here, dry off, then help yourself to hot coffee and sandwiches. There's a mixture there, so you're sure to find something to your taste."

As Shona towelled off, Rory started rummaging in his hold all, looking for dry clothes. He announced he was going for a shower, and issued a warning that was only half in jest, that he expected some of the sandwiches left for him. While she poured herself a coffee and helped herself to some of the sandwiches, Shona started to unpack the laptop and printer. The coffee was hot and she felt a pleasant sensation as the warmth hit her throat and stomach. Once she had the equipment connected, she switched them on. Suddenly, as the laptop was booting up, she asked Chisholm "Has the hotel got an internet connection?"

"Yes, free wi-fi. Do you need it?"

"No, not for printing off the rest of the folder. Not even if Rory has to work on more codes. But remember back at the lodge I said there was one more thing I could give you? Well, I need to be on the internet for that."

As Chisholm nodded in vague understanding, Rory came out of the bathroom, dressed in fresh clothes, and looking a whole lot better than he had done ten minutes earlier. He made straight for the remaining food, but not without watching Shona as she started up the laptop. Less than three minutes later she announced that everything appeared to be translating into English using the same code as before. Rory gave a grateful laugh, and lay back on the bed nearest the window. Within seconds, he was asleep. It was the first proper sleep he had had in three days. The printer chuntered on. It was a top of the range model, fast and quiet. The paper came out far too fast for them to read, and Shona contented herself with collating the paper into bundles. Soon she had fourteen bundles of paper one for each of the fourteen files in the folder, each neatly piled up in order, on the bed that Rory was not lying on. Then she inserted a USB stick into the side of the laptop, and copied all of the files onto that. Finally, she created another paper copy of each of the files. In the meantime, Chisholm had used paper clips to attach the fourteen files, and was now starting to read them. Most of the files were of similar size, perhaps fifteen to twenty pages long, but one file was much bigger, containing seventy two pages. As Shona watched the last of the paper come off the printer, she was aware that Chisholm had gone very quiet. When she looked at him, he had also gone very pale. The colour had drained from his face. "What's wrong?" she asked.

Chisholm shook his head. "Good grief, Shona." His voice was a barely audible whisper. "Just read this stuff. It's too hot to handle." There was something so compelling in his voice that Shona just picked up her bundle of papers to read. They both read in fascinated silence for the next two hours, exchanging occasional incredulous glances. Rory slept. It was nearing eleven o'clock when Shona broke the stillness that had descended. "Well, what do we do with this, Mr Chisholm? Any ideas?"

"No, Shona. This is almost too much. How can we make this public? How much of it should we make public? Who can we take it to? These are the questions going round in my head."

"Well, I can answer one of these for you. All of this should be in the public domain. This is what our government and one of its agencies are doing to us. They are meant to be there for our benefit. We should be able to trust them. This all has to be put in front of the public. As to how you do that, well, I'm not sure. We can place it on the internet, but it will take days to get people switched on to what has gone on. People do not open big files that look boring. They want short sharp bits of entertainment. I'm no expert on news agencies and TV channels, but we must get it out there in the public domain." She was surprised herself at the determination in her voice.

Chisholm raised a hand for silence. "Just hang on a minute, Shona. Let's slow down and think about this. There is a lot of material here. If we just hand it over to someone, it will take them ages to go through, and to look for verification of it all. Perhaps we should take some time ourselves to sift through it, to really understand it, and to edit it and sort it into a more presentable fashion. If we could make it more succinct, it would be easier to present."

Shona looked doubtful. "I don't know about that. Look, the referendum is on Thursday, two days away. We have got to find a way before then. All of the material is damning, so what do you think we should edit out?" This last sentence contained a note of confrontation.

"Look, Shona, some of this doesn't affect the way the voters have been influenced. I'm saying we should remove those bits so that the rest of the material has more impact. That is what is important." Chisholm's manner suggested that he had made up his mind and was not prepared to discuss the matter further. He rose, and went towards the bathroom, as a way of ending the conversation.

Shona would not let it go, however. Suddenly she felt that she needed an ally. She continued, "Rory is as much part of this as you and me. He needs to see this." With that she started shaking the boy awake.

Rory, for all his lack of sleep in the preceding days, was in the deepest sleep. However he woke quickly, with Shona urging him to look at the printed material. She went back to the laptop and stated booting it up. Rory took only a moment to sit himself upright on the edge of the bed and pick up one of the bundles of papers. As he absorbed himself in this, he was aware of Chisholm looking on disapprovingly, but saying nothing. Eventually Chisholm turned to Shona and asked what she was doing.

"I'm putting two more copies of the folder onto USB sticks so we have a copy each. We are partners in this in a way, and we should have the same information." Shona and Chisholm both knew that she really meant that if they each had a copy, no one of them could without the agreement of the others, omit or delete some of the material. He let it pass.

Rory had read the first few pages, and looked up, from one to the other asking, "Is this for real?"

* * *

In the Lawson cottage, Hardie, or Constable Brown, as he had called himself had long since been relieved and replaced by a WPC. This was Kate McLean, and she was a local girl, well known to the Lawsons. Her father ran the chemist's shop in Plockton. Fair hair, fresh face and blue eyes, she was full of genuine sympathy for the three people in the room. She had been at school with Angus, albeit she was a couple of years older. She sang in the same choir as Flora Lawson. She knew Rory, too, but not well. Earlier in the evening, under the pretext of tending to his livestock, Hugh Lawson had gone out with his son. He had taken the opportunity to tell Angus all that he knew. The reaction was as he had expected. Angus was wholeheartedly behind the adventure, pleased that his family could be associated with such matters. He had proposed, "Dad, Kate is here. We can trust her. Why don't we tell her everything, and she can speak to her superiors. She could get them to call off the search. That would leave Rory and his two companions a clear run."

Hugh Lawson replied, "I've been thinking about that for a while now. It pains me to be deceiving Kate like this. If we told her, she would be duty bound to report it up her chain of command. They might believe her, they might not. Remember, they are acting on information from MI5. They are not going to discount that very readily. All we would do is put poor Kate in an awkward position."

When they got back into the house, Angus went to the kitchen to make some tea and sandwiches. He suggested to Kate that she come to help him. Once there, he told Kate that his parents just needed five minutes alone together. Kate indicated that she understood. Once Angus and Kate had left the room, Hugh started explaining to Flora exactly what had happened. Any hopes that he held out that she would approve faded as quickly as her brow furrowed, and her gaze hardened. She let Hugh finish, then said carefully not raising her voice. "You mean that you thought it was alright to let our son get mixed up in this? Hugh, this is unbelievable. Did you never consider the risks? How stupid can you be? I could expect Rory to get involved in this, this mad adventure. He's just a boy with no experience of the world. You should have known better, and stopped this. You should have sent those two away. They had no right involving Rory in any of this. What were you thinking of?"

Hugh had been married to Flora for twenty six years, and had known her for ten years before that. He had never seen her so angry. He said lamely, "I just think that some risks are worth taking. I know you don't agree, but please go along with this for now."

"No risks are worth taking when it involves our boys. Go along with it? Do I have a choice?" Flora was incandescent with rage. Hugh was preparing himself for a further outburst when the kitchen door opened and Kate, followed by Angus appeared, carrying cups, plates of sandwiches and a tin full of chocolate biscuits. The atmosphere was decidedly frosty, and Kate put that down to the natural anxiety of the whole family for Rory's wellbeing.

* * *

In the Stag's Heart Hotel, Rory was still reading the material. He was more than half way through, and apart from the occasional exclamation of astonishment, he was reading avidly and in silence. Shona had given him a USB stick with the entire folder copied onto it, and he had stuffed that deep into a pocket. She had given one to Chisholm, who had accepted it with a cool grace. The third one, she had kept to herself. Now, as it approached midnight, she was logging onto the internet. Chisholm asked her what she intended to do.

"I'm going to find out exactly who created these documents, and which computers were used for their creation. That will be the piece of evidence that demonstrates beyond question that these documents are genuine. That will mean nobody can question the authenticity of what we have, so there will be no need for the media to go through a lengthy validation process."

Chisholm was taken by surprise. "You can do that? How?"

Shona didn't stop work as she replied. "We know the names of not just the files, but all the individual documents. They will have a history which will include the author's name, the machine on which it was created, the date it was created, and the date of any amendments. I will just have to get into the MI5 system again. Now I know how to do that through ASS, it will be easy."

Chisholm fidgeted. "Surely they will have worked out how you broke in the last time and will have closed that gap?"

"Maybe, but I don't think so. It would need a significant rewrite, and this is an internally designed piece of software. They have not had much time, and I'd bet that most of their IT people have been busy all weekend working out how we broke into the system. I don't think they will have had the chance to rewrite the software, test it and install it. Anyway, it is worth taking the chance."

"Shona," Chisholm said after a moment's consideration, "Don't do it. Don't take the chance. They will be looking for any attempts to breach their system again, and they will use that to track us down."

Shona replied irritably, "There is little risk of them finding us. They won't even know that I have been into their system this time. Do you not trust me to get the evidence, Mr Chisholm? You came to me asking for help to get evidence, and that is what I'm doing. We need all the evidence, not just some of it. You are the trained law officer; you should be urging me to get as much evidence as possible. Why are you suddenly reluctant to gather all the evidence?" She pressed a key on the keypad, and leaned back, arms folded.

"I'm not reluctant." Chisholm said defensively. "It's just that we have so much that I don't want to put it all at risk by going back for more. We are so close. I don't want to chance us getting caught at this stage."

"That is just as well," said Shona as the printer kicked into life. "That's it done, and they will never know. Well, not until we go public and tell them. Then they will know."

Chisholm shook his head. "That is all it took? Just seconds?"

"Yes," replied Shona with a grin. "Just seconds. That is all I needed the laptop and printer for," and she started closing down the computer. She disconnected everything and packed them in their carry bags. "Let's get rid of these." She and Rory carried the equipment to the Volvo, via the fire escape. Thankfully, it had finally stopped raining, but the car park was wet, with large puddles for them to negotiate. They placed the equipment in the boot of the car, and returned to the room the way they had come. Once they were in the room and seated, Chisholm spoke to them both, addressing Rory first.

"Have you read all the material yet, Rory?"

"Not quite. I've got one more file to go. It's amazing stuff though, isn't it?"

"Yes, Rory, it certainly is. We have to decide what to do with it. Shona thinks we should just present it to someone as it is, warts and all. I suggest we, or rather I, do some editing work on it – cut out some of the less important things and make it snappier to present. What do you think?"

Before he could answer, Shona interjected. "Some of the material might not be as important as other bits, but all the material together adds up to the whole story. Even the bits that are not so important are bad enough in themselves. Then there is the issue of timescale. As you say, Mr Chisholm, there is a lot of material. How long would it take to edit it? The referendum is only two days away. So even if we did want to edit this, how could we do it in the time we have? And we still have to decide how we are going to release it to the public."

Rory looked from one to the other and rubbed his chin thoughtfully. "It looks like I have the casting vote here."

They debated animatedly for another half hour before coming to an uneasy truce. The discussion had swung between Chisholm and Shona as each reinforced their argument. Rory, in the main, listened and said very little, but what he did say was telling. Eventually, exhausted, they prepared to sleep, Rory insisting he would be able to sleep on the floor, with the aid of a pillow and a sheet pulled over him. They made sure that various alarms were set for eight o'clock, Chisholm had an alarm built into his wrist watch, Rory set the alarm on the mobile phone that Chisholm had given him back at the cottage, and Shona set the alarm function on the TV. They all knew how tired each other was, and were determined not to oversleep – tomorrow promised to be a busy day. Within minutes, all three of them were sound asleep.

Chapter Eighteen

Preparation

It was the morning of the debate. Penny Carter had set her bedside radio alarm for six o'clock. This was a day she was looking forward to. It was the culmination of weeks of work. As she went through her customary morning routine, she went over everything in her mind. All the components were in place. Her session with Richard Hume had gone well, and he could hardly be better prepared for the debate with Alistair Morrison that night. Systematically, she reviewed all the actions she had been involved in since the Prime Minister had instructed her only ten weeks earlier to take responsibility for ensuring that the Scottish independence debate resulted in a vote in favour of maintaining the Union. Mentally, she ticked each one off, and smiled to herself in satisfaction. She had kept the Prime Minister fully informed, and she knew that he had, in turn, kept the Leader of the Opposition informed. All the feedback she had received indicated that they were happy with the progress she had made. Once showered and dressed, she took herself to the small room in the flat that she used as her office, and went through the various notes she had, sorting out those that she might need at the meeting later that morning. Those that she considered she might need were placed in careful order in her briefcase. She was sure that she didn't need to refer to them personally – she knew the contents in meticulous detail. Others, however, might want to check a detail here or there. Besides, it was much more businesslike for her to carry a briefcase than a handbag. When the time came, she left her flat and walked, confidently the short distance to Downing Street.

The dewy morning light shone weakly through the window of the Prime Minister's office. Seven thirty was unusually early for a meeting, and consequently, a tray with breakfast tea, coffee, bacon rolls and Danish pastries lay across the smaller of the two tables in the meeting room. All the crockery was delicate bone china, with a subtle blue pattern. Nigel Braithwaite, Richard Hume, Stephen Halford and Penny Carson were enjoying their breakfast in good mood. Braithwaite, dressed in shirt sleeves, with his shirt open at the neck, was feeling particularly buoyant. Good news had been in short supply lately, but the recent round up of a gang of international forgers and people traffickers had been widely regarded as a major success, and by association, his government, and Braithwaite personally had received some of the credit. He was expecting the Scottish independence referendum to bring more good news. Sir David Lee and his people were the main bright spot in his life at that moment.

Across the table from him, Penny Carson was looking as she always did, immaculate and confident. Braithwaite wondered idly how long she had been up to get that level of grooming in place. She smiled at him casually as she sipped her Darjeeling and bit demurely into a pastry. For her, he thought, this was the end of a long, tiring project and it was about to come to a very successful conclusion. Braithwaite thought, not for the first time in his career, that she was his most invaluable ally. The Leader of the Opposition, Stephen Halford, formal as ever, sat between them, dressed for business, white shirt with blue striped tie; he had hung his suit jacket on the coat stand by the door. If he felt uncomfortable sharing breakfast with the leader and deputy leader of his political opponents, he didn't show it. He enjoyed being in the place that he very much hoped would one day be his home. On the fourth side of the table was Richard Hume, the Deputy Prime Minister. Independently wealthy, the former barrister prided himself on his dapper appearance. His thinning black hair was in part the product of a chemical, and was slicked back hard into his head. He wore a blue striped shirt with a white collar and white cuffs, and a carefully chosen matching tie. Unlike Halford, he had not removed the jacket of his pinstriped suit, yet his gold cuff links were visible beneath his sleeves. His expensive cologne was just a little too powerful. He had bright black eyes that danced around the room missing nothing, high cheekbones and a slightly hooked nose, over a rather thin mouth. He was tall, over six feet in height, and very slim. He was somewhat stooped, and altogether presented as a rather cadaverous vulture. He drank black coffee and resisted the food. He habitually skipped breakfast, fearing that he might put on weight.

The Prime Minister had no need to introduce the participants – they already knew each other – so immediately after a few words of welcome he raised the business that they had gathered for. The relationships between them, with the exception of that between Penny and him, were such that idle chat was not likely to take place in any event. "Richard, I understand that you are fully prepared for the debate tonight, up in Scotland. Is that right? Is there more support we can give you, anything at all that you might need?"

Hume, his fingers steepled in front of him, replied in his usual clipped, precise tones. "I have everything I need. Penny has seen to that. We have been through the brief. It is very clear, and very complete. The tactics are very obvious, and classical, working up from points that are merely embarrassing to those that are completely devastating. The last part, which people will remember longest, is the most shattering. Whoever pulled the brief together is very skilful, and Penny has been an excellent support in going over it and in getting clarification where needed. We have been most thorough. There are no gaps and no omissions. Getting the outline of Morrison's presentation last night was also really helpful. I don't know how you managed to do that." His last remark was accompanied by a meaningful glance towards Penny.

"There are some things that you don't need to know, Richard." Penny Carson was enjoying her privileged knowledge concerning MI5's informants. "Suffice to say, it came from an impeccable source. That information can be trusted completely."

"I'm sure it can." Hume continued in the same vein as before. "As I have said, having that last night was helpful. It has enabled me to adjust the brief slightly so that the line of cross examination can follow Morrison's presentation more closely. I have all the ammunition I need to destroy every element of his case. Believe me, the cross examination will be child's play. However, Morrison will think that it has been a blood sport. He will feel like he has been hit by an express train." He gave a malevolent grin which revealed a set of slightly uneven but brightly polished teeth. "For me, this is a return to my background. Trial by jury. The audience shall be the jury, and everything will be directed to expose Morrison to them."

Nigel Braithwaite showed no sign of emotion, but instead, he pushed on. "Good, Richard. If ever there was a time to live up to your reputation as the most feared cross examiner that the Old Bailey has ever seen, tonight is it. You will not let us down. I have every confidence in you, as does Stephen here. You are without question, the best man for the job. Remember that both our parties have a vested interest in destroying the separatist movement. Let us be resolved. We know that the latest opinion polls indicate the separatists will do very badly. We must, none of us, ease up. This is the time to go for the jugular – to kill them off once and for all."

When Halford spoke for the first time, it was with feeling. "Richard, it is good to be on the same side for once. I know that you will be more than a match for Morrison, even without the assistance you have been given. I know better than most what it is like to face you across a debating chamber. I wish I could be there in the audience to witness the downfall of the separatists. I wanted to be there, but I agree with Nigel's reasoning. You will be better than he would be at tearing Morrison to pieces. Your cross examinations are legendary. If Nigel's not there as leader of his party, then as leader of my party I can't be there either. It's pity, for this promises to be an historic night. Please don't think that you have to show any mercy to Morrison." Halford realised as he said it, that his final exhortation had been completely unnecessary. He had never seen Richard Hume show any mercy in the debating chamber, and he, Halford, owed his position as leader almost entirely to the effects of Hume's savage exchanges that caused the previous leader to step down. He had witnessed at first hand Hume's acerbic put downs, his withering looks and his acidic wit when debating with an opponent. There was no doubt in his mind that Richard Hume would grind Alistair Morrison into the dust, and that the Scot would be humiliated in front of a large home audience and a much wider international one. That would surely put an end to the separatists' aspirations.

Braithwaite continued, "Stephen that brings us nicely to the next point. As you know, Richard, the two debaters, you and Morrison, have been allocated three seats each in the front row of the invited audience. These are not people who take part in the debate; they are there for moral support. Seated in the front row, we can expect them to be picked up in various camera shots. That is why I have decided that Edith Bannon should be there. As Secretary of State for Scotland she will be instantly recognised, and it is really giving her what should rightfully be her place. The second person will be Penny. She is hardly well known to the media, but she knows more about this campaign than most. She can be a source of information right up to the start of the debate. The last seat, I've given to Stephen. That will show that our parties are united in the campaign to stop the separatists. As he has already explained, Stephen cannot take up the seat personally."

Braithwaite nodded towards Halford, indicating that he should speak.

"That is correct. I have agreed that George Graham will join you. He is a Scot, and something of a populist figure. He has, as you know, a high public profile and a large personal following. He is particularly well known in Scotland, as you might surmise. His presence there will send out the right messages." Halford smiled at the thought of anything uniting the suave and urbane Hume and Graham, a grizzled veteran who had managed to get a substantial amount of air time over the years. They were poles apart in their backgrounds and political beliefs.

"Are all your travel arrangements in place, Penny?" asked the Prime Minister.

"They are. We will meet Edith and George later this morning and after lunching together in the House of Commons restaurant, we will fly up to Edinburgh. We'll be met by a car. We have to be at the studio for half past six, but the debate doesn't start until an hour after that. The hour is to go through make up, and get any final briefings on the studio layout, test microphones, check camera positions and so on. The debate will last for an hour. We should get away from the studio about nine o'clock, and by ten o'clock we'll be on board the light aircraft standing by at the airport. We'll be back in London in time to join in the celebrations by midnight." Penny was trying hard to contain her feeling of self fulfilment at a job well done. Her part was over, and she knew that the battle was already won. There was only this final act to be played out, and that would be down to Richard Hume. She had prepared him to the point of readiness. She felt fully entitled to congratulate herself. Tonight would be the public defeat of the separatists, and the man Morrison would be made to look an incompetent fool in front of millions of viewers. Her tongue slowly ran along her lips in an involuntarily act of anticipation of the thought of Morrison's impending demise.

Penny felt that she had one more piece of information that she should share. She had been considering how to phrase this so that she could derive as much satisfaction as possible from telling the others. She felt it was important that all present appreciated how completely crushed Morrison had been. It extended the time that she could reflect contentedly on his demise. "Prime Minister, I understand that Morrison is so bereft of support that he intends his three places to be taken up by his wife, his Communications officer and his Transport Minister, who is just a junior Minister, not even in the Scottish cabinet."

Braithwaite smiled indulgently, and replied, "I don't think it will make any difference who he has in the audience, his fate is sealed."

Stephen Halford drained his coffee, excused himself and rose to leave. He understood that the other three might have party business to attend to and that he should leave them to it. He had no wish to spend longer than necessary in the Prime Minister's company. As he left, pulling on his jacket, he called back, "Good luck, Richard!"

Hume raised a hand in acknowledgement and said to Braithwaite as the door closed behind Halford, "It isn't a question of luck, you know. This isn't in the lap of the gods, or down to some roll of the dice. It is all down to good planning and preparation. We have done that. I'm really rather relishing the opportunity to smash the separatists." His sardonic expression left no-one in any doubt that he meant that.

Once the Leader of the Opposition had left them, the Prime Minister said to Penny "I take it that there are no last minute hiccups. There is nothing at all that we should be concerned about? Our friend has no worries that there is anything else that should be covered? I must say, I can't think of anything. This looks like a job well done."

"No, sir. There is nothing of concern to report. I met our contact last night when we got hold of the outline of Morrison's presentation. It was business as usual. He seemed very confident. I think we have all the bases covered."

"Penny, I want you to know that you have handled this assignment expertly. You have shown a lot of skill and good judgement. It is myself and after tonight, Richard, who will get the public credit, but be assured,

I know how much we owe to you. Hurry back after the debate. I'll have some good champagne chilled and waiting for you both."

"Thank you, sir. You know that I'm not looking for public recognition. It is enough that you trust me as you do and that you believe that I have done well. To be fair, I must point out that our contact has also done remarkably well." Penny Carter felt that she could afford to be generous, for she was the main recipient of the Prime Minister's favour, and being present to witness at first hand Morrison's downfall would be sufficient reward for her. That this project had also resulted in the impending demise of Sir Michael Hammond, the Home Secretary, was for her, an unexpected and welcome bonus. She had never thought to analyse why bringing down men whom she perceived to be powerful gave her so much pleasure.

Richard Hume raised an eyebrow by a mere millimetre and concealed an amused smile. All this talk of "our contact" or "our friend" was for his benefit, as though he hadn't worked out much earlier who the contact was. Still, as Penny had said, there were some things he didn't need to know. As far as he was concerned, all the information he had been passed had come from the Prime Minister's adviser. He knew that Penny Carter was the go-between, but that she had not created any of the papers herself, and that the documents she had given him access to would not be all that had been created.

Richard Hume and Penny Carson left 10 Downing Street together, stepping out of the famous black door into the bright sunlight, just as a TV crew started filming their political reporter doing a live link from Downing Street to their studio for the eight o'clock news bulletin. At the end of Downing Street, without speaking, they went their separate ways, having previously arranged to meet outside the House of Commons Restaurant at half past eleven.

Chapter Nineteen

Break-in

It had been a little after one o'clock in the morning when the three of them had reached a decision. It was a decision that had come out of the blue, based on a suggestion from Rory. Shona had immediately supported the idea, but Chisholm had been much more reticent. He had seen problems with the idea itself, and couldn't see how they could hope to implement it. Eventually, he had agreed in principle with Rory's suggestion, but still held real reservations about how practical the idea was. He had to admit eventually that he had no better proposal. In theory it might work, but the timescale to put this into operation effectively meant that they had only a few hours to achieve their goal. That left him with no time to edit the material, and he remained uneasy about that. His other concern was that their proposed action could well involve a degree of physical risk for them, especially Rory and Shona, and he wasn't sure if they fully appreciated that. Certainly, neither of them had any training in the kind of activities that might be called for. He himself had been away from field operations for too long and worried that he had lost his edge. He wasn't fully convinced yet, but he could see no other way that offered a better chance of success.

All of them had been exhausted, even Rory. Despite managing to sleep for a couple of hours as the others read the first prints, his sleep loss over the previous days meant that he was ready to sleep some more. They had all agreed that they needed to be fresh and ready for action. So they had set alarms and gone to sleep. The first alarm to go off was Chisholm's wrist watch at 7:58, followed seconds later by the much louder phone alarm that Rory had set. All three were awake, but not properly awake. They were in that place somewhere between deep sleep and consciousness, that warm

194

fuzzy, friendly place that they didn't want to leave. Something at the back of Chisholm's mind kept pulling away from that comfort, telling him there were things that needed to be done. At length, he stretched out a lazy arm and switched on a bedside light. The harshness of the light after the darkness of the room stung their eyes, and, at that instant, the television alarm also went off, switching almost immediately to the hourly news bulletin. Groggily, they each sat up, feeling that they could have slept on for hours. The noise from the TV made sure that they would not fall asleep again. Rory started making stretching motions and yawned loudly and prodigiously. Chisholm, who was gathering his wits, exhorted the boy to quiet. There might be something on the news bulletin about the alleged kidnap. They should watch that before rising.

When wakening up from a deep sleep, there are few stimulants that can speed up that process. One of them is hearing your name, particularly from an unexpected source. Another is seeing your face where you least expect to. When both of these happened more or less instantaneously, the three people in the room immediately propped up where they lay, alert and attentive. It was the first item on the news. The news reader had introduced the item with a grave, concerned tone. "Police forces all over Scotland are hunting a couple who abducted a teenager from near his home, by the highland town of Plockton. Fifteen year old Rory Lawson was snatched sometime yesterday morning." A photograph of Rory in his school uniform flashed up on the screen. "He is described as five foot nine, of slim build, and when last seen was wearing jeans and a navy blue hoodie. Police believe that the couple who abducted him are connected to organised crime, and belong to a gambling syndicate. The suspects are David Chisholm, who may be using the name David Lee, and Shona Murray." At that, the screen changed, with Rory's picture being replaced by a split screen showing a photograph of Chisholm and Shona. "Police are advising the public that they are thought to be armed and dangerous. Any member of the public who thinks they may have seen anything that can help the police should make immediate contact. The public are warned that under no circumstances should they approach the suspects themselves."

As the news reader drifted on to the next item, Rory stood up, grinning. "Well done, Dad. He's thinking how he can help us. That school photo he has given them was taken eighteen months ago and is nothing like how I look now. I had long hair then. He knows that I don't have a navy blue hoodie but that's what he has told them I'm wearing!"

The other two looked at him with some surprise, before Shona said, "Well I hope that I don't look anything like the picture of me they are using. That was taken while I was in prison, with cropped hair. It's not very flattering." The other two laughed and assured her that she looked much better than her photograph.

Chisholm was thoughtful. He concluded that the release of the photographs forced his hand. "It's an old work photo of me too, I'm much greyer now. It certainly helps that they are using poor pictures of us. There are two important things we have learned from that broadcast. Firstly, they know, as we suspected, exactly who we are, and that I have created a second identity by using the name Lee in certain transactions. More importantly, by telling the public that we are armed and dangerous, they are in fact saying that any police who approach us will be armed. They will have been told to take no chances, so they will shoot given any reason, or suspicion that we might do something to resist."

Shona let this sink in for a moment, then asked "You're not armed, are you, Mr Chisholm?"

"David, please, I keep telling you, it's David. All I'm armed with is a folder full of information. No guns, no knives, no weapons of any sort, I promise."

Rory was on his feet now, and started to boil some water in the kettle that came with the tea and coffee facilities. "So what does that mean for us? How can we do what we agreed last night?"

Chisholm rubbed his chin in contemplation, weighing up the options. He was aware that the other two were looking to him for guidance. "OK, here's what I think we should do. It's a bit risky, so if you're not sure, just say so. Everything depends on us getting to Edinburgh. We had planned to go together, but people might recognise us and the police will be on the lookout for a couple with a teenage boy. The three of us together would attract a closer look, and while they are not good, the photos that have been released, if someone really studied us, they would recognise us. So we will travel to Edinburgh individually. Nobody will be looking for us as an old man on his own, a teenager on his own, or a young woman on her own. We go by train, but we sit in different compartments, and leave the Volvo at the station here. We would probably never get parked in Edinburgh anyway. I'll give you money to buy your tickets, and we don't go up together to buy them. At Edinburgh, we get off at Haymarket station, and make our way to Princes Street, meeting at the corner of Charlotte Square. We each carry a copy of the folder on the USB stick Shona gave us. At least one of us must get through. On the train, try not to look suspicious. If you are recognised and challenged, don't resist, but try to direct them away from the rest of us. How does that sound?"

Rory and Shona exchanged long looks before nodding. Rory said, "There is just one problem. I don't know my way around Edinburgh. Where is Charlotte Square?"

The kettle was boiling, and Chisholm was starting to pour the water into the coffee cups as he explained to Rory how to get from Haymarket station to the rendezvous point at Charlotte Square. As they got ready, taking turns in the bathroom where Chisholm took his time shaving, they helped themselves to coffee and got dressed. They finalised their arrangements and made ready to leave. The room had been paid for, so there was no need to check out. They gathered their belongings and Rory opened the door just enough to poke an enquiring eye round so that he could see along the corridor. There was no-one around. He signalled to the others and they hurried to the fire escape, Chisholm pausing to put the room key in the door, so that it was visible from the corridor. The rain of the previous night had given way to a bright, crisp morning. They made it to the car without passing anyone, loaded their luggage into the boot, and drove off. As she had done the previous night, Shona lay flat along the back seat. It was 9:15 a.m. The journey to the station was short and uneventful. The car park adjoining the station was almost full, but Chisholm found a vacant space. They had agreed on the way there that Shona would go first.

Although she knew that wasn't the case, as she walked the thirty yards from the car to the ticket office, she felt fully exposed, as though everybody was taking an interest in her. She was aware of everyone, and thought they were all looking at her. Shona knew that it only needed one person to recognise her and she could be stopped. She forced herself to stay calm, and walk at a normal pace, controlling her breathing. She wanted to run, to reach the relative safety of the crowd where she could mingle and stay hidden. Out here in the open, she felt certain someone would recognise her. The thirty yards could have been a mile, for it seemed to her that it took an age to reach the ticket office. Finally, she reached the small queue and bought her ticket. She went to the newsagent's kiosk and hurriedly chose a magazine. She wasn't interested in the magazine, but they had agreed that having something to put in front of their face while on the train would reduce their chances of being recognised. As she walked back towards the platform she saw Rory making his way across the car park. He was walking too fast, almost running. He would draw attention to himself, she was sure. She forced herself not to stare, but kept walking to the platform. Once there, she could see the queue at the ticket office. With relief, she saw that Rory had made it that far. Shona opened up her magazine and pretended to read. Every few seconds she stole a glance in Rory's direction, trying to be as unobtrusive as possible. He was at the kiosk now, selecting a magazine. A few seconds that seemed like a lifetime later he passed her without acknowledgment, and walked to the far end of the platform. She had just a glimpse of his magazine – Advanced Sudoku Puzzles, and permitted herself a wry smile.

The train was due in less than five minutes, and the platform was filling up. The more crowded it got, the less exposed Shona felt, but there was a new anxiety enveloping her. Where was Chisholm? She hadn't seen him in the queue at the ticket office. He should have been there minutes ago. What could have happened? Momentarily she considered whether she should investigate, but remembered Chisholm's own exhortation that at least one of them should make it all the way. She had lost sight of Rory in the crowded platform, but that did not concern her. He was safe, at least for the moment. Now the platform was busy as people moved around, trying to find a part of the platform where the rows of people waiting for the train were thinnest. Her view of the ticket office and its queue was obscured as people passed in front of her. For a moment she thought she saw Chisholm at the front of the small queue, but she couldn't be sure. The next time she got a good look at the ticket office he wasn't there.

The train pulled up and the doors opened. There was a surge of bodies all along the platform, and Shona felt that she was more swept on board the train than she had stepped on board voluntarily. Quickly, she found a seat and opened her magazine. An elderly man sat beside her, and paid no attention as he read his morning paper. The two seats opposite were occupied by girls, both aged about twenty, and they clearly knew each other. Each had an iPod, and had text books open in front of them. They were obviously students, catching up with class work, Shona decided. She relaxed a little, aware that nobody was paying her any attention, but there was no sign of Chisholm and she wondered whether he was on the train.

Two carriages ahead, Rory had managed to find a seat at a table for four, sharing it with a bedraggled mother and her two young children. Rory estimated that they were possibly five and three years old. He had helped her place the three year old's buggy in the overhead storage space, and was already working on the Sudoku puzzles as the train pulled away from the station. By the time they reached the outskirts of Edinburgh, the three year old was crying. His brother had hit him, and was being scolded by his mother as she tried to console the younger boy. Rory was already on his fourth puzzle. They really were too easy. He was relieved too, that the woman sitting beside him had other things to occupy her and was taking no interest in him. He assumed that his two colleagues had managed to get on board the train with as little trouble as he had experienced.

As the train pulled into Haymarket after the short fifteen minute journey, many passengers prepared to get off. Haymarket is the second station in Edinburgh, after the bigger and better known Waverley Station, but trains at this time frequently carried many passengers who would go no further than Haymarket, as it suited those who were heading for offices and colleges. Shona tried to keep to the centre of the group getting off from her compartment, and once on the platform, she shuffled slowly with the others towards the stairs that led to the automatic ticket barrier. As she approached the bottom of the stairs, she caught sight of Rory at the top, approaching the ticket barriers. She knew that if a watch was being kept it would be at the barrier. As she made her way up the stairs, she lost sight of Rory, and when she approached the barrier, no more than a dozen paces away, she realised that on the other side of the barrier, directly opposite her, there stood a uniformed policeman. She wanted to turn and flee. Never before had she felt the need for flight so strongly. The crush from the passengers behind her thrust her forward though, towards the barrier, and towards the policeman. She felt the panic rising within her as she frantically tried to turn. It was no use. She was being driven forward. She held her ticket out, trying to find a way out, somewhere to run. What saved her at that moment was a large overweight man in a loose, billowing coat who pushed his way aggressively ahead of her using his elbows like weapons as he cleared his path. Behind him, she was effectively obscured from the policeman's view. This gave her a couple of seconds to gather her thoughts. She realised that if she tried to turn and run she would only succeed in drawing attention to herself, and she realised that the policeman was standing there quite calmly. He wouldn't be doing that if he had recognised Rory passing through the barrier a few minutes earlier. Rory must be past him, he must be through! The thought hit her like a thunderclap, and strengthened her resolve. Keeping behind the large man, she inched her way to the barrier, and quickly she followed him through. The policeman appeared not to notice her, and suddenly, she was out of the station and into the bright sunlight of the street.

With a deep sigh of relief, Shona started to walk quickly away from the railway station. In spite of herself, she couldn't resist the temptation to look behind her to see whether she was being followed. There was no sign of the policeman, and she hurried across the road. Nobody paid her any attention. There were plenty of pedestrians and many of them seemed to be walking purposefully, going about their business. There were a few tourists, meandering along, consulting street maps and admiring the Georgian architecture. She found it quite easy to blend in with them, to become anonymous on these pavements, yet her nerves were taut, like violin strings. She expected any minute to be stopped or to feel a tap on her shoulder. She turned into Princes Street, and then into Charlotte Square. Immediately she saw Rory standing at the agreed meeting place. He was looking pretty self conscious, pretending to take a great interest in the statue of Prince Albert on horseback in the centre of the square. She hurried over to him. Rory was reassured at the sight of her. He sounded nervous, more so than he had been at any point previously. "Am I glad to see you, Shona. I was beginning to wonder where you were, or whether I was in the right place. Have you seen any sign of Mr Chisholm?"

"No, Rory, I haven't. I'm not even sure that he got on the train." Without realising it, she had joined in with the boy's role play, and she was pointing at the statue as she spoke. "From where I was standing on the platform I had a pretty good view of the ticket office, and I don't think he got on the train. We give him two or three minutes and if he hasn't turned up by then, I think we should go on without him. What do you say?" Shona had been thinking about this possibility during the train journey, being fairly sure that Chisholm, for whatever reason, hadn't been on the train.

Rory considered this. "I'd feel a lot better with him here, but you're right. We should keep going without him if he doesn't show up soon. I feel really silly standing here pretending to be a tourist."

Simultaneously, they noticed a man coming in their direction from the other side of the square. It would have been surprising if they had not noticed him. He was dressed in bright pink trousers, and wore an equally bright yellow windproof jacket which bore the logo of the Boston Red Sox, the American baseball team. The same logo appeared on his baseball cap. He wore wraparound sun glasses, and round his neck swung a camera. As he approached them, they could see he was vigorously chewing gum. An American tourist surely, and he was heading straight for them. He stopped only a couple of feet away, and looked at them closely. For a moment, both of them were taken by surprise, and then the same thought occurred to them. This tourist had seen the news bulletin, and had recognised them. The man spoke, and they immediately recognised the voice. "Pretty good disguise, isn't it. I avoided anyone looking at me closely by dressing to attract attention, but in a way that would make people think of an American with no dress sense rather than a dangerous kidnapper. It is quite a standard practice in our business, a way of wrong footing the opposition. I didn't tell you back in Livingston because I didn't have the kit to change both of your characters. This gear was in my overnight case, and I changed into it as soon as I saw Rory reach the ticket office. Anyway, we've all made it here safely. Let's get on with what we have to do."

Shona and Rory looked at each other in astonishment.

They walked slowly round Charlotte Square three times, stopping frequently as Chisholm pretended to take photographs. Sometimes the other two would pose; sometimes he lined up a shot meticulously of a building or took a picture of the statue from yet another angle, all the while taking his time to ensure that the camera would capture his subject to his absolute satisfaction. He was beginning to wonder how much more time they could spend in the square without attracting comment. It was just after ten o'clock when he learned what he wanted to know. A woman that he didn't recognise, but was in fact, Margaret Morrison, the wife of the First Minister left Bute House. He wasn't interested in her, though. What he had learned was that there were two security men stationed by the door, just inside. Undoubtedly, on a detail like this, they would be armed. This might present a problem, but it wasn't unexpected. He had been thinking how he might deal with a situation like this. Fearing that if they spent more time in Charlotte Square they would attract attention to themselves, Chisholm moved them back onto Princes Street, and crossed into the gardens beyond. There they found a bench under the shadow of the battlements of the awe inspiring castle which dominated the skyline, where they could sit and talk. He needed them to be absolutely clear about what they were going to do next. In many ways this would be the most dangerous step they had taken. There would be no room for errors, and one of them, at least, had to get through. They had come too far to fail. As he explained his plan, the others nodded in understanding, and asked a number of questions to clarify certain points. Chisholm made them both describe in minute detail their part in the plan, first Rory, and then Shona repeated their own individual roles, and then the three of them went over the plan, each describing their parts, but this time in the sequence they intended to carry out the plan. Finally, Chisholm was satisfied that they all knew what they had to do. He was uncertain, however, whether they would be able to hold their nerve when it came to putting the plan into practice, but he could see no alternative. It was expecting much of these two untrained civilians, and Chisholm concluded that it said much for the trust and respect he had developed, for both of them, that he was even considering this course of action. They all understood that the key was to have the door open. Chisholm had explained clearly that since their faces had been splashed all over the press, and if people thought they were armed and dangerous, that would influence how the security men would respond, but that it was something he intended to use to their advantage.

As agreed, they approached Bute House simultaneously, Rory and Shona from the north, and Chisholm from the south. As they approached, they saw a heavily built, dark haired big man speak at the intercom. The door opened and he went inside. They were too far away to take advantage of the open door. To their surprise, instead of closing the door, one of the security men came out, and stood on the top step, looking about him. Rory made up his mind in an instant. Without taking time to tell Shona what he intended, but praying that she and Chisholm would react, he starting running as fast as he could towards Bute House. He only had fifteen yards to go. He was shouting at the top of his voice "Help, help! Let me in! They're trying to kidnap me!" as he bounded up the steps, two at a time.

The security man at the top step had only a second to react as he turned to see where the shouts had come from. Rory was at his side, panting "Let me in, they're after me." and pointing in the general direction of Shona. The man regained his balance quickly. This was the boy he had seen on the news. He put a protective arm round Rory and pushed him towards the open door. At that instant, his colleague stepped into the doorway to investigate the noise. Rory saw him coming, and using the impetus from the push crashed into the guard, bending low as he did so, taking the man in his stomach with his shoulder. The man, caught off balance with one foot still in the house and the other on the step, toppled over backwards, Rory on top of him. In the same instant, the man on the step was reaching inside his jacket for his gun. He had heard that the kidnappers were armed and dangerous. He was looking in the direction that Rory had pointed, and saw Shona running towards him, then skidding to a halt, no more than five yards away. That was when Chisholm, unseen approaching from the other direction, hit him hard in the back, sending him onto the ground, face first, and sent the gun spinning out into the street.

Meanwhile, the second man was winded, but was struggling to get out from under Rory. Rory wasn't trying to hold him down, he was just making deliberately clumsy attempts to get up, which had the effect of completely defeating the man's efforts. Rory could however, feel the strength of the man below him as he finally pushed the boy to one side. Rory rolled away, and climbed nimbly to his feet. By this time Chisholm was standing over the man, and he said quietly to the prone figure, "You know who I am. Reach very slowly into your jacket, and bring out your gun. Then slide it over towards me." The man was tough, but he knew, or believed that he was dealing with a dangerous professional criminal. Chisholm wasn't holding a gun, but his right hand was in his jacket pocket, which clearly contained something that was the size of a small hand gun. He reached very slowly into his jacket, and brought out his gun holding it gingerly between his thumb and middle finger. Then he slid it over towards Chisholm's feet. Chisholm kicked the gun to one side, sending it underneath a small table, and said to the man in his most threatening voice "Get out, now."

The man did so, stumbling, without really getting fully to his feet. Chisholm pulled the door closed behind him, and applied the security lock. Shona meanwhile had run in past them and was already exploring doors on the ground floor. She opened one – a toilet. The next was a sitting room but with no-one in it. Quickly she moved to the next one. She opened the door and was met with the indignant glare of the First Minister, and a startled reaction from the other man in the room, whom she recognised as the man who had entered minutes before. She called out over her shoulder, "In here. He's here!" She held the door open until Chisholm and Rory entered, then closed it. Chisholm took command of the situation. Rory jammed a chair against the door, effectively preventing anyone from entering. "First Minister, do you know who we are? Good, I see that you do. Do not try anything stupid. Who is this, with you?"

Morrison was indignant, but like everyone he had seen this man and his accomplice demonised in news bulletins. Despite his outrage, he controlled his response, wondering why these people should turn up here. "This is Donald Barrie, my Communications and Press Officer. Now, if you don't mind, we are trying to prepare for a very important television debate."

Chisholm laughed out loud. "In that case, Mr Barrie, you should stay. Neither of you are in any danger from us let me assure you. If you doubt it, just ask Rory. He has not been abducted, nor is he here against his will. However, I am armed and very dangerous should anybody try to come in. Do you understand? Good. It seems that we have come at exactly the right time. I will be keeping guard on the door, so I suggest you phone whoever you need to and tell them that we are not to be disturbed. Then you will spend the next two hours listening to everything my two young friends here have to tell you. I see that you have a laptop with you, Mr Barrie. I take it that it has a port for a memory stick? Good. Please boot it up. Believe me, First Minister, you will not be in a position to prepare for your television debate until you have heard what my friends will tell you, and seen the details they will show you from their memory stick. What you are about to see will completely change that debate and how you prepare for it."

Alistair Morrison was wrong-footed by this unexpected turn of events, but he used the internal phone on his desk to call, Chisholm listening in carefully to every word. He did as instructed, and said that he wanted no heroic storming of the room, and at prompting from Chisholm, said that he wanted a media blackout on the situation. Satisfied, Chisholm pulled a seat over to the door, and sat there, hand in the pocket of his yellow jacket, where something was bulging out. Morrison took this to be a gun of some sort. Meanwhile, Donald Barrie had set up his laptop, under the watchful eye of Shona Murray. She inserted the memory stick, and seconds later a folder bearing the legend REFERENDUM appeared on screen. Shona invited Morrison to sit alongside Donald Barrie, in a position where they could both see the screen.

Chisholm had been mistaken. Morrison and Barrie did not spend two hours listening to Shona and Rory. It was three and half hours later that they stopped listening. They had gone through a range of emotions. Fear had given way to disbelief, to astonishment, and on to incredulity. Anger had changed to rage and then to resentment. Finally, a cold fury descended on the room. They had lost all track of time, and Morrison had forgotten that they were apparently being held hostage. By now, he knew that Chisholm was not armed and that the bulge in his pocket was a camera. Morrison had, with Chisholm's approval, arranged for a tray to be brought in with lunch for five people. It fell to Rory to explain the plan that he had proposed to Chisholm and

Shona in the bedroom of the Stag's Heart Hotel. Donald Barrie had some reservations, but Alistair Morrison liked it a lot.

Chapter Twenty

The Studio

WPC Kate McLean was back at the Lawson cottage. She had been relieved by a colleague from Portree about eleven o'clock the previous night, but had returned at lunchtime. For her, this was more than a question of duty. The Lawsons were her friends, and they were in trouble. There wasn't much she could do to help them practically, but she had managed to chase off several reporters and one television news crew. The sight of her uniform, and some well chosen words from her had been enough to dissuade any intrusion. She had spotted in the distance a camera man with a telephoto lens, the lens reflecting in the mid afternoon sun, and had got one of her colleagues to pick the man up and confiscate the memory card from his camera. At least she could protect their privacy at this trying time. She had helped Flora prepare an evening meal while Hugh and Angus busied themselves with some essential work with the livestock. Over the meal the tension between the Lawsons was palpable. It hung in the air like a pall of dark, rancid smoke. Kate wondered if this was a normal reaction. This was the first time she had dealt with an abduction, and had no yardstick to measure things by. She was sure that Flora was blaming someone, either herself for being away from home when the kidnap had occurred, or Hugh for not doing more to prevent it. However, she realised that it might just be the inevitable anxiety of very worried parents. During the day, even Angus had seemed to allow his spirits to dip, gradually changing from reassuring everyone that things would work out alright, to a quiet, withdrawn reticence. The evening meal had passed in almost total silence, and now Angus was helping his mother to clear up in the kitchen, while Hugh was in the sitting room with her. He was staring absently towards the door.

That was when the radio attached to the front of her uniform went off. She excused herself, and went into an adjoining room in order to be out of earshot, as police protocol demanded. She was gone for just over three minutes, during which time, the house landline also rang. The handset was in the hall, and Flora rushed to answer that, drying her hands as she went. She picked up the handset in a quivering hand. Angus joined his father in the sitting room, and the two of them exchanged puzzled looks, without comment. Kate came into the sitting room first, wearing a broad grin "Good news! He's safe!" At that, Flora came in, looking as though a massive weight had been lifted off her shoulders, her eyes moist. Kate continued, "Rory's safe. That was my headquarters. They don't have any details yet, but he is safe. He is in Edinburgh. I have to stay with you until we can arrange a reunion. This is just great." Kate felt that a great stress had been removed – she had been asking herself how she would handle things if there was a bad outcome, and she was left to break the news to the Lawsons, and now that was not going to happen.

Flora, tears of joy and relief now running unashamedly down her face, said, between sobs, "That was Rory on the phone. He says he is OK. He said he didn't have much time to talk, but he is looking forward to seeing us all soon. He sends his love. He says we have all to watch the independence debate on the television tonight. He was most insistent. Then he said something really strange. He said we've to tell Iain Beag that he has to watch it too. What has any of this got to do with Iain?"

Hugh shrugged, pulled a face and raised his palms in a gesture that indicated he had no idea what Iain Beag's involvement might be.

"The debate starts in just over an hour," Angus observed.

Amid much hugging and backslapping, Hugh poured four rather large whiskies to toast Rory's health. On duty or not, Kate accepted the drink – it would have been churlish to have refused. In any event she shared the sense of relief in the room. Alone amongst them, she believed that there had been a genuine kidnapping by armed and dangerous gangsters, and had been dreading the possibility that she might at some point have to break bad news to the Lawsons. She felt sure that should her sergeant ever find out that she had accepted a drink he would understand completely. Hugh turned to Kate. "Thank you for all your support, Kate. You have been tremendous. We, or rather, I have a confession to make to you, though. We all feel bad about not sharing this with you earlier, but I think it would have made things very difficult for you." He started to tell her about the late night visit from Chisholm and Shona, as Angus extricated himself from his mother's hug, excused himself and phoned Iain Beag.

* * *

Richard Hume arrived at the studio in Edinburgh in the same limousine as Penny Carson, Edith Bannon and George Graham. He was met by one of the researchers for the programme, who directed his three companions to a lounge area where they could have coffee and biscuits. Hume was shown into a private room, where he was joined by an open-shirted man carrying a clipboard, who introduced himself as the floor manager. He explained the format of the programme, and that he would shortly be required to come to the podium on the stage that had been set up for the debate so that the engineers could complete a sound test. Then a girl from the make up department would visit, to ensure that he looked perfect, and that the bright studio lights would not reflect off his face. He went on to describe that his own role would be linking with the producer, and Sue Farquhar who was the anchor for the transmission. He would be responsible for moving cameras around, and audience control, signalling when to applaud and when to stop, and so on. Then he was gone, saying that he had to go over the same information with the First Minister.

The same researcher that met Hume on arrival collected him, and took him to the wings of the platform. He and Morrison were to enter simultaneously to their respective podiums from opposite sides of the stage, place any notes they had on a small table beside the podium, then meet in the middle to shake hands, before taking up position for the debate. Hume could sense the buzzing atmosphere, the expectation in the three hundred strong studio audience. He could see Penny seated in the front row, flanked by George Graham and Edith Bannon. Across the platform, he saw Alistair Morrison waiting in the wings, stony faced, and wearing a tie with a saltire motif. Signals went up, and the floor manager was waving the audience into a round of applause, and then, as Sue Farquhar moved to the centre of the stage, clutching a clipboard full of notes, he signalled for the applause to stop.

Sue Farquhar was, as always, well prepared, calm and when she spoke, very clear. She looked directly into one of the cameras, and read from the autocue. "Good evening, and welcome to the Independence Debate. On Thursday, Scotland goes to the polls in a referendum that will decide the future of our country. This historic occasion will determine whether Scotland will become an independent nation, or remain as part of a union with the other nations of Great Britain. This debate is obviously of great interest here in Scotland, but it has attracted interest from all over the world, and the debate is being screened live by a number of television companies to over ninety countries around the world. So we extend a welcome to them."

She paused, and then continued, looking into a different camera. "We have a studio audience here in Edinburgh gathered to hear the final arguments in the debate. The purpose of this is to help people across Scotland decide how to cast their vote on Thursday. We are going to have the case for independence put by Alistair Morrison, leader of the independence movement, and First Minister of Scotland, and the case against will be put by the Right Honourable Richard Hume, MP, the Deputy Prime Minister of the British government. Please, welcome them both on stage."

The stage manager waved the audience into loud applause and urged Morrison and Hume onto the stage. The two protagonists, walked smartly to their podiums, every step followed on camera. Morrison deposited a thick brown folder on the table by his podium. Hume did the same with a much slimmer blue folder. Then both men continued a few paces until they met half way. As they gave a perfunctory handshake, Hume said quietly to Morrison, so that the microphone would not pick up his voice "May the best man win." Morrison gave him a disarming smile, and whispered back, "Rest assured, Richard, the best man will win." Then both men returned to their respective positions, Hume wondering briefly about Morrison's enigmatic remark.

As the applause died down, Sue Farquhar continued with her introduction. "The format for tonight's debate is straightforward. We have Alistair Morrison proposing the motion that Scotland should be an independent country. He will have five minutes to make his case. Then Richard Hume will have ten minutes to cross examine him. This will consist of putting questions to Alistair Morrison, not making a speech. Then the roles will be reversed. Richard Hume will have five minutes to make the case against independence, and Alistair Morrison will have ten minutes to cross examine him. Then there will be a period of questions from the audience, before first Alistair Morrison and then Richard Hume sum up the debate. Of course, the real outcome of the debate will not be known until after Thursday's votes have all been counted.

"I call on Alistair Morrison to open the debate by making the case for Scottish independence."

As the floor manager once more indicated that the audience should applaud, Alistair Morrison took hold of the edges of the lectern on his podium, and slowly looked round the audience, noting the identity of

Hume's three supporting guests. As the polite applause died away, Morrison turned and looked directly into the camera.

"Before I start to make the case for Scottish independence, I wish to take the opportunity to share with you some good news, which I am sure you will all rejoice to hear. Everybody here will be aware of the manhunt that has been going on over Scotland to find the abducted schoolboy, Rory Lawson. Well, I can announce that Rory is safe and well. In fact he is here with us tonight, sitting in the front row."

A camera panned along the audience, and there was Rory, seated between Donald Barrie and Margaret Morrison, the First Minister's wife. He was grinning broadly, and waving to the camera, and giving the thumbs up sign. In response to prompting from the floor manager, who had received an instruction from the producer, Rory stood up, and turned briefly to face the audience, before resuming his seat. The cameraman, on instruction, zoomed in for a close-up of the boy. The floor manager had no need to invite applause – there was a spontaneous outburst of cheers and clapping from the audience, all of whom had believed the boy to be in the clutches of a desperate and dangerous gang. Morrison held his hand up for silence. "As you can see, Rory is perfectly alright. In fact, he had never been abducted. That means that no crime has been committed, and the two suspects, David Chisholm and Shona Murray are no longer wanted in connection with the alleged crime. Mr Chisholm and Miss Murray were merely making it possible for Rory to be my guest at tonight's debate. There has been no crime committed. There has only been a misunderstanding between one law agency and the police force. These two people are neither armed nor dangerous, contrary to earlier reports. As a consequence, police forces across Scotland have been advised to call off the manhunt."

There was a gasp, and some clapping in the audience. Taken by surprise, they didn't know how to react. Hume exchanged looks with Penny Carson who just gave a puzzled shrug. She had, of course heard about the hunt for Rory Lawson – it had been on every news bulletin throughout the day – but she had no reason to connect it to the debate that was about to unfold. She thought that it must be Morrison's idea of a publicity stunt to win back some lost ground. Unworried by this, she settled down to watch the demise of the separatists.

At the sight of Rory on his television screen, Iain Beag, picked up his dog, Shep, and did a little jig around his sitting room. A few miles away, in the Lawson cottage, there were shouts of glee, Angus pointing at the television, and cheering. Even Kate, who now knew much of the background to Rory's appearance in Edinburgh, and wished that she didn't, couldn't help but join in the cheering.

Morrison started to lay out his case for independence. He gave a good performance over the next five minutes, as he covered a lot of the usual ground in the arguments that had been developed over the years, before exhorting the voters to vote in favour of independence. He had fallen just a little short of his own exceptional standards of oratory. Only occasionally throughout his address had real passion and zeal shone through. Penny Carson and Richard Hume had both studied hours of footage of Morrison addressing audiences, both noted this marginally below standard performance. They both reached the same conclusion - Morrison knew he was on his way to disaster in Thursday's polls, and in the circumstances it would have been strange if his performance wasn't affected to some extent. In fact, Penny was mildly surprised at how much fight he had managed to put into things. Both of them were satisfied that his speech had followed the general outline that they had been given, and had been pleasantly surprised that some of his specific references led directly into Richard Hume's cross examination. Apart from his little theatrical stunt with the kidnapped boy, there were no surprises.

The applause was generous, but hardly rapturous. As the floor manager signalled for quiet in the audience, the cameras panned away from Alistair Morrison, and focused on Sue Farquhar, clutching her clipboard. Keeping her expression neutral, she addressed the camera. "Thank you, First Minister, for that statement, making the case for independence. We are about to find out how strong that case is as I invite Richard Hume, Deputy Prime Minister, to cross examine you, and test the arguments you have been making. I call on Richard Hume to begin the cross examination."

Hume was not a popular figure with the Scottish public, many of whom regarded him as being from a privileged background, and rather aloof. The applause he received reflected this.

Chapter Twenty One

Cross Examination

There was a pause, a split second when there was total silence in the studio. Penny Carson, Edith Bannon and George Graham all had their attention focused on Richard Hume, full of anticipation. Penny glanced at Morrison. He seemed somewhat detached, a lonely figure by his podium, apparently too relaxed, as he looked around the studio audience. She wondered with a sense of cold detachment whether he had any idea, any hint, of the extent of the damage this cross examination was going to cause him personally, or how much it was going to harm the cause he held so dear. She smiled to herself. It pleased her to think that she had been part of his downfall, and she believed that it was her right to be here, to witness at first hand his final demise. Her expectation of the end of Morrison's dream consumed her. This was something she had worked hard to bring about. The moment of ultimate triumph had arrived, Hume could not fail.

Hume cleared his throat, and looked momentarily at one of the cameras. There was now one camera focusing on him all the time. Another was trained on Morrison, and two others were concentrating on shots of the audience. He took a final fleeting look at his notes, although he knew perfectly what they contained. Then he was ready. He fixed his gaze intently on Morrison, who was pouring himself a top up of water. "Well, First Minister, let me congratulate you on your presentation. You have made many bold claims and you talked about having evidence for them. You talked about trust and competence. Let us see if your evidence stands up to some scrutiny or whether your entire presentation was a fabrication, a fantasy version of a future that can never be. Does your presentation belong to the same fantasy world of the discredited tales of Ossian?

"First, I want to examine the claim that you made at the start of your presentation about wanting to retain the monarchy. You say that, but is it really true? Perhaps on a personal basis you believe that, but isn't the truth that you head a party of republican fanatics? That you would ditch the monarchy at the first opportunity and set up instead some presidential style arrangement, no doubt designed to keep you in office? First Minister, you talk about evidence. The evidence in this regard is a matter of public knowledge. Can you deny that your branch in Glenturrach was debating this very issue only a matter of weeks ago, and we are grateful to the press for revealing the true and extreme sentiments of your party on this issue?"

Morrison, blinked and smiled across at the Deputy Prime Minister. He hesitated for an instant before replying. "Richard, this is a democracy. Party members are free to hold whatever views they wish. Debate is a cornerstone of democracy. We would not wish to stifle open debate. Every political party has elements that are on the fringes, representing minority views. In your own party there is a known minority who advocate leaving the EU. Yet you don't classify yourselves as an extremist party. Some of your members are on record as disagreeing with your policies on reducing greenhouse gases. That does not make your party an extremist one. It is my duty, and it should be yours, as a politician to preserve democracy, to put the facts simply and honestly to the people. We should trust the people. We should seek to stimulate debate. Freedom of speech is of vital importance." Hume turned away from Morrison, until he was facing the audience. Pointing at Morrison, he said. "The First Minister talks about truth. Well, at least he spares us the lie of denying that there is a strong republican element in his party. We all heard the tapes of his members using their freedom of speech, as he puts it, to run down and criticise the monarchy, to demand that their very houses be taken from them, in a modern day equivalent of the overthrow of the Russian Royal Family. We all know where that led."

Turning back to face Morrison, he continued jabbing his forefinger at the other man, "So you don't deny that these discussions go on within your party? How can you deny it?"

Morrison just smiled, and replied mildly, "Of course I don't deny that the debate that was taped and then passed to the various news agencies took place in a branch of my party. As you point out, how could I? Everybody has seen the evidence." Alistair Morrison caught sight of Penny Carter just at that moment. She had worked herself up into a frenzy of excitement. This was going even better than she had hoped. Morrison was putting up no defence at all. This would be a massacre! She almost fell off her seat as she struggled to contain her exhilaration.

Hume nodded, satisfied that he had scored a major blow, and was about to move on to his next and yet more damning point, when Morrison continued, "I have to say that I wondered at the wisdom of holding such a debate, and I wonder how you would react, Richard, if private debates within your party were recorded and given to the press. When we look in detail at what happened there, some interesting things emerge. You can clearly hear someone talking on the tape, and it is obviously mainly one person. Certainly, you can hear a couple of others cheering. The person speaking was a new branch member, who joined only a fortnight earlier. He proposed the debate for the agenda, and he led the debate. Our membership records show him to be called Walter Wilson. He has had no more contact with anyone in the party since the debate. In fact, we cannot contact him. There is no record of him living at the address he gave when joining. In fact the flat that the address relates to had been taken out on a two month lease by someone called Allan M. Whittle. There is no forwarding address, but I have evidence that it was this Allan Whittle who passed the tapes to the press. Indeed, I have reason to believe that Walter

Wilson and Allan M. Whittle are one and the same person. It is very difficult to track down Mr Whittle, but I suspect his name might crop up again.

"So Richard, you ask for evidence. There, you have all the evidence. Someone using a fictitious name joins a branch, leads an inflammatory debate, then sends copies of that debate, knowing how damaging it will be, to the press. He subsequently disappears. Why would someone do that? What do you make of the evidence?"

Richard Hume gave a mirthless laugh. "What I make of it is the same as everybody in the audience will conclude. This mystery man, this Wilson, or Whittle, or whatever name you want to use, is pure fantasy. This story is a fiction, a fairy tale, dreamt up to give you a response to the indefensible. You really should stop, First Minister, while you still retain some of your credibility. Surely the people of Scotland will not want to be led to independence by someone who is apparently having difficulty separating the real world from a make believe world. Or do you think this is Scotland the Make Believe?"

It wasn't a great joke, but the audience laughed, a muted, rather embarrassed snigger. None of them, even those who opposed him could quite believe that their First Minister was standing there, being humiliated in this way in front of a huge audience. This was the man who had stood up to some big challenges over his political life, and who had always been able to defend himself and his policies from attack. This was the man who had put his party in the position where their desire for independence had come close to realisation. What had happened to him? There was embarrassment too, in the audience, that he was being treated this way, being made fun of, by someone who wasn't a Scot. In some way, this was beginning to look like a national defeat, a national humiliation.

Alistair Morrison pulled a face and gave a shrug. He still seemed detached. In the control room the producer could sense that something major was happening to Alistair Morrison, and he instructed the cameraman to get closer, and to miss nothing of Morrison's reactions. Hume swivelled on his heel so that he was facing Morrison directly. He pulled himself up to his full height, to create an even more intimidating appearance. He knew that when he had a witness on the ropes, he should follow up quickly, allowing no thinking time, no recovery space. What Richard Hume saw when he looked at Morrison was disconcerting. Morrison, looked unconcerned, and was even smiling. Hume had cross examined enough witnesses to know when someone looked worried. Morrison didn't: he appeared untroubled. The thought occurred to Hume that perhaps Morrison's mind had just shut down. It could be a reflex action. The enormity of the defeat awaiting him had just hit home, and his brain was shutting it out. He had heard of such things. The brain tries to protect the person by closing out reality. That must be it. Still, he had a job to do. Now was not the time for sympathy. Rather it was time to press home the advantage, ruthlessly.

"Let us move on, and try if we might to get back to reality. Mr Morrison. You claim to head a government of competence. You put great store by the way you and your team run things. I want to examine if that is borne out by the evidence. Would you say that your Finance Minister is one of your most trusted colleagues?"

Alistair Morrison was looking at a point on the ceiling of the studio, almost appearing to be bored, when he answered. "Indeed so, Richard. Christine Milne is an exemplary Finance Minister with an unblemished record."

"Very commendable loyalty, First Minister, but do you not recall just a few short weeks ago, in this very studio, I believe, in a debate that Sue Farquhar here was chairing, she couldn't get even the most basic facts right from a straightforward report. Tell us, is this what you mean when you talk about, an exemplary record, and about competence in government? Ministers who can't quote from reports?"

Morrison looked down at his lectern, then up, not to Hume, but to Sue Farquhar. "Sue, you were chairing that debate. Did you notice anything strange? No? Oh well, I guess I'll have to explain."

Hume cut in brusquely, "What is it going to be this time, First Minister, a UFO?"

Morrison appeared not to notice Richard Hume. "Christine Milne is an excellent Minister, and I have never known her to be wrong. Yet, at the debate that you refer to she quoted figures that were very wrong, as Edith Bannon, the Secretary of State for Scotland in the British government who is with us tonight in the front row, was quick to point out on the night. It is indeed devastating when the numbers quoted are wrong. As I said earlier, democracy depends on politicians telling the truth and being honest with each other and with the public. On that night, Christine was wrong. There can be no doubt about that. She quoted the wrong numbers. Edith Bannon pointed that out. If you look back at footage of that debate, you will see how quickly Edith moved to point out the error. Too quickly, in fact. The evidence is all there, it is on the tape. She was reacting before Christine offered the wrong figures. You can see that if you look closely at the footage. The camera is focused on Christine, but Edith can be seen in the background." Morrison paused, and switched his line of vision to the front row, and looked directly at Edith Bannon. "Edith, you knew that Christine was about to make a gaffe, didn't you? You knew because Penny Carson, the Prime Minister's advisor, who is also here this evening told you that she would. Penny knew this because she had received a briefing from a senior civil servant to the effect that a copy of the report had been amended to include the wrong figures, and that copy had been circulated to the Scottish cabinet. The name on that briefing was Allan M. Whittle - that name again - wasn't it, Penny? Mr Whittle knew that the wrong version had been circulated to the Scottish government because another civil servant that he was blackmailing, one holding a senior position at Holyrood,

222

had assured him that this was the case. The civil servant being blackmailed had been involved in a procurement scandal at the Ministry of Defence some years earlier and his part in it had been covered up to avoid a public humiliation for the government of the day. Before George Graham there gets too smug, let me tell you that incident occurred when his party was in power."

One of the cameramen who had been taking shots of the audience had now been instructed by the producer to get down to the front and to concentrate on Edith Bannon and Penny Carson. He was just too late to catch their initial shock at Morrison's accusation, and they had regained some of their composure by the time the producer managed to cut to a shot of them both. For all that, they still both looked extremely uncomfortable. Penny Carson was furiously trying to work out how Morrison could have known that, and if he knew that, what else did he know?

"So you see, Christine Milne is an exemplary and competent minister who was deliberately supplied with erroneous information so that she would look foolish in front of a television audience. Since we have Edith and Penny with us, and since we are all agreed that we are seeking evidence and truth, perhaps either or both of them would wish to tell the Scottish public exactly what they have been up to?"

Richard Hume interjected, "It is you, First Minister, who is being cross examined here, no-one else. So far every time I ask you something, you just come up with an ever more unbelievable tale. You have nothing to hide behind but a web of deceit. You have invented this bogey man, this Mr Whittle, and you seem determined to lay the blame for all your misfortunes, all the inadequacies of your case, at the door of this fantasy character. I put to you that this nonsense must stop, First Minister. We are here to hold a serious debate, and you are turning it into a farce with your completely unsubstantiated claims. In any case, to return to the issue of competence, you raised the matter of the A9.

Surely you recognise that this is hardly a matter that you should be using to demonstrate competence. At this moment, we have the main contractor describing this project – your government's major flagship project – as over budget and behind schedule. Not by a trifling amount, but six months behind schedule, and £5 million over budget. Yet you and your ministers insist there is no problem. You say the contractor has got it wrong, but I say that you have got it wrong. It is absolutely not in the contractor's interest to highlight problems on a project where they are carrying out the work. Why, First Minister would they do that?"

Alistair Morrison continued to smile benignly at Hume. "Why indeed? Richard, why don't we ask Penny Carson, she knows the answer? Sorry, I forgot it is me who is being cross examined. Let's not allow a search for the truth to interfere with your cross examination." He paused.

This time the camera was focused on Penny Carson as Morrison referred to her, and there was no missing her expression. She was taken aback. This was not supposed to happen. How could she be exposed like this? Underneath her well manicured appearance, she was flustered. Her eyes had narrowed and her mouth tightened. Her brow was furrowed as she realised with sickening certainty that Morrison knew exactly what was going on, and she was the only other person in the room who had the same information. But how could he possibly have obtained his information? She fought to control the rising tide of nausea, and she could feel the taste of bile in her throat. Frantically she tried to think. Was there an alternative strategy open to her and Hume, and how could she tell Richard Hume what was going on?

Morrison continued, "You see the difficulty here, as you put it, Richard. Why would a contractor like Readybuild issue a report that showed them, at least by association, in a bad light? Intriguing, isn't it? Well, the answer lies in that word, intrigue. What would make them issue a report they knew to be wrong? Well, maybe a big enough incentive would do the trick. Perhaps the certainty of future work and large contracts would secure their cooperation. What would serve as sufficient incentive? Well, how about the promise of two really big contracts, such as the new network motorway, the so-called super motorway proposed to link four major English cities, and the project to create a new university campus to replace three London University campuses? The estimated combined value of these two projects is £80 billion. That was enough for John Webster, the Readybuild chairman, when he met with a man he believed to be a senior civil servant called," here he paused for dramatic effect, "Allan M. Whittle."

Morrison held his hand up to prevent an interjection from Richard Hume. "I know that you will say that I am blaming Mr Whittle again. I don't blame him for anything, for the very good reason that he doesn't exist. There is no such senior civil servant. You are absolutely right, Richard when you say he is a fantasy figure. However, he is not in my fantasy. You said, Richard that I am making unsubstantiated claims, unsupported by evidence. If that was true, I would just have slandered John Webster, but I have not. I have all the evidence I need, all the evidence that anybody will ever need, in this file here." He tapped the brown folder that lay on the table beside him. "Perhaps since you accused me of being somewhat of a fantasist who offers no evidence to support what he says, you will permit me to demonstrate that all that I have said is absolutely true."

Morrison opened the folder. It contained fourteen other folders, each neatly bound. Thirteen of them were quite slim, and one was rather bulky. Morrison picked up the top folder. "This contains details of the operation to place Walter Wilson inside one of our branches. It contains documentation of the expenses and receipt of the flat rented in the name of Allan M. Whittle. It describes the plan to make the recording of the meeting and to release it to the press." He laid the folder to one side.

In the control room, the producer was trying to think clearly. He had four cameras, one each trained on Morrison and Hume; the other two were concentrating on Penny Carson. Hume looked puzzled and crestfallen, Carson's face was contorted in discomfort, and Morrison held the floor in a way that compelled attention. Somehow, he had to capture all of this. It was clear to him, watching the reaction of Hume and Carson, that Morrison's revelations were true, and devastating. The size of the folder Morrison had opened meant that there was much more to come. He spoke urgently to Sue Farquhar through her ear piece. "Make sure Morrison gets to continue. Forget the debate schedule. This is bigger. Don't let anybody interrupt him." He could see her nod her understanding. Then he returned to his control panel, and concentrated on switching shots between Morrison, Hume and Carson, trying to anticipate where the best reactions and most telling images would come from at any point.

Morrison picked up the second file, and waved it towards the camera. "This file contains details of a briefing prepared under the name of Allan M. Whittle, and passed to Penny Carson for onward transmission to Edith Bannon. It details the difference between the two versions of the Taxation in Inner Cities report. The one which came to the Scottish government contains a deliberate error, that had been inserted, and which made it inevitable that we would use the figures from the version we had to counter certain arguments. All Edith Bannon had to do was to raise those arguments, and sit back waiting for Christine Milne to respond. This file," he continued holding up the next file from his desk, "holds the details of the procurement scandal and how it was being used to blackmail the civil servant in Edinburgh."

The camera close–ups of Penny Carson, who was used to staying out of the limelight, and Edith Bannon, were dramatic. Neither could control their facial expressions. Their reactions were a mixture of shock and apprehension.

"This next file contains details of the discussion between Whittle and Webster. It includes the confidential information about other contracts that Whittle used to convince Webster that he could deliver on his promise of ensuring that he be awarded these two huge contracts. It also contains evidence about who authorised the release of these confidential documents, and the report that was passed to Penny Carson, confirming Webster's agreement to the subterfuge.

"Now lest anyone has any doubts, Penny Carson, who is not a known public figure, is the personal adviser to Nigel Braithwaite, the Prime Minister." The camera zoomed in even more closely on her. She was covering her face with her hands, and shaking with a mixture of fear and fury. "Is it conceivable that she was acting on this without her master's consent? Well, no, this next file holds details of a request made by the Prime Minister himself, with full agreement and cooperation from the Leader of the Opposition, Stephen Halford, to mount an operation to discredit me and my government and to derail the move towards Scottish independence." He looked at the opposition MP sitting in the front row. "I believe that George Graham there knew nothing of this."

However, the camera had panned across to Graham in time to pick up his astonished and pained reaction to the news that his own party leader was implicated. Up to this point, he had been merely incredulous as detail followed detail. The entire audience were spellbound. They all knew by now that Morrison was producing evidence that would have consequences beyond the impending referendum. This would strike at the very heart of government in Great Britain. He had their full attention. Sue Farquhar was almost willing him to continue to see what the next revelation would be.

Morrison continued, his voice hard, now, as he pulled a file from the bottom of the folder. "Ah, yes, this is the file that contains the brief that was prepared by the man calling himself Whittle, and given to Richard, here, by none other than Penny Carson. It contains his presentation, but also gives him instruction on the points for cross examination." He opened the file and extracted a typed sheet of paper. So, Richard, next you were going to quiz me on the article attributed to the late Hank Warren, the Texan oil tycoon, where he is alleged to have said that oil companies would pull out of a newly independent Scotland. Let us examine this file. Who was the journalist, Richard? When did the interview take place, given that Mr Warren was very weak slipping in and out of consciousness in the months before his death? Well, I have a file here that shows that the article was put together by a certain Allan M. Whittle, using source material from an interview and four articles attributed to Hank Warren in the 1970s. What he has done is to pour over these sources, and select anything that could be of use to him. The material is old, and has been misquoted and phrases and sentences used out of context. Parts of sentences from one article have been joined to parts from another, and so on. Is there no end to the depths of immorality you will sink to, Richard? An old dying man, yet all you see is an opportunity to misquote and misrepresent him for your own purposes, knowing that he was about to die and would be unable to correct the record.

"But why, you might wonder would an organisation like Sir Nigel Hardcastle's media group accept and publish such an unauthenticated article?" He took his time, and selected the thick file. "This is the dossier that Sir Nigel was promised in return for publishing the article – he has already been given half of it. It contains enough evidence to bring to an abrupt and inglorious end the career of a prominent cabinet minister. There are expense claims, insider information to friends, some undeclared but pretty obvious conflicts of interest, and some interesting snippets of his private life. So to perpetrate a lie, the Westminster government was quite prepared to send one of their own to the wolves." Morrison looked at Richard Hume, who was now avoiding eye contact and looking increasingly as though he wanted to leave the platform. Morrison decided to take a chance, "I'll bet they never told you the name of that cabinet member, did they, Richard?"

Hume looked up, startled. Could he have been betrayed and set up in this way? In desperation he looked to Penny Carson. She saw him, and realised what he was thinking. Forgetting that there was a camera trained on her, she mouthed to him "It's not you." When he still looked bewildered, she added, still mouthing "It's Sir Michael Hammond." The camera caught every exaggerated mouthed syllable. There was no room for doubt, and any viewer watching knew in that instant that, incredible as it seemed, all that Morrison was saying must be true. The producer was torn between cutting between shots of Hume and Carson, but in the end, decided to concentrate on the distraught Penny Carson, whose reactions and facial expressions were, he thought, worth thousands of words.

Morrison paused long enough for this to register with everyone, and when he continued, he was like a man transformed. All the passion and zeal that had been missing earlier had returned. His delivery held the audience as though transfixed. "But that wasn't enough for your people, was it, Richard? You had to take out an insurance policy, and that is what you were to quiz me about next, wasn't it? Just in case we got a statement refuting the Hank Warren article, you tried to cover the issue of oil revenues from another angle. Hence the hugely unbalanced article that appeared in the Economics Review magazine, claiming that a surplus of income would be damaging to Scotland's wellbeing. It will come as no surprise to you that the author of that article was none other than Allan M. Whittle. This file here contains the article as written and details of the discussions with the proprietor and editor of the magazine. It shows that they initially refused to take the article, but were then threatened. They were told that certain powerful foreign governments would be upset and would be advised that the magazine had accessed confidential financial documents from those countries. What Mr Whittle didn't mention was that these documents were fakes, and had been supplied earlier by his own organisation. Details of these fake documents are in this next file.

"I think that leaves us with the task of unmasking the mysterious Mr Whittle. This last file has only one sheet in it. It shows where and when all of the other documents in the other files were created. Most of them were created on the same laptop. All the articles and the two files used to blackmail one man and betray another were created on this laptop. The machine in question is assigned to Norman Williams, Section Head and Deputy Director of MI5. Allan M. Whittle is, in fact, Norman Williams."

He paused to let this information sink in. There were gasps from the audience, and Sue Farquhar and the floor manager both signalled for silence.

"Let me sum up, then. Two months ago, it looked like a racing certainty that the Scots would vote for independence. We were well ahead in the opinion polls, and gathering more support by the day. The British government were faced with two choices. They could let democracy have its way, and wish Scotland good luck as we took our place among the nations of the world. Or, they could interfere with the democratic process, and try to prevent us from leaving the Union. This is what they chose to do. Ironically, as they chose to lie and cheat, they made their case against independence based not on the benefits of the Union, but on the pretext that we, my colleagues and I, were unworthy of your trust. They sought to show us at every turn to be wrong and incompetent. They sought to show us to be mistaken and opposed by expert opinion. To do this, they resorted to bullying, to bribery, to blackmail. They have distorted the truth beyond recognition. They invented evidence and changed official documents. They have reached the bottom of the pit of immorality, and they have ruined lives and reputations in the process. All of this comes from a government that claims moral authority when dealing with other supposedly less democratic regimes across the world.

"I say to you tonight, that the case for Scottish independence has been made. Many people supported it a few short weeks ago. The reasons why you supported it then are still valid. In that sense, nothing has changed. The events that had many of you considering shifting your support were orchestrated dishonestly to get you to change your mind. It is those events which have now been fully exposed tonight that should be discounted from your considerations when you come to vote on Thursday. However, I ask you to consider whether you want anything further to do with this set of people who would go to such lengths to deceive you. Throughout the campaign we have had no arguments of any substance forwarded in support of the Union. Those who oppose independence have chosen instead to base their campaign on negative issues, scaremongering about the effects of independence. We have shown tonight that these tactics are not based on fact. Richard Hume accused me of living in a fantasy world. I ask you to judge now whose version of our future is based in reality and who has presented a case based on fabrication and deceit. To our friends in the rest of the UK, I will tell you, that you need more than a change of government, you need a change in the morality of your leaders, a change in the type of people who are allowed to become leaders. Scotland has many friends in the rest of these islands, and an independent Scotland will offer every assistance to them to clear up this sorry state that they find themselves in, and to help them re-establish a credible democracy.

"I urge you in the name of Scotland, its future, and for the sake of future generations, to choose to be an independent country. Let us choose to take responsibility for ourselves. Let us choose to rejoin the international community. Let us choose to be a nation that creates an equal society, that is progressive in its thinking, and that aims to lead the way in a modern 21st century world."

The audience sat in stunned silence for what seemed like minutes. They all knew that they had seen history taking place before their eyes. Finally, lead by Donald Barrie, clapping started, and grew louder, and louder, reaching a cacophony of applause and cheers. Rory Lawson was on his feet, cheering one minute, and without knowing how, the next he was at the podium, shaking Alistair Morrison vigorously by the hand, still cheering deliriously, and punching the air with his free hand. Sue Farquhar and the floor manager were desperately trying to restore some semblance of order, although the producer was also thinking about the startling effects of the images his cameramen were capturing. Finally, it was Morrison, with hands raised, ushering Rory back to his seat, that called for quiet. It took a few seconds as he tried to make himself heard over the noise, and once every one settled down, he said, "We have a debate to finish. I don't know about the rest of you, but I'd quite like to hear if Richard has any arguments at all in favour of us staying with the Union." He looked at Sue Farquhar, who took her cue from him rather than her producer.

"Quite right, First Minister," She searched around for a camera to talk into. "You have put the case for independence, and answered the questions put to you during cross examination. You have done so in a most unusual and unexpected way. The next stage in the debate is for Richard Hume, Deputy Prime Minister, to put the case against independence. I call on you, Richard Hume to present the case."

Richard Hume looked desperate. He knew this had turned into a disaster. He was shell-shocked. His face was devoid of colour. His composure had gone, and he was struggling to respond. This was all too much too quickly for him to take in. He was being called upon to present his case. Automatically, he reached for his notes. The words swam in front of his eyes. He could hardly think, but he knew that he had to continue. He started reading "Ladies and gentlemen, the people of Scotland have been part of a political union with the other nations on this island for over three hundred years. During that time, we have developed many bonds and shared many institutions. Together, we have played a magnificent role in world affairs." He became aware of an echo of his own voice, but couldn't locate it immediately. His first thought was that it must be some feedback from the sound system. He continued, however. "Together, we built an empire." The echo was Alistair Morrison's voice. In unison they read. "We have stood together through two world wars. We have shared good times and bad times."

Hume stopped, and stared at Morrison. "What is going on? What do think you are doing?"

Morrison smiled, and said sedately, "Richard, have you forgotten? I told you that I had the file prepared by Williams or Whittle, if you prefer, that had the cross examination and the presentation that he prepared for you."

Hume was more than beaten, he was broken. He didn't gather up his notes, but tore off his microphone, and strode off the platform without a glance in any direction. Penny Carson, followed closely by a tearful Edith Bannon, rose and quickly made their way after him. George Graham stayed where he was, frozen to spot, his face like stone. He didn't know how to react.

The producer was happy that he had captured all of the drama as it unfolded, but there was still air time available. He was urging Sue Farquhar to engage the First Minister for more details. He directed one of the cameras to capture her in close up.

"Well, I guess that concludes the debate part of the programme, unless, First Minister, you would like to deliver Richard Hume's presentation, since you seem to have it to hand."

"No, Sue, I'm sure you will understand that I really don't want to do that. I don't think it would add anything new to the discussion anyway." Morrison replied with a laugh.

"Tell me, First Minister, when did you become aware of this evidence and why did you decide to reveal it tonight?"

"This evidence was extremely difficult to come by, and I only had it presented to me this morning. Tonight is the first opportunity I have had to make the evidence public. Incidentally, I have to thank an Englishman and a democrat for presenting it to me. This is a man who tells me he is no supporter of Scottish independence but who does possess the moral decency and commitment to democracy to ensure that these attempts to thwart the democratic rights of the people of Scotland would not succeed."

"What happens now to the evidence?"

"Well, Sue, the file will be placed in the hands of the Director of Public Prosecutions in England, and the Lord Advocate here in Scotland already has a copy. It seems certain that criminal charges will arise from this. However, I believe that the people have the right to know exactly what has been going on and what has been done by their government. For that reason, we are working now on creating a link from our website to enable anyone who is interested to view these files. That will be put in place overnight. We will make all the files available and the only thing we will delete is anything that can be used to identify the blackmailed civil servant. This is an example to governments and regimes all over the world of what can go wrong without openness and transparency. That is a message that will not be lost in an independent Scotland."

Sue Farquhar, on the instruction of her producer, rounded up the programme, thanking Morrison for presenting his case, and referring to the historic nature of the programme. She thanked Richard Hume in his absence for his participation in what she described as a "night of revelations." She concluded "Scotland goes to the polls in less than thirty six hours, to vote for the future of our nation. We have seen history being made here in this studio in Scotland tonight. Surely there can be no doubt that we stand on the brink of another historic day for Scotland as people across the country go to vote on Thursday."

* * *

In a little flat in the centre of London that he used during the week when Parliament was in session, Alex Watson had gathered with a small group of his colleagues to watch the debate. They had come together with a sense of despair and despondency. Alex had received a message that the First Minister had been trying to contact him, but by the time he was free to respond he knew that Morrison would be on his way to the studio. He knew now what Morrison had wanted to tell him. Seemingly unaware of the excited and animated babble of his colleagues, Alex stood in front of the television screen, mouth open, repeatedly clapping a clenched fist into the palm of his other hand. What he had just witnessed was the most incredulous event of his political life. For a long time words failed him.

Chapter Twenty Two

Aftermath

The Prime Minister was alone in a private office at Number 10 Downing Street. He held in his right hand a crystal glass that contained the last drops of what had been a very large brandy. He was seated at his desk and staring absently at nothing in particular. He had been there for over twenty minutes, trying to work out the implications of the debate that he had witnessed earlier. The debate had finished less than an hour earlier, and his initial shock and outrage as the debate had unfolded, and had turned – from his perspective – into a debacle, had subsided into a cold fury. He had been unable to reach either Richard Hume or Penny Carson. Apart from the implications for the outcome of the independence referendum, he was considering the implications for him, and for his government. Clearly, the consequences would be enormous, and he had to work out how to manage them to limit the damage as much as possible. It said much for his judgement and ability to operate in a crisis that he was already beginning to think through his options. However, he had needed the brandy to steady himself after what was the biggest shock of his political career. His concentration was broken by the ring of the telephone which cut into the silence like a chainsaw. When he picked up the handset, a female voice said, "Prime Minister, I have the Leader of the Opposition on the line. Will you take the call?"

Nigel Braithwaite considered this. It was inevitable that he would have to speak to Stephen Halford at some stage. He wasn't ready to have that conversation, but he acknowledged that Halford would be angry, and that there was little to be gained by keeping him waiting. Indeed delaying speaking to him was likely only to add to his anger. He decided to accept the call. "Stephen, good evening. I take it that you saw it all. I'm furious. I'm sure you are too. I am looking for answers."

"Furious isn't a strong enough word for how I feel." Halford paid no heed to convention, and couldn't bring himself to address Braithwaite by name, far less as Prime Minister. "You realise of course that we are both finished. I trusted you and look what has happened. How stupid could I have been? These files, what do they say? Are they as damaging as Morrison made them sound?"

"Stephen, I haven't seen the files. I have left messages for Sir David Lee to contact me urgently and provide me with a copy. Of course I'll share it with you. Lee seems to be out of direct contact, but I'm told that his office can reach him."

Halford gave a mirthless laugh. "There's no need for that, if we can believe Morrison. It will soon be on the internet, and then we can all see it. Maybe Morrison will get it to you more quickly that your own sources. What a mess this is!"

"Look, Stephen, we are in this together. It is both our futures that are at stake here. We need to act together to salvage things. How about we meet tomorrow over lunch? We will have had a chance to assess what is in those files, and I'll have Penny and Richard back from Scotland to get their input. We will be able to work out something. Look, Stephen, this is an MI5 operation that has gone wrong, that has got out of hand. We may be able to transfer the heat to Sir David."

Halford's disposition hadn't changed, but he recognised that he would get no further change out of the Prime Minister for the time being. "I don't think so. Your fingerprints are all over this, and to a lesser extent, so are mine. I will come over to Downing Street tomorrow for lunch, but I don't expect an easy solution, and maybe it is already too late for us. You do know that the whole world will be waiting to see this posted on the internet?"

"Right, Stephen, we'll talk tomorrow. I see there's another call waiting. Hopefully that will be Sir David. If he's got the files I'll get them copied to you."

It wasn't Sir David Lee who was calling. It was an indignant, enraged and fuming Home Secretary, Sir Michael Hammond. He launched into a furious tirade. "What do you think you are playing at, Braithwaite? You think I'm expendable in your little plans to hold on to Scotland! How dare you, you upstart! You think that you can give the press the dirty on me? Well, you forget that we share a number of secrets. If I go down, you will be right alongside me. Don't try to deny it. The whole world saw Morrison say it and your bitch Carson confirm it was me you sold out. You're nothing but a slimy weasel! I know enough about you and your dealings to blow the lid right off this government of yours, and don't think that I won't do it. I don't know how you sleep at night, or how you can live with yourself, to do this to a colleague! Goodnight, Prime Minister." With those final three words dripping with white hot hate, without waiting for a response, Sir Michael slammed the phone down. The Prime Minister had not said a single word; he hadn't been given the chance. He wondered if Sir Michael had drawn breath during the call.

When Sir David Lee called, it was almost midnight. The Prime Minister's mood had not improved. He was, by his standards, strangely uncertain. He could see no plan of action, and this worried him. What he was sure of was that the leaking of this information must come from Sir David's organisation, and just maybe that would give him some room for manoeuvre. "Sir David, where have you been? I have been trying to contact you ever since that debate finished. What is going on? I need a report."

Sir David's voice came over as calm and clear. He seemed completely unruffled either with the events in Edinburgh or the Prime Minister's curt greeting. "Prime Minister, it would appear that somebody has managed to hack into our internal system, copy the file, and pass its contents to the First Minister. I have been busy setting our IT team on working out how this could have happened. We had taken every precaution, and the contents of the files were protected by encryption and were stack coded. This means that they would be virtually impregnable, even if someone did manage to access them. The first thing we need to do is establish how the breach happened, and then we can consider what to do about it."

Braithwaite listened with growing impatience. "So you admit that the security breach happened in your organisation? I told you not to keep files."

"Prime Minister, it does look as though the security breach was indeed at this end. But sir, you were well aware that we had files on this. We had to have files. We created, and you knew that we did, the dossier on Sir Michael Hammond, and the blackmailed civil servant. You knew that we created the article attributed to Hank Warren and so on. How else did you imagine we had material to put into the public domain? You must have known this, and certainly Penny Carson did. I was given to understand that she was reporting everything back to you, and that you were keeping the Leader of the Opposition informed. Is that not correct?"

The Prime Minister could feel himself being boxed in. There was a hint of desperation in his voice when he spoke. "Yes, yes. You had to create these documents. I understand that. I told you expressly that there should be no record of my involvement. Why did you ignore that?"

Sir David's tone did not waiver as he replied, "You are suggesting, I think, Prime Minister, that although you ordered this operation, that I should deny that. That I should present this as an adventure dreamt up and carried out by my organisation without sanction: that you escape public scrutiny by claiming no involvement, and no knowledge of any of this. Prime Minister, you must consider me to be extremely naïve. The information is out there in the public domain, and there is no way of retrieving it."

Nigel Braithwaite poured himself another large brandy, his third of the night. There seemed that he had no way out of this.

It was just after midnight when Richard Hume and Penny Carson arrived at Downing Street. There was no champagne waiting for them. Indeed, there was nothing to be said. On the journey down from Scotland they had hardly exchanged a dozen words and were still too bewildered to offer any meaningful explanation of what had happened.

* * *

At five thirty in the morning, Margaret Morrison nudged her husband awake. She knew that he was exhausted and needed to sleep, but this was his office phone, and even at this hour, his calls would be filtered. Slowly, Morrison roused himself from the first deep and contented sleep he had experienced in weeks, and answered the phone. He had not managed to get to his bed until well after midnight, as colleagues and supporters had contacted him, to congratulate him and express their astonishment at what had been revealed to the public during the debate. The voice at the other end was apologetic and excited at the same time. "I'm sorry to waken you at this ungodly hour, First Minister, but I think you will want to take this call. I have the President of the Unites States on the line for you." Morrison shook himself fully awake and moved into an adjoining room, absurdly and automatically tidying his hair with his hand as he went. "First Minister, I hope I didn't get you out of bed." The distinctive American accent was unmistakable.

"Mr President, no, it is quite alright," Morrison said, now fully alert.

"Well, it is just after midnight here, and it takes something very special for me still to be working at this time. First Minister, tonight you gave us something very special indeed. My advisors have been going over the recording with me, and we are assessing the implications. I see that the files you promised to put on the internet were posted about ninety minutes ago, and my people are still pouring over them. It is clear that you have done democracy a great service by exposing these underhand things in the name of democratic government. All these actions you have brought to the world's attention so spectacularly can only be described as anti-democratic. Let me assure you, First Minister, that America is a friend to all who would promote and defend democracy and will give no succour to those who oppose or abuse democracy. I look forward to having the nation of Scotland as an ally in our work to promote democracy and human rights. Tomorrow I will speak to Prime Minister Braithwaite and leave him in no doubt of my displeasure. I will advise him that the last American President to disgrace our nation was impeached and removed from office. It is not for me to tell Great Britain, or what remains of it after Thursday, how to run her affairs, but no government can behave in this way and expect any support from America."

Morrison had not expected this ringing endorsement, and was slightly abashed. "Thank you, Mr President, for you support. I very much hope that Scotland will be able to support democracy and human rights, as you say, from the status of an independent nation. I hope, too, that as an independent nation, we can develop trade and cultural links with America that are even stronger than those that already exist between our countries."

"First Minister, the bonds between our counties are strong, and can only become stronger, I am well aware of the part played in American history and development by the Scots. People like John Muir, Alistair McCallum, William MacLure and Andrew Carnegie are lasting testimony to the debt that America owes to Scotland. Of course, as you will know, Thomas Jefferson, the principal author of our Declaration of Independence had visited Scotland and was greatly influenced by your own declaration, some centuries earlier. Our nations have much in common. Get Thursday's referendum out of the way and my people will be in touch to arrange a state visit to Scotland, where we can discuss properly the links between our countries. I wish you and your nation well. God bless Scotland!"

Morrison said, almost in wonder, "Yes, Mr President, and God bless America."

Morrison was excited when he went back to bed, thoughts were whirling round in his head, and he was desperate to talk but his wife was asleep. He knew better than to wake her.

* * *

At 7:30 a.m. Sir Nigel Hardcastle entered his board room. Already gathered there were six members of his senior management team – the directors and editors of his newspaper empire. There was an awkward silence as he sat down, with only one piece of paper in his hand. When he spoke, it was with lowered head and in hushed tones. "Ladies and gentlemen, you will all be aware of the content of last night's televised debate from Edinburgh, and you have probably all read by now the relevant part of the material posted by the Scottish government on their website overnight. I have prepared a press release, but I have asked you all here because you deserve to hear it first. This contains all I intend to say on the matter."

He cleared his throat, sipped water, and started reading from his single sheet. "Having made a serious error of judgement in the matter of accepting for publication an unsubstantiated article that I had reason to believe was fabricated, it is impossible for me carry on as owner and proprietor of any news agency. That this error of judgement was compounded by accepting material designed to discredit a cabinet minister, and accordingly it is clear to me that my position as owner and proprietor is untenable. I wish to make it clear that these errors were mine, and mine alone, and that no other person from this organisation was involved. The blame and the responsibility lie entirely with me.

"Accordingly, I have today sold my entire interest in the agency to News Canada, who will, I am sure, be excellent proprietors. I expect that the sale will go through quickly, dependent upon the usual regulatory checks being completed. In the meantime, I will have no more contact with the agency, and pass the day to day management over to Simon Telford, the current editor-in-chief. He will take control of the business in the interim until the sale is completed. I wish to take this opportunity of expressing my apologies to all those I have hurt or let down by my actions."

With that, Sir Nigel rose, and left without another word, leaving an astonished and speechless boardroom behind. No-one was more astonished than Simon Telford.

* * *

At 8:15, the First Minister sat down to his usual frugal breakfast in Bute House, unusually in the dining room. The reason for the change of venue was that he had company, and some business to attend to. In spite of his lack of sleep, there was a spring in his step, and a jauntiness that had been missing from his manner over the last two months. Round the table were Donald Barrie and Gavin Cabrelli, Q.C., the Lord Advocate of Scotland, the most senior law officer in the country. Cabrelli was the grandson of an Italian immigrant, and his hair colouring and complexion betrayed his Mediterranean origins. His accent, however, revealed an upbringing that could only have taken place in Aberdeen. They were joined by Chisholm, Shona and Rory, who each had been found a bed in Bute House. They were enjoying breakfast, although Rory and Shona looked extremely self conscious in this company, and beyond answering politely to enquiries about how well they slept, they said nothing. The First Minister put down his cup, and turned to the Law Officer. "Thank you for coming here this morning. We have a little legal problem to deal with that requires your expertise."

"First Minister, it is always a pleasure to come here. Of course, my assistance in legal matters is at your disposal. What is the nature of the problem?"

"Well, Gavin, you are well aware of the events that unfolded here yesterday and at the debate last night. You will by now have had time to look at the folder of evidence that I had delivered to you yesterday afternoon. None of that would have been possible without considerable help from our three friends, here. I cannot overstate their contribution. That brings me to the immediate problem. Shona is currently serving a period of probation, and part of her probationary condition is that she has no access to a computer or to the internet. Clearly, in order to access this material she has violated those terms, and so something must be done." He smiled to Shona, who was listening in increasing dismay. Surely she would not be sent back to prison?

"Shona has, by breaking the conditions of her probation done the nation a great service, and has indeed done a great service to democracy itself. It would seem ludicrous if she was to be punished for this. In any event, she did not believe that she was acting as a private individual in this instance." He pulled out a piece of paper and passed it to Cabrelli. "You will see from this, it is a solemn statement from David Chisholm that he recruited her, leading her to believe that she was working for the state. You will see that she knew, or thought him to be a senior operative in MI5, and that he needed her to work with him on one of their operations. Gavin, I was hoping that you could suggest some legal way in which we could ensure that Shona's honourable breech of her conditions does not work to her detriment."

The Lord Advocate read the paper in front of him, and considered for a long time before he spoke. "I am familiar with the background to Shona's conviction. It received a lot of publicity at the time. I have to say that breaking probation conditions is a serious matter, and one that I cannot condone. There does seem to be unusual and overpowering mitigating circumstances in this case however, and Shona's actions were certainly for the public good. I am sure that I can square this with the probation service."

Shona let out a sigh of relief, as the First Minister conveyed his thanks to the Lord Advocate. Donald Barrie interjected, "While we are on the subject, a newly independent nation will, I believe, need to use all its talents to the maximum. In Shona, we clearly have someone who has exceptional IT skills, yet we have banned her from using them. Could we find some compromise? For the duration of her probation, could her terms be amended so that she can access a computer and the internet, but only under license and control of someone responsible? For instance, I have a need for a top class research assistant, and I would be happy to offer that to Shona, and to be her supervisor. That is, if she is interested."

This was all happening almost too quickly for Shona to take in. Rory nudged her, and signed to her that she should accept. Cabrelli said, "I think that could be done." All eyes were on her. Almost in a dream, she nodded, and said simply "Yes." While Donald Barrie shook her by the hand, Rory slapped her back, and beamed his infectious grin at her. Shona was bemused, but happier than she could remember, as she looked from one to another round the table, before breaking into a grin, big enough to match Rory's.

After a few minutes, Gavin Cabrelli took his leave. Then Chisholm said that he too had to be going, that he had other places to be, and that he needed to get back to his house in Gloucester. He made to leave, and the First Minister shook him warmly by the hand. "You are an example of why there will always be warm relations between our two countries. You are indeed an honourable man, and I wish you well."

Chisholm replied, "I was just doing what I've tried to do all my working life – protect democracy." Rory and Shona had both risen from the table as he made his way to the door. He looked from one to the other "I could not have had better help or asked for better companions. You two are precious people, and I hope that your new Scotland takes care of you both."

Rory raised a hand in salute, "Mr Chisholm, thanks for everything."

Shona added "I have certainly had a bit of excitement over these last few days, thanks to you. I wouldn't have missed it for the world. Take care of yourself, David." With that, Chisholm, bowed slightly, in an old-fashioned kind of gesture, turned on his heels and left them.

Morrison and Barrie were already in conversation, almost oblivious to the presence of the other two. Barrie was informing the First Minister. "I've been up almost all night. There is no end to the number of news agencies interested in this, from all over the world. You could spend all day just doing interviews on this, but I've held off arranging any. You already had a full day of campaigning lined up."

"Indeed, Donnie, and I've seen the early morning news bulletins. The fall out from last night's debate is everywhere. It was a good decision to post everything on the internet. That means we are putting everything in front of the public, and it also means there is plenty for the media to get their teeth into without needing interviews. We need to keep focused on the main objective, which is to secure a vote in favour of independence. Yet this scandal is linked to the referendum. I need to do the campaign, but we need to push the message that this whole sorry episode only happened because they had no answers to the case we were putting forward in support of independence. They couldn't hope to win by fair means so they tried to win by foul means. Prepare a ten minute brief for me along those lines Can you arrange a press conference in time to catch the evening news bulletins, and I'll fit it in."

Shona found her voice. "Since I am now working for you, Mr Barrie, maybe I could start by working on developing a strategy and the First Minister's brief for the press conference. After all, with the exception of

Rory, nobody knows the material better than I do. My degree from Edinburgh University was in media studies, so I know what to do, and I understand from what the First Minister has just said what line you will want to take. I can have it ready in good time for you to check it over."

Rory chimed in. "I can help her."

Morrison and Barrie exchanged looks before saying, in unison, "Aye."

The telephone rang, and Barrie picked it up. He spoke for a few minutes then turned to Morrison. "Ally, that was Mary Ford. She wants you to know that half an hour ago, Reginald Small handed in his resignation."

"Well, that simplifies one aspect, I guess," Morrison replied. Turning to Shona and Rory, he said with a wink "If you will excuse us both, we have a referendum to win, and you have a brief to prepare."

* * *

At half past ten, Alex Watson strode through the corridors of the House of Commons. There were very few people around at that time, other than officials, but no-one attempted to stop him or to engage him in conversation. He had the look about him of a man on a mission. He made straight for the office of the Speaker of the House. The Speaker is the presiding officer of the Parliament, and he determines debates, who has the right to speak, maintains order, and has the right to punish those who break the House rules. He knocked once, and was immediately asked to enter. The room was surprisingly small, and dominated by a large desk in the centre of the floor. The speaker rose from behind the desk and came to shake hands. "Alex, I was expecting you. After last night, you had to come to me." The speaker was Arfron Jenkins, a genial Welshman who enjoyed the respect of the whole House. He had a well earned reputation for fairness, but would stand for no nonsense. He had a rare ability to keep order using his infectious sense of humour, but this did not stop him from dealing harshly with Members of the House when the occasion demanded.

"Thank you Arfron," Alex Watson shook the hand of the small, silver-haired former coal miner warmly. "As you can guess, I am here to seek to move a motion of no confidence in the government and in the Prime Minister in particular."

"Ah, Alex, what can I say? I have been checking the timetable in expectation of just such a motion. Next Tuesday afternoon can be freed up for this as an emergency debate. We can move the two debates we had scheduled back to a later date. I think in the circumstances, your request will take precedence over debates on changes to the dog licence and whether we should increase the penalty for dropping litter. I take it you will want to lead in the debate."

"I certainly do. Thank you, Arfron, as always you have been very helpful."

The Speaker had a twinkle in his eye. "As you prepare, Alex, you might want to concentrate on the government more than the Prime Minister. By Tuesday he might no longer be a target waiting to be knocked down."

Alex left the Speaker's office, wondering what Arfron Jenkins knew. Jenkins was the kind of man who always knew what was going on, and would not drop hints unless he was certain of his information.

* * *

At eleven o'clock, Nigel Braithwaite was in his study, alone, re-reading the files that implicated him so badly, when one of his aides, knocked and entered. "I'm sorry to disturb you, Prime Minister, but I have to tell you that you have been summonsed to the Palace. Your presence has been requested for ten o'clock tomorrow."

Braithwaite looked up, eyes flashing. "What do you mean? Summoned? I don't get summoned to Buckingham Palace. I request audiences with the Royal Family." Even as he spoke, Nigel Braithwaite could feel the noose tighten, like some death grip, noting the term "summoned" had been used rather than the more conventional "invited".

The aide replied "Sir, there may be no modern precedent for this, but nevertheless, you have been summoned. I fear that it would seem rather disrespectful to refuse. How should I reply to the Palace?"

"Tell them I'll be there," growled Braithwaite.

* * *

As Braithwaite received his royal summons, the Lawson family were being reunited in the sitting room in Bute House. There was much hugging, and backslapping. Tears were shed. Angus was desperate for his brother to tell the whole story in every detail. Flora could hardly bring herself to speak at the sight of her son, safe and happy. Hugh couldn't get the grin off his face, the same grin he had been wearing during the long drive down from his cottage that morning. Rory, for his part, was delighted and relieved to see his family, but was keen to get back to helping Shona. To him, the job was not yet quite complete. He had arranged with Margaret Morrison, at her instigation that the family would lunch together in private in Bute House. He eventually extricated himself from their embraces, saying that he had a bit of work to finish, and then he would take great delight in filling them in on every detail over lunch.

* * *

At twenty minutes after midday, Penny Carson, Richard Hume and Stephen Halford were shown into a room next door to the Prime Minister's office, where a sandwich lunch had been prepared. Almost at once they were joined by Nigel Braithwaite. Penny Carson, for once, her immaculate grooming having failed her, and she still looked rattled, like a rabbit caught in the headlights, had been waiting for her opportunity. Drawn and pale, she looked as though she had not slept. Her eyes seemed curiously sunken, and there were lines round them that had not been evident a day earlier. She was, however, quite determined. "Prime Minister, this was my task. It has gone horribly wrong. That is my responsibility. My letter of resignation is here."

"Penny, that is very noble of you. There will be a number of people falling on their swords, and your sacrifice will not save the rest of us. Morrison has made sure of that by putting the whole lot on the internet. However, please let me bring you all up to date with the latest developments. Sir David Lee has no idea how their security was breached. He is determined that MI5 will not take the wrap for this, and he has enough information to implicate all of us, other than perhaps you, Richard. I've been through all the material, as I'm sure you have. I can see no way out. Just over an hour ago I received a summons – note, a summons – to attend the Palace tomorrow. I can only think that it will be to seek my resignation. I know that this would be unprecedented. However, I cannot see this being merely a request for an explanation. The separatists have already arranged for a vote of no confidence for next week. Just a few minutes ago I spoke with the American President. He is furious. He says that his whole foreign policy is built round spreading democracy and encouraging ethical government. He considers that we were seen as his closest ally, and that now he feels we have betrayed him. He says that he is compelled to take the strongest actions open to him, and we can expect representation from his ambassador here in London over the next couple of days. Throughout the morning, I have been receiving calls from heads of government, particularly in the Commonwealth, registering their lack of support, and distancing themselves from our actions. I have no option but to offer my resignation tomorrow when I go to the Palace. Like me, you will have seen the news reports. My Press Office people tell me they have never been so inundated for interviews and statements. Stephen, I know we have had our differences, but I ask you to believe that I am truly sorry that this has all come out, and probably means that you will have to resign too. What I propose is that we keep this quiet until I return from the Palace, but that tonight, we convene a meeting. Five people from both of our parties should meet here to prepare an outline arrangement for a provisional government to try to restore some confidence."

There was silence as they all tried to take this in. Richard Hume, as Deputy Prime Minister might have expected to take over from Nigel Braithwaite, but he had become the public face of the scandal by virtue of leading the debate the night before. Nobody could suggest an alternative, and with a shrug of resignation, they all agreed to meet that night with their respective teams. He realised that he might be able to ride the media storm that was already gathering force, but he was too damaged to hope that he would be a candidate to become Prime Minister.

* * *

At five o'clock precisely, Sir David Lee left his office and drove through the congestion of Piccadilly, out of London, initially following the A4, and then picking up speed as he joined the M4. He had been driving for almost an hour and a half when he turned off the motorway, continued on for another couple of miles, and then pulled into the courtyard of a red–bricked country pub. The sign above the door indicated that the pub was called the Fox and Hound. He parked his car and went into the empty lounge. He ordered two large whiskies, and found the most secluded corner he could. He could hear voices coming from the public bar, and the distinctive noise of pool balls striking each other, but he was satisfied that the lounge was empty. He had to wait only a couple of minutes until the man he had come to see entered. The newcomer looked about himself, located Sir David in the shadows, and walked purposefully over, arm extended, and hand held out to invite the handshake.

Sir David rose, and took the man by the hand. There was genuine warmth in the handshake. "David, how good to see you. We have something to celebrate. Here, have that malt. Speyside, I seem to recall was your preference. We have to toast this in finest Scotch. After all that is the most appropriate thing we can do."

David Chisholm picked up his glass, and touched it to Sir David's, as both men said, "Cheers!"

Sir David looked appraisingly at his former colleague. "That was rather close. I thought that you weren't going to get the material in time."

Chisholm smiled ruefully into his glass. "We didn't have enough time. I couldn't get to the material early enough to edit out any reference to you, and as you saw, I had to abandon the plan to give it to the media. In order to get it out in time, I had to hand it over to Alistair Morrison instead."

"Don't worry about me, David. I'll be alright. If you read the files closely, I'm not really incriminated. I brought back an instruction from the Prime Minister supported by the Leader of the Opposition which I said on record I considered to be illegal and unethical. My doubts are on record, alongside the origin of the order. Then at every stage of the operation, you will see Williams has proposed actions which I expressed concern over. None of his actions were actually approved by me. It was an inspired move to give it to Morrison. I thought he handled it rather well. A bit theatrical, but that's what I'd expect."

"So, Sir David, it is Norman Williams who is being sacrificed?"

"Well, yes, in a way. But it has cost me a peerage, you know." Sir David gave a little laugh, and Chisholm looked at him enquiringly. "Braithwaite was going to give me a peerage. That would be the price of my silence. I would have to resign from active duty of course, and Williams would be promoted into my job. I couldn't have that. On top of everything else, I couldn't have that. Williams is not the man for this. He is not like you and I. He enjoys destroying things, and has no

252

powers of judgement. Of the small band of people who knew about this project, apart from him, he had two researchers working on this - he was the only one who didn't question it. He just wanted to get on with breaking things down. He relished blackmailing the civil servant, preparing all that stuff on the Home Secretary, bullying that Cole girl who edits the Economics Review, and so on. I know he does it well, but he does it for the wrong reasons. For him it is about destruction, not preservation of society and democracy. I will be meeting him tomorrow to review his future."

Chisholm considered this. "I could still have done with an extra two or three days."

Sir David smiled. "I know that you could. I was worried that you would run out of time, but there was no point breaking into our system before all the material was lodged there, and that meant waiting until Williams had cleared Richard Hume's briefing. The code was always going to be the problem of course. That was the one thing I couldn't help you with. It would have been far too suspicious if I had asked our coding team how to decipher it. By the way, it was a brilliant move to find the Lawson boy. How did you come up with that?"

"I didn't. That was Shona Murray. When she couldn't break the code herself with the software at her disposal she knew that she had to think laterally. As you say, though, brilliant. They both were. What happens now, sir?"

Sir David was silent for a long time. When he spoke, it was with infinite sadness. "The politicians who forgot that they are where they are because we are a democracy will not be there by this time next week. Maybe they will even be gone by tomorrow. They made the mistake of asking us to put their needs before the needs of the people. People like you and I will always protect democracy from attacks from any source, even our own politicians."

The two men sat in long, satisfied and companionable silence until their glasses were empty.

Lightning Source UK Ltd.
Milton Keynes UK
UKOW03f0304240414

230503UK00002B/23/P